THE
THINGS
NOT
SAID

LANDRY YVES

Copyright © 2022 Landry Yves

All rights reserved

No part of this book may be reproduced or transmitted in any form or by any means, electronic or mechanical, including photocopying, recording, or by any information storage and retrieval system without the written permission of the author, except for the use of brief quotations in a review.

This is a work of fiction. Names, characters, places, and incidents are either the products of the author's imagination or are used fictitiously. Any resemblance to actual persons, living or dead, business establishments, events, or locales is entirely coincidental.

Editing: Elaine York; allusionpublishing.com and M. Taylor; ataylorededit.com
Cover Design: Kari March; karimarch.com
Formatting: Champagne Book Design

For Chloe, Louie, and Moxie.
You will forever hold a piece of my heart.

THE
THINGS
NOT
SAID

ONE

GASP FOR BREATH, FORCING OXYGEN INTO MY LUNGS in burning pulls. Several moments pass before my constricted throat relaxes enough to properly inhale. I gulp in the chilled air and hold it in my lungs as I blink sleep from my eyes. The room is dark and my sheets, damp from sweat, are tangled around me. The shadowed outlines of objects come into focus as my heart beats violently against my chest. I slowly release the held breath just as my fingers tingle with numbness.

I focus on repeating the process, the deep breaths cleansing me of my residual panic with every exhale.

In and out.

In and out.

I can practically hear my Pilates instructor providing instructions in a sing-song voice, *focus on your breath, always come back to your breath.*

After several moments of this exercise, I feel my heart rate slow. But as the adrenaline subsides, my mind returns to the dream I'd just woke from. Tendrils of dread knot in my stomach as I think of the glorious oblivion that managed to embrace me during sleep. The knots continue to tighten until my stomach hollows. Like a jack-o'-lantern, my warm and gooey insides are scooped out the moment reality chases away the sweet reprieve of the dream, its imprint evaporating like mist until I am once again cold and numb.

I run a hand over the top of my nightstand, sending an object careening over the edge. The loud clang of a book hitting the floor jolts me awake. My fingers finally find the cord of my cell phone charger. I follow it until I clasp the thin rectangle, illuminating the screen—2:16 stares back at me. *You've got to be kidding me. I've only been asleep for two hours? Please don't let this be another sleepless night; not tonight.*

I straighten my sheets and beat my feather pillows, now flat and lifeless, into submission. Dropping onto my back, I try to relax into the cloud of down cradling my head.

Closing my eyes, I focus on relaxing my body. Starting with my head, I make my way down to my toes, relaxing each muscle along the way in a weak attempt to allow sleep to find me. After the fifth relaxation wave, I realize it's pointless. The jitteriness of drinking two cups of coffee remains.

Surrendering to the fact that any chance of falling back to sleep disappeared the moment I woke, I open my eyes and stare at the ceiling. My thoughts idly turn to my dream—like a stubborn weed growing out of concrete, remnants of the dream threaten to break through the mental shield I've painstakingly constructed over the past nine months.

My subconscious is an addict searching for a fix, yearning to bask in warmth and once again feel alive, to feel whole. Even if only for a moment. Even if the respite I may feel by reminiscing will make my cold, hard reality so much more painful.

Out of habit, I force my thoughts away from what was and turn my attention to what is … my morning meetings.

Knowing sleep will elude me, I toss my comforter aside and escape the warm cocoon of the bed.

I hardly register the bite of the cold from the hardwood floor on my bare feet as I walk down the hall. Entering my home office, I settle in behind my desk, pulling my legs up as I snuggle into the oversized, tufted office chair. I flip the switch on my desk lamp and press down on the track pad of my laptop to illuminate the screen. I instantly feel better; a level of misplaced normality clutched in my fist.

If I can't sleep, I'll be productive. Turning lemons into lemonade, or whatever the ridiculous saying is.

* * *

"Ms. Tate!" My assistant's voice shouts from the phone intercom on my office desk. "Mr. Thompson is about to enter your office. I'm so sorry, I tried to stop him, but—"

"It's fine, Darcy," I interrupt. "Thank you for letting me know."

Yet another interruption, albeit a welcome one, as I've been staring at the same document for the past thirty minutes. Waking up when the majority of Manhattan is lying down to sleep has provided a productive morning. Even if I am beginning to feel the heaviness of exhaustion settle over me.

Benjamin Thompson interrupts my thoughts as he throws open my office door and saunters in. "I would ask how our fearless leader's first week back at Tate is shaping up, but it's fairly obvious. You look like hell, Elle."

Wow, that didn't take long. "Well, thank you. It's wonderful to see you too, Benjamin." I purposely use his full name to piss him off.

My general counsel and best friend, at least when he's not insulting me, doesn't hesitate to walk behind my desk. Grabbing my shoulders, he lifts me out of my chair and pulls me in for a hug. I feel my body go rigid as his embrace tightens. As grateful as I am for his support, I am not in the mood today—my nerves are too fried. Still, I wrap my arms around the torso of his six-three frame.

Ben moves his hands to my shoulders and guides me back to look at my face. "Another sleepless night, doll?"

I raise a questioning brow. "It's that obvious?"

He pulls me in for another brief squeeze and walks to the front of my desk, tossing a manila folder on top of it before unbuttoning his suit jacket and sitting in one of the two adjacent chairs facing me. We stare at each other for a moment before he places his elbows on his knees and leans in, sitting in his traditional *we are about to have a serious conversation, whether you want to or not* position.

Shit, we don't have time for this now… especially with my lack of sleep already putting me off-kilter. Still standing, I place my hands on my desk and lean forward. "Before you start, we don't have time, we need to discuss our 12 o'clock."

Ben smirks. "You think you know me so well."

I match his smirk with one of my own. The truth is, I know Benjamin Thompson better than I know myself right now. I can't help but smile as I think about the day we met so long ago.

The crowd continued to grow in my parents' backyard, making it difficult to navigate the sea of bodies. As soon as I dodged one boring adult, another would pop up, telling me how much I'd grown. I couldn't help but think of the Whac-A-Mole game at the fair as idle conversations continued to pop up, regardless of how many I was able to smack away. When I managed to reach the edge of the beach abutting the property, I looked back toward the house, sweeping my eyes across the mass of people congregating on the lawn. My parents' Fourth of July parties were legendary, the number of partygoers a sure sign this year would be no different. The crowd thinned the closer I got to the seawall separating the manicured lawn from the sand. I scanned the beach—plastic inflatable toys littered the area in front of our home, remnants of a long day in the sun. Shielding my eyes, I looked toward our summer neighbors and family friends, Theo and Margaret Murphy's house. Several partygoers spilled onto their back lawn, enjoying the seasonal Long Island July day as a group played croquet.

Drawn by the laughter and lighter crowd, I began to walk toward the croquet match on the Murphy's back lawn when movement caught my eye. Three boys stood facing each other in front of a large oak tree on the opposite side of the property, one boy noticeably smaller than the other two. They were too far away for me to hear anything, but their body language made it clear something was wrong. I began to walk closer when one of the larger boys pushed the small boy. I watched wide-eyed as the small body flew backward, landing on his back.

Before I could think about what I was doing, I started sprinting toward the trio. As I drew closer, I recognized Richard, the son of one of my father's colleagues. I remembered my lack of surprise at seeing him; Richard had always been a coward masquerading as a bully.

As I neared the group, the smaller boy pushed himself to his feet. My own feet pounded over the grass, propelling me closer. The small boy stood, and Richard immediately pushed him into bully number two.

Adrenaline pumped through me as I covered the remaining distance.

Three heads turned my way when I screamed, "Leave him alone!" My breath had caught at the sight of the small, beautiful boy who looked so lost.

I'll never forget the humorous attempt at an insult that left Richard's mouth when he sneered, "Go back to your daddy's party, little girl. I'm teaching Prince Humperdinck a lesson on manners."

I placed my hand on my hip and cocked my head to the side before responding, "Really, a character from *The Princess Bride*? Surely you are more creative than that?" Moving my hand from my hip to place a finger to my lips in an act of contemplation, I continued, "Actually, never mind, I already know the answer to that."

Richard's expression transformed from a scowl to detached, all emotion erased. The sight was unsettling. He turned from me, walked up to the small boy and took his shoulders from bully number two, who was still holding him. I watched in disbelief as Richard's arm cocked back before his fist connected with the boy's middle. He managed to land on his bottom this time, his head bowed as he clutched his stomach until the small boy slowly raised his broken eyes to look at me.

I. Saw. Red.

A rage unlike anything I had experienced before consumed me.

Before I could register my response, my fist connected with Richard's nose and a sickening crack echoed around us, the self-defense classes my parents had forced me to take finally paying off.

Richard's eyes filled with tears and both of his hands

clasped his nose, blood oozing between his fingers. He turned and ran toward my house with bully number two following closely behind, screaming expletives until we could no longer see them.

The small boy stood, brushing dirt off his shorts. He stuck his hand out, as if he was an adult and not a ten-year-old kid, and said, "Hi, I'm Ben," as if nothing had happened. I gave him my hand, trying not to wince as he gently squeezed. "It looks like I owe you, Tyson. Come on, let's find some ice for your hand."

We've been inseparable from that day forward, our friendship continuing in the same way it had throughout our childhood into our adulthood. With each of us taking care of the other in our own way. He has been the one constant in my life since that day.

"Hello, are you with me, Elle?"

Still smiling at the memory, my eyes focus on Ben, who is far from the small boy who was bullied. He has towered over most people since his teenage years, and his cut muscles, high cheekbones and natural smolder make him look more like a model than an attorney. "I think I know you fairly well after twenty years."

Ben grins, his dimples flashing as his hazel eyes study me. After what feels like several minutes, but must only be seconds, I see him acquiesce, the intensity of his gaze easing. "Fine, this conversation can wait, but we do need to talk. We're worried about you."

The last thing I want is to make Ben and his partner, Jackson, worry, but irritation crawls up my throat. I am giving my all just to move through the motions. The energy to get out of bed in the morning, to shower, to dress, to attempt to work—it's taking everything in me. Everything. At least

I'm no longer drifting in the dismal state I have been in for the past several months. I'm trying, damn it!

"Look, I appreciate the concern, I truly do. I don't know what I would do without you and Jax, but I have things under control. It's just …" I pause as I try to find the right words. "I was out for too long. It's forced me to spend my time playing catch up."

Ben raises his hand to interrupt. "That's exactly the problem. It's only been a week and already your life has become work. It doesn't take a shrink to realize it's a coping mechanism."

Ice coats my stomach. I can only imagine what Ben sees in my expression when his eyes soften before he adds, "Look, I'm simply making an observation. If you don't realign your priorities, you're going to end up having a breakdown—or worse, you'll become a recluse with twelve cats."

I stare, unblinking, waiting for him to finish, not caring that he is trying to lighten the mood with a clichéd cat joke.

"Let us in, Elle. Let us help you. I hate to break it to you, but you are not Teflon, you can't continue to repel everything having anything to do with Al …"

My eyes widen as I silently dare Ben to continue. "Don't. Not today," I interrupt, unable to hide the bite in my voice. What the hell is he doing? This is neither the time nor the place.

Ben shrinks back at my reaction and my anger is doused, the ice in my stomach thawing to a sludge of guilt. I shouldn't lash out at Ben; I know he's only trying to help, but his help is unwarranted, not to mention unprofessional, at the moment.

I make myself smile for Ben's benefit, but I know it doesn't reach my eyes. "Look, Ben, you're wrong. I'm not a fan of cats so you don't have to worry about me turning into a crazy cat lady." And because my stomach is still sour, I add, "I get it, I do. And we will talk, just not here, and definitely not before our meeting with TA Holdings."

Placated, Ben smiles and leans back, crossing his legs. I feel myself relax knowing he is dropping this … at least for now.

"So, our 12 o'clock." Ben relaxes farther into the chair, not a care in the world, as the sentence hangs between us like an unwanted visitor.

Right. Shit. I feel my shoulders tense.

"Elle, how are you going to meet with TA Holdings when you go nuclear if someone says *his* name?"

I don't miss the emphasis on the word *his*. I take a deep breath while unceremoniously collapsing into my chair. Leaning my chin on my hand I try, once more, to placate my friend. "Ben, it's not an issue," I respond. "This meeting is strictly business, not personal. And I am a gem at compartmentalizing."

"Yeah, you're a gem at repressing and ignoring. One of these days it will catch up to you."

My jaw clenches. "I thought we just covered this. Can we please move on? Do I need to remind you how important this meeting is?" I feel my pulse throb at an increased tempo as my blood pressure rises. We've only discussed this a minimum of ten times. "We are a breath away from reclaiming the majority stake of Immunotech. We need to get our shit together."

Ben shifts back, his eyes widening in surprise. I lower my head, deflating as I take a breath to calm my ever-fraying nerves. Looking up, I allow my vulnerability to show as I look him in the eye. "I owe him this, Ben. I can't begin to imagine how irate he would be to know his life's work is becoming nothing more than a revenue stream bankrolling an asshole he despised. His vision was to make a difference, to save lives. Not for his company to be a cog in the wheel of a financial scheme."

Ben leans forward, giving me his full attention. "I know, doll. I have no doubt you'll get Immunotech back on track. I just want to make sure your head is in the game and hearing his name won't send you spiraling." In a whisper he adds, "Especially now that you're starting to show signs of the old Elle."

I force a smile and nod. Fake it 'till you make it, I suppose. I love Ben, he truly is like a brother and his concern for me is endearing, which is why I don't want to disappoint him by stating what I know to be true: I will never find my way back to my old self again. I couldn't be that person if I tried because I no longer know who she is. The old Elle has been replaced, on a cellular level, by a cold, numb shell.

Recognizing the need to regain control of my thoughts, I force myself to focus on the impending meeting with TA Holdings, the majority shareholder of Immunotech. "Were you able to find out anything more regarding TA's motivations to hold on to Immunotech?"

Ben leans back in his chair. Arching his eyebrows, he answers, "Actually, yes. I've learned a few interesting tidbits."

Oh, Lord. I brace myself.

"Apparently, Theo has been somewhat operationally inactive."

I shake my head, not understanding. "What the hell does that mean, he isn't working?" That isn't like Theo at all. In fact, I don't recall a time when Theo Murphy wasn't working; him and his wife Margaret joining dinner dates with my family late or canceling weekends away because of his work. We all forgave him because no one could ever be angry with the kind and generous Theodore Murphy. Plus, Theo's workaholic habits allowed his business partner, my father, time to be with my mother and me.

"Yes, that's exactly what it means. I'm afraid our assumptions are proving to be correct. The board has given Richard Dorn free rein. Theo has been pulling back in preparation of his retirement.

I cringe. Richard, the devil incarnate, involved in *anything* without a babysitter is sure to lead to disaster.

Ben notices my expression and adds, "Trust me, I know. Dorn at the helm coupled with the financials these past few months ..." Ben pauses and shakes his head in disbelief.

"Wait, what?" I ask ineloquently. "So, it's true?"

Ben narrows his eyes. "It appears so. As you know, Immunotech profit took a nose-dive, even though prescription volume has doubled, but that's not all." Ben pauses and I nod my head impatiently, urging him to get to the point. Humor glints in his eyes as he basks in the drama of drawing this out, and I ask the universe for patience.

Taking his precious time, Ben leans forward, capturing my full attention. "Capital expenditures have nearly tripled since Al ... ah, in the past three quarters. We were finally able to get our hands on the CapEx line items this morning—Genevieve is combing through the documents as we speak."

The guilt blanketing me becomes suffocating as my confusion turns into understanding. How could I have allowed a hugely successful biotech firm to fall apart in less than a year? I curse under my breath. This is my fault. This is the result of my absence these past nine months. If I could have pulled out of my state of self-pity sooner, TA would never have had to step in to help. Furthermore, Richard Dorn wouldn't have had the opportunity to gain control and the company would still be thriving under the tutelage of Tate, Inc.

I feel an internal flame light from a dormant place I thought no longer existed. Not yet a fire, but kindling in anticipation as an intrinsic instinct to protect Immunotech kicks in. There is no way I will allow a multimillion-dollar company that was painstakingly built by one of the most brilliant people I've ever known—a company that is now his legacy—fail.

Standing from my chair, I begin to pace. "I don't want to know how you managed to get the CapEx details, but I'm glad you did. If anyone can figure this out, it's Genevieve. I want to hear from Gen the minute she's finished with her review."

Ben winks. "She's already planning to update you by the end of the day, boss."

"Fantastic, then I will choose to ignore your sarcasm."

The corner of Ben's lip lifts. "In light of this new information, how do you want to handle our 12 o'clock with Theo?"

I stop pacing and stand in front of Ben, crossing my arms. "We are going to ask him why the hell a company I trusted him with is under financial scrutiny and why the fuck he didn't involve us sooner."

Ben smiles. "There she is. Nice to have you back, Tyson."

I scowl in response. "Shut up."

Ben's eyes light with mirth. "I do have one suggestion."

My eyebrows raise, and he continues, "Perhaps you lose the F-bomb when you address your godfather?"

The itch for me to take action overrides any retort I would have slung at Ben. Grabbing my phone, I dial Gen's extension.

Gen's lilting voice answers, "It took you long enough. I expected a call ten minutes ago."

"Ben just updated me. Have you found anything yet?"

Ben's eyes look to the ceiling before he shouts, "I told her you would update her at the END of the day."

Hearing him through the phone, Gen breathes out a laugh. "Haven't found anything yet, but I'll have a list of expenditures to you before your meeting with TA Holdings."

I look at the clock. "That only gives you two hours."

"Then you better let me go so I can get on with it" Gen retorts, the smile still present in her voice.

"Fine, bye." I lean back in my chair and mentally catalog what this new information could imply. A myriad of questions filter through my mind. Chiefly, why are profits dwindling when volume has increased? Costs should be decreasing with scale. This leads to a host of different questions I would rather not consider, such as, why the hell hasn't Theo involved us? The last question causes my stomach to turn. I can't bring myself to consider a potential betrayal by a man I not only consider family, but who has been a rock through so many chapters of my life. Through celebration and tragedy. A man who taught me to keep living when my heart was ripped from my chest, and I wanted to lie in bed under a mountain of covers forever. A man who walked me down the aisle on the happiest day of my life because my own father, the A in TA Holdings, wasn't there to do so.

Ben scoots his chair closer to my desk. "I know what

you're thinking, Elle, and there is no way Theo knows what's going on. Just give him the benefit of the doubt before you even go there." With his brows raised, he waits for me to nod before tapping the manila folder he entered my office with. "I took the liberty of asking your security team to begin compiling background information on Richard, since he is now running the show at TA."

The reminder makes me shake my head in disbelief. "I can't believe TA has allowed Dorn such autonomy. That man needs a handler."

Ben exhales his frustration. "As I said, leadership has practically given him the keys to the castle with Theo stepping back, which leads me to believe there's more to the story."

Could this situation become any more confounding?

Ben continues, "We need to look deeper into Richard. I've always thought something was off with him."

"Oh, really? Did you come to that conclusion after the asshole accosted you when we were children, or was this realization within the past decade?"

Ben looks up in thought. "You know, it should have been when we were ten, but I think it was right after college when you both went for the analyst position at TA."

I nod my head in agreement. Dorn was such a dick during that process, and an even bigger dick when he wasn't selected.

"Alright, tell Nik to focus on Richard." If anyone can uncover dirt on that maniac, it's my head of security. "I would like a full dossier as soon as possible." I rub my temples in an attempt to fend off an impending headache. The stark realization that we've only scratched the surface of this mess causes a feeling of unease to uncurl in my stomach.

The only thing I know with absolute certainty is I will not let Immunotech fail. "Ben, I need to know who exactly has been babysitting my company these past nine months."

"Got it, I'll find Nik. In the meantime, a general background summary on Richard is in the envelope."

I grab the yellow pouch and slide its contents onto my desk. The first page is a general summary on Richard with his photo, which looks like a Brooks Brothers ad. My lip curls at his arrogant smirk. Below the photo is information on Richard's education, including an unimpressive GPA and career summary. All information that is easily found online.

Ben grabs the stapled sheets, flips through a few pages and sets the stack in front of me with a page labeled *background check* on top. I scan the page until I reach the section Ben wants me to see. My eyes shoot up to meet his in surprise as, "Yes, we need to dig deeper into Richard's background," leaves my mouth on a breath.

Ben leans forward, reaching across my desk to squeeze my hand. His eyes display conviction, and in this moment, I know we will get Immunotech back.

TWO

A SHARP PAIN PULSES OVER MY RIGHT EYE, KEEPING time with my heartbeat. I apply pressure to my temples to alleviate the nauseating hammer that pounds against my skull. After spending the past two hours digging through research on TA Holdings, including a last-minute meeting with Nik, head of Tate security and begrudging pseudo-family member, my impending headache has made its grand, debilitating debut.

Walking to the private conference room adjacent to my office, Ben hands me three pills and a bottle of water. I swallow the tablets, drinking heavily from the proffered bottle as we enter the room.

An assortment of charcuterie, imported cheeses, various breads, fruit, and bottles of sparkling water have been placed at the far end of the room, but what draws my eye are the two men seated toward the head of the long conference table.

What the … I'm not sure how, but I manage not to choke on the water I'm drinking, though I do freeze at the doorway. Schooling my features into a mask of impassivity, I remember to place one foot in front of the other, taking steady, even steps toward them.

As I walk to him, Theo stands, embracing me in a hug the moment I'm within distance. "It is such a pleasure to see you, Eliana."

Theo is one of the few people who call me by my full name, which I allow because he's family. He gives me one more squeeze and releases. Taking my hands in his as he pulls back, his expressive eyes show concern as he studies my face.

"It has been far too long. Margaret insists you accept one of our dinner invitations soon. She threatened to physically drag you to our home herself next time you're invited."

I smile as my old friend guilt twists my stomach into knots. "Theo, it is wonderful to see you as well. I've missed you both and I must admit, I especially miss Margaret's cooking. I promise to clear my evening the next time I'm extended an invitation."

Theo's eyes smile at my response. "Margaret will be delighted. We would love nothing more than to spend time with you. We have so much to catch up on."

I give Theo's hands a squeeze. "Speaking of catching up." I shoot a pointed look at his companion, who is now standing rather awkwardly behind him, waiting for his fatherly affection to end. "I wasn't expecting Dick to be joining you this afternoon." I am mildly impressed with my calm tone as my inner voice is screaming, *why is Richard fucking Dorn in my office?*

Richard's face turns red at my use of the shortened version of his name. I look back at Theo to see an apology in his eyes. Richard offers his hand to shake while adding, "You know I prefer Richard. Nice to see you, Eliana."

My brows raise as I offer a plastic smile. "A pleasure, I'm sure."

Ben steps forward, effectively cutting the tension as he embraces Theo. "Please tell Margaret I will be incredibly jealous if Elle gets to enjoy her delicious cooking without me. Besides, she knows I'm the fun one," he adds with a wink.

Theo chuckles, slapping Ben on the back. "Of course you're invited, Benjamin. What would an evening be without you to keep us entertained?"

Ben gives Richard a slight nod of his head. "Dick," he says before turning on his heel and walking to the food. He spears fruit and cheese onto his plate and continues to the other side of the table, taking a seat across from Theo and Richard with dramatic flair.

Pursing my lips to fight a smile, I raise my hand to offer the spread of food laid out in the corner. The three of us fill our plates and I claim my seat next to Ben.

Once we are all seated, a moment of awkward silence ensues as we look across the table at one another. The silence and tension thicken until it's tangible. This is ridiculous; there is no way I will be able to fake pleasantries with Richard, so I might as well dive in.

"Let's get down to it, shall we? What will it take for you to relinquish control of Immunotech?"

Theo's eyebrows raise in surprise as Richard wipes his mouth, placing his napkin back in his lap before clearing his throat. "You certainly don't beat around the bush, do you, Eliana?"

"You can call me Ms. Tate, and no, I don't. I feel transparency is best when a flourishing company is suddenly and inexplicably in the red. You know my intentions. I want my company back and I want my position as chair of the board reinstated."

Richard raises his brows. "Is that all?"

I smile in return. "No, Dick, that's not all. I also intend to buy back the Immunotech shares Tate sold to TA Holdings nine months ago."

Richard leans back, his lips spread into a serpentine smile that makes my skin crawl. Why does this guy have such a serial killer vibe?

"Your candor is appreciated; however, we aren't convinced we should sell any of our shares to you. In fact, we think it's in our best interest to ensure control remains with TA Holdings."

Theo's head snaps to Richard in surprise as his nostrils flare.

The corners of my mouth turn up slightly. I'm certain the fire in my stomach is reflected in my eyes. This guy thinks he can justify stealing Immunotech out from under me while I was away grieving. Game on, asshole.

"Let's be realistic, Richard. Sell me back my shares and you can use the capital to purchase a substantial stake in the generics company you've been eyeing. Biotech is far from the expertise of TA Holdings. You could do far more with a generic pharmaceutical manufacturer than you could with a company focused on immunotherapy, especially one you want for all the wrong reasons."

I feel Ben's shoulders move in silent laughter. He knows exactly what I'm doing as I throw out a proverbial carrot to gain information. Richard's ego is far too big for him to sit quietly while I bait him. The more he talks, the more leverage we will have.

Theo nods in agreement, but as he begins to speak, Richard bulldozes over his words.

"I'm not sure I know what you are referring to.

Immunotech is our only interest in the health science space at this time."

My eyes narrow at the liar sitting in front of me.

"Furthermore, we have more than enough expertise in the biotech sector to effectively maintain and grow the business," Richard continues.

"Is that so? Then please explain how Immunotech has posted a loss the past three quarters?"

I see Richard's jaw clench as he leans forward and tilts his head to the side, pasting on an expression of artificial concern. "I know these past few months have been … difficult for you. Perhaps you should take some more time off. I'm sure Ben is more than capable of continuing to run things at Tate, and TA can continue to turn Immunotech into the blockbuster company it is destined to be. Think about it, this is a win-win scenario for you."

Every word he speaks makes the fire in my stomach blaze hotter. An inferno ready to be unleashed. Ready to engulf anyone in my path.

Richard clears his throat. "Don't personalize this. The fact remains that Tate wasn't able to hold on to Immunotech before. You should be grateful we graciously stepped in to help."

Ah, there it is. Richard's final blow in his attempt to maim me. Is this lunatic for real? I take a cleansing breath to regain my composure before speaking. "You helped? Is that what we're calling it? You mean you helped yourself to an attempted hostile takeover. It's unfortunate your efforts will have been in vain."

Richard side-eyes Theo. "Yes, well, you can thank Theo for that. He seems to have a soft spot for you. However, I fear he may not be able to help you moving forward, *Ms. Tate.*" He spits out my name as if it's a bitter taste in his mouth.

What the hell does that mean? I quickly run through various scenarios I may not have prepared for, but I'm at a loss. I look between the two men, my confusion evident. Theo looks incredibly uncomfortable, his normally rosy complexion exceedingly pale as he looks at Richard in disdain.

"I apologize for my colleague; he appears to be a bit delusional this afternoon." Theo's face scrunches up as he turns toward Richard and removes all pretense. "What the hell are you playing at, Dorn?"

The men glare at each other in what appears to be a battle of wills before Theo turns his attention back to Ben and me. "I apologize, we wasted your time today. I was ill-informed that Dorn had an ulterior motive for this meeting." He slants a glare back to Richard. "Why don't we reschedule once our side is aligned?"

Richard's smug expression is made even more disconcerting by the malice in his eyes, and I realize we were just played. Richard wanted this meeting delayed because he knew TA leadership, with Murphy at the helm, would vote to sell the shares back to Tate. He's biding his time.

I feel blood rush to my head, and I welcome the pulsing ache behind my eye, allowing it to center me.

Richard shakes his head back and forth. "Alexander would be rolling over in his grave if he knew how little regard you have for his lifetime achievement."

I suck in a shocked breath.

Ben tenses next to me, ready to spring to my defense, but it's Theo who jumps up, his chair rolling backward and hitting the wall. Looking down at Richard he roars, "ENOUGH!"

The blood rushing to my head a moment ago is replaced with ice that spreads throughout my body, making my limbs numb. I try to focus on maintaining a calm and unaffected façade, channeling my inner ice queen when I give Richard a condescending smirk.

"I appreciate the concern, Dick. Fortunately, these past months have provided all the motivation I could possibly need to ensure the things most important to me receive my undivided attention. Regaining control of Immunotech before you run it into the ground is priority number one."

Richard's fists clench and his scowl deepens.

My hands begin to shake and I move them to my lap. I need to leave this conference room before my mask shatters and I reveal that I'm hanging on by a thread, pretending to be the person I once was.

I look at Theo to apologize or thank him, not sure which is appropriate at this point, and my lungs seize. Theo's face is pale and waxy. Little beads of sweat glisten on his forehead and upper lip as one hand is planted on the table to support his weight and the other grasps at his tie, trying to loosen the knot.

I jump out of my chair and run to Theo's side. Grabbing the chair beside him, I wheel it around and help him sit, placing my hand on his shoulder in a poor attempt at comfort.

"Theo, are you okay?" I squeak out, my voice tight with panic. Ben is on the other side of Theo, trying to push a glass of water into his hand. I kneel when he doesn't respond to see his face pinched from pain, his complexion becoming grayer by the second.

Oh no, no, no, this can't be happening.

I look at Richard, who is calmly sitting in his chair, observing the scene, as if he were watching an interesting Nat Geo show on primates. My ice queen veneer shatters into a million pieces as I'm taken back to that summer day so long ago when I punched Richard in the nose. He's lucky he isn't in striking range.

"What the hell are you doing? Call an ambulance!" I shriek at the imbecile, gesturing with my chin to the phone in front of him. He reaches for the phone and holds the receiver to his ear.

"No dial tone."

Standing, I grab the phone from his hand and press several buttons, trying to get it to work. Nothing.

"Go tell my assistant to call an ambulance." Richard doesn't move. "NOW!"

With the typical speed of an arrogant prick, Richard stands and begins to saunter to the door.

Screw this. I look at Ben…as always, he knows what I need without me saying a word. He simply nods. "Go, I've got him."

I race past Richard, making it to Darcy's desk before he makes it out of the conference room. "Darcy, call an ambulance, Theo isn't well."

Darcy dials and hands me the phone once the operator is on the line. I am so focused on answering the emergency dispatcher's questions, I don't catalog the minutes as they tick by. Finally, Max, the front office receptionist, passes me as he leads four paramedics to the conference room. I drop the phone and follow the group.

When I reenter the conference room, I see four large men huddled around Theo, effectively blocking my view as they attend to his medical needs. I stand back, wishing there was something, anything, I could do as the static threads of anxiety build, multiplying into a web that soon becomes a noose around my neck.

Sliding my diamond pendant back and forth on its chain, a nervous habit I adopted when my life imploded nearly a year ago, I try to focus on Theo. Kind, caring, selfless Theo.

A succession of childhood memories flip through my mind. I think of all the times he brought me Toblerone chocolate bars when he returned from traveling to one country or another. As a young girl, I thought the milk chocolate was an exotic delicacy only found on other continents. The novelty lasted for a couple of years until I saw the confection at a JFK duty-free store when I was six. Still, I always cherished his thoughtfulness, which is why the gift never lost its magic.

The strangled noise of Theo fighting for air interrupts my thoughts as the noose of panic constricts my throat. I feel the delicate thread precariously holding me together tighten, and I vaguely wonder what will happen if it snaps. It's at this moment I smell the familiar clean scent of fresh linen with a hint of citrus as Ben wraps his arm around my shoulder. I melt into his warmth, allowing him to physically hold me together.

"He'll be fine, doll. You know Theo, there's no way he's going down like this."

I'm unable to respond as I try to swallow past the massive lump in my throat. If I could talk, I would tell Ben how much his comfort means to me. Tell him I was a moment away from shattering. That I'm always a moment away from shattering, and this reality may be my new normal. I would explain the amount of relief his words bring me. But I don't because my nearly closed throat prevents me from speaking.

One of the paramedics notices us and walks over. "He's stable. We're taking him to Sacred Heart," he explains in a gruff, no-nonsense voice. I release the breath I was holding. Thank God. I send up a silent prayer of thanks.

My voice cracks when I say, "I'm going with him. I'll call his wife on our way to the hospital."

The paramedic shoots me a look of skepticism. "Are you family?"

"Yes, he's my uncle," I squeak out before adding, "practically," under my breath. He nods his head in agreement and I turn my eyes back to Theo as he is being strapped to a stretcher.

The lump in my throat manages to grow larger as the group files out of the conference room. I squeeze between two paramedics to see Theo. His eyes focus for a moment as he reaches for my hand. I bend to whisper in his ear, "I'm right behind you. I'll ride to the hospital with you, and we can call Margaret on the way."

He gives me a small nod. I watch as his pinched face relaxes before releasing my wrist as he's wheeled away.

My feet are frozen to the floor as the paramedics exit the room. How the hell did a lunch meeting end with Theo being carted off to the hospital? My eyes scan the room, trying to make sense of the past ten minutes. Ben is the only person remaining, staring at me like I'm an injured animal he doesn't want to spook.

Relief from seeing Ben rips me from the fog. I walk over and wrap my arms around his waist.

"Thank you. Just—thank you."

Ben returns my hug and kisses the top of my head.

"He's going to be fine, Elle. Now get your skinny ass down to the ambulance before they leave without you. I'll meet you at the hospital."

Ben turns me toward the door, and I begin to exit the room in the same way I entered: one foot in front of the other my only goal.

I'm almost to the doorway when I turn back to Ben. "Where the hell is Richard?"

Ben shrugs his shoulders. "He followed you out and never came back."

I eye the phone on the conference room table before rushing over to lift it up. Sure enough, the phone cord falls onto the table because it wasn't plugged in all the way. I throw my hands up in exasperation, "Can you please update Nik? I want someone on Dorn twenty-four-seven."

Ben nods, his expression solemn as he stares at the errant phone cord before returning his attention to me. "Out of curiosity, what was that about the generics company?"

I avert my eyes. "We may have uncovered email correspondence."

Ben places his hands on his hips and looks to the ceiling as he exhales a rather loud sigh. "Elle, you know how this works. As your general counsel, the less I know the better."

"I know, but Genevieve discovered that the bulk of Immunotech capital expenditures is being funneled to a shell company. I asked Nik to investigate, and he may have uncovered email correspondence between Richard and the CEO of Zenra indicating TA is pursuing an acquisition."

Ben looks bewildered, his prior consternation forgotten. "What is he up to?"

I shake my head because at this moment, I don't care. "Look, I need to get downstairs. I'll keep you posted on Theo."

Ben closes the distance between us to usher me out the door. "I'll meet you at the hospital after I speak with Nik."

With a final nod of agreement, I run through the office to catch up to Theo.

THREE

B LINKING MYSELF AWAKE, I SLOWLY RAISE MY HEAD from the precarious angle it had occupied for far too long, if my stiff neck is any indication. One eye peels open a crack before slamming shut again when I'm assaulted by piercing white light. I try a second time and manage to squint at the LED bulbs hanging from the ceiling. My stomach churns as the light causes the lingering pain from my earlier headache to flare.

I shift in the uncomfortable plastic chair I've occupied the past few hours when a familiarity inches its way forward from my subconscious.

Oh my God. My eyes fly open as realization of what woke me hits like a bolus shot of epinephrine. Bolting upright and spinning around to survey the room, I see that I'm alone in the hospital waiting room, but the faint masculine scent of spice and leather, with a hint of sweetness, assaults my senses. My heart beats against my chest as if I've just run five miles.

I jump up, untangling my legs from a faded blue blanket as I run out the open door to scan the hallway.

Empty. My head swings back to the waiting room. Still empty.

Bracing myself against the doorway while I try to calm myself, I can't help but wonder if I'm finally losing my mind. Not only can I not stop dreaming about him, but I'm now smelling him in public places? I make a mental note to schedule a session with Dr. Wickham tomorrow.

Inhaling deeply, I try to capture remnants of the now-fading scent. God, I miss that smell. I miss the comfort and yearning from breathing him in. But most of all, I miss home. *He* was the scent of home.

My mind goes to the folded T-shirt currently in a Ziploc bag under my bed. The same bag I opened just last night, pressing my nose against the preserved cotton and slowly inhaling, as if it were a fine wine.

Shaking my thoughts away, I return to the chair and fish my phone out of my bag to check the time: 8:05 p.m. I've been at the hospital for nearly seven hours. My adrenaline evaporates as I think of Theo lying in a hospital bed down the hall.

The ride to the hospital was as uneventful as a ride transporting a loved one with a failing heart could be. I sat beside Theo and held his hand as the paramedics placed sensors on him to monitor his vitals. I called Margaret who, as expected, was distraught. I can't begin to imagine the number of traffic laws her driver broke to get her to the hospital shortly after us.

Nausea builds as I think about the argument that led to Theo's hospital stay. If I would have harnessed my theatrics with Richard, Theo wouldn't have gotten upset and would be home with Margaret instead of hooked up to machines in a cold hospital room. I tried to apologize during the ambulance ride, but Theo wouldn't have it, shaking his head and tightening his grip on my hand. His eyes pleading with me to stop. I know Theo would never blame me, but he should.

I begin to scroll through the several missed calls and text messages I've received over the past several hours, selfishly wishing Ben and his partner Jackson were still with me. After sitting with me for most of the afternoon, the two needed to get home to walk Jasper, their Great Dane. I insisted they go, but I wish they were here. I feel lost without them, like a fraud continuing to act as if she has her life together. But the truth is, I am unraveling at the seams.

Tossing my phone back into my bag, not wanting to deal with the missed calls and messages quickly multiplying, a puddle of blue on the floor catches my eye. I reach down to pick up the blanket I kicked off during my sprint to find the phantom, yet all too familiar, scent. My fingertips touch the worn satin edge and I freeze. I didn't have a blanket before falling asleep, and Ben and Jax had already left, so this couldn't have come from either of them.

Cautiously, as if it might bite, I pick the blanket up with two fingers and stare, searching for answers. When none come, I fold the blanket and place it on the chair next to me.

Who would have covered me? I cross my arms in front of me, hugging my middle, to fend off a chill. Perhaps one of the nurses provided the blanket when they noticed I was sleeping. It's a plausible explanation. I force myself to shake off my unease; clearly my paranoia is ratcheted from the stress of Theo being in this hospital. Still, I continue to eye the blanket.

Perhaps now would be the perfect time to check on Theo I think to myself before grabbing my bag and bolting out the door.

* * *

Margaret is sitting in a chair beside Theo's bed. Both of her hands are clasped around his right hand, as if she's afraid he might disappear. Her head is resting on the bed as she stares at her husband's face. It's a beautiful sight, the love surrounding them.

I lean against the doorframe, feeling like a voyeur as I watch the two of them. I allow myself to remember what that felt like. A love so unique, so rare, few people ever experience it. Two souls braided together in a beautiful kaleidoscope of color, fitting together as one. The kind of love that results in the feeling of having been together a thousand lifetimes.

I feel the corners of my lips turn up as I watch the two of them. I'm so damn grateful Theo and Margaret have each other. Warmth coats my nerves like syrup, replacing my instinct to find the nearest exit.

Margaret must feel my eyes on her because she turns her head toward the doorway. A smile lights her face as she sits up and holds out an arm, indicating I join her. I walk over and bend down, allowing her to embrace me in a tight hug, a hug that continues for a full minute before she releases me. Now that it's just the two of us, I expect her to tell me how much she misses me and that I don't come around enough, twisting the knife of guilt deeper, but she doesn't. Instead, she looks at me, her warm cognac eyes penetrating to my soul. Feeling a bit unnerved, I turn my eyes to Theo.

"How is he? Any updates?"

Margaret squeezes my hand and then wraps her arm around me. "The doctor said he'll be just fine. They had to place a stent to open an artery, but he won't need bypass surgery, at least not in the foreseeable future."

Oh, thank God. The relief at hearing this news allows me to relax into Margaret's embrace.

We sit in companionable silence, watching as Theo's chest moves up and down with each blessed oxygen-assisted breath he takes. I'm glad he doesn't have to breathe in the chemically tainted hospital air. The slight sting of bleach and disinfectant invades my nostrils with each inhale.

Margaret continues to hold my hand as I rest my head on her shoulder, enjoying the familiar comfort only she can bring. It takes me back to my sophomore year of college.

My family always spent Thanksgiving skiing in Colorado—it was a tradition that dated back to before I could walk. But as Thanksgiving approached, so did finals. I was panicking over my economics final; my professor was impossible, and there was a true possibility this class would blemish my GPA. Getting a poor grade in the class would, in my twenty-year-old brain, make it impossible for me to get into a top business school, which would subsequently result in me never landing a job and winding up homeless, my life effectively ruined by one class in undergrad. Overly dramatic, I know.

I was discussing my current grade with the professor when his gorgeous TA, Alexander, overheard and offered to help me study over the holiday break. I would miss out on skiing, but I'd be preparing for my final exam with one of the most gorgeous men I'd ever laid eyes on. It was a no-brainer. My decision to stay on campus over the break ended up being the best decision of my life … and the worst mistake I've ever made.

The evening of Thanksgiving, I spoke with my parents

before they left for dinner. Both were in good spirits, even though there was a slight damper to the energy as we were missing not being together. My mom swore she understood, but it didn't mean she and my dad weren't disappointed I wasn't there. I promised to make up for my absence over winter break, when we would have two weeks together. We said our goodbyes and planned to speak again the following evening, after they were finished skiing.

Campus was deserted. My friends were with their families for the Thanksgiving break, so I ended up having an impromptu dinner with the cute TA turned econ tutor. We ate at a French restaurant catering to those of us who were displaced for the holiday. The dinner lasted hours, both of us learning about the other. I had laughed until my stomach muscles were sore. The evening ended with Alexander walking me to my door and, to my disappointment, giving me a kiss on the cheek goodbye. I remember thinking perhaps he thought I was too young for him and went to bed feeling slightly dejected.

The next morning, I was awoken by my doorbell. Anticipation filled my stomach with butterflies. Had Alexander come back to rectify his mistake from the night before? I threw on my robe and ran to my bathroom to brush my teeth and throw my hair up in a messy bun. I was opening the front door in under two minutes. I remember jumping back in surprise when I saw Margaret and Theo standing in my apartment doorway. From their expressions, I instantly knew two things were certain: something horrible had happened, and whatever it was would irrevocably alter my world.

I'll forever remember the look on Theo's face; he was entirely gutted. His eyes, normally so warm and expressive, were simultaneously tortured yet empty. Margaret told me we needed to talk and led me to the living room. Theo followed behind. I sat on my couch in a daze, my heartbeat blocking out all other noise.

Margaret sat next to me and clasped my hand as Theo explained that my parents hadn't made it home from dinner the night before. A large delivery truck lost control on black ice and plowed into their SUV as they were driving back up the mountain after dinner in town. I was told there wasn't anything either vehicle could have done differently to prevent the catastrophe. Neither of my parents survived.

My world fractured into a million pieces. At the time, I truly thought I would never experience a pain so acute, so numbingly severe, again. I was so very wrong.

Luckily, I had the Murphys, Ben and eventually Alexander. They were the sparks of light that guided me through that very dark time in my life.

Margaret sighs, bringing me back to the present. "I don't think you've allowed me to comfort you since you were in college."

I smile in response. "I was just thinking the same thing, and yet I should be the one comforting you." I motion toward Theo's form in the bed. "I wouldn't have survived that first year without you and Uncle Theo, and now …" My throat closes as unshed tears prevent me from finishing the sentence.

Margaret squeezes my hand. "You would have been just fine, you always are. But know we love you and want to be there for you, just as much now as then."

Warmth spreads throughout my chest. Another layer of ice melting. "Thank you, you don't know how much that means to me."

The vise around my throat tightens as tears gather at the corner of my eyes. Taking a deep breath, I look up toward the ceiling, willing the tears back. *The last thing Margaret needs is for me to lose it when she needs me most.* I start reciting the Pledge of Allegiance in my head, a surprisingly effective tactic for getting your thoughts out of a grief spiral. My throat begins to relax as my emotions recede back into their bottle.

With my eyes still turned toward the ceiling, tears clearing, I notice a small black square. What the … I stare at the object as my mind pieces together whether or not it is what I think it is. My wet eyes forgotten, I stand and carry the chair I was sitting on to the foot of Theo's bed.

Margaret's expression morphs from confusion to alarm, no doubt thinking I've officially lost my mind. "Elle? What's wrong, dear?"

I don't reply, too focused on my task. I climb onto the chair and stand on the tips of my toes, reaching up to grab the small black square. I stretch but it's still over a foot away. I'm scanning the room for a taller chair to stand on when Theo's nurse walks in. She looks up at me and freezes, her expression a mixture of confusion and trepidation. I can't eloquently explain what she walked in on, so I simply point at the black square. "I need a ladder."

Five minutes later, Margaret, the nurse who introduced herself as Julie, and a middle-aged hospital maintenance worker join me as I stare at the small black eye now laying on Julie's cart.

Ted, the hospital maintenance worker, scratches the gray scruff of a beard on his chin. "What is it?"

Not knowing how much to say, I remain quiet. I

already texted Nik, who is on his way. He'll be able to play interference.

Margaret's face pinches in confusion. "This looks like the security cameras we have at home, but a smaller version." She looks up in alarm. "Is that what this is? Why would a surveillance camera be in Theo's room?"

Margaret is a smart woman, but I don't want to confirm her suspicions. She has enough to worry about without adding this to the list. Theo's nurse, standing beside Margaret, begins to shift from one foot to the other, clearly uncomfortable with what is unfolding in front of her.

I look at my watch; Nik should be here in sixteen minutes. "Margaret, I'm sure there's an explanation. Who knows if the device is even picking up a feed? It's wireless, which means it would have to be charged. If this is a camera, it could've been used when someone else was in this room and left behind when they were discharged. Maybe the prior patient's family members were unable to be with them and wanted to keep watch."

Margaret visibly relaxes. "I suppose that would make sense." She pats my hand before returning to the chair she vacated, a look of unease on her face as she resumes her vigil.

I don't blame her. My suspicion remains as well—I saw the small blue indicator light prior to it going dark. The device was on when we first removed the camera, but the light no longer glows. I look at my watch. Thirteen minutes.

Nurse Julie moves to stand next to me as we both inspect the device. "I think I should call my supervisor; she'll want to alert hospital administration."

Shit, the last thing I need is for the hospital to try

to make this all disappear before I can have the evidence analyzed.

"I understand, Julie, but I really don't think that's necessary. This device, whatever it is, could have been here for months for all we know. I'm not sure it would be wise to alert anyone now. Especially while Theodore Murphy is occupying this room. Can you imagine the negative press the hospital would receive if this leaked? I would hate for you to be in the middle of a public relations nightmare just because the device was discovered on your watch. That's not fair to you."

Julie's expression shifts to understanding as she processes the ramifications if this were to get out. Understanding turns to resolve—Julie would make a terrible poker player—before she responds, "Yes, you're right, this could have been here for ages."

Neither of us believe it, but it has bought me more time. I look down, seven minutes. I need to get Julie and Ted out of the room.

"Well, now that the show is over, can you please return the ladder, Ted? And Julie, would you mind getting some water for Mrs. Murphy? I think all of this is taking a toll on her."

Ted and Julie move to complete their tasks. The beauty of dealing with an unknown situation is there's no prescribed method of how it should be handled. No indication of what is socially acceptable, which lends to people responding well to direction.

Ted follows Julie out of the room, the ladder slung over his shoulder, and I release a breath as I turn to see Margaret once again clutching Theo's hand.

"Margaret, you've been in here for hours, why don't

we grab a coffee. I saw a Starbucks downstairs." Margaret looks at Theo and purses her lips. It's obvious she's about to object. "It will be good for us both to stretch our legs, and coffee will help us stay awake."

Margaret's eyes remain on Theo as she answers. "That might be a good idea, the doctor said he most likely won't wake again for a few hours, and I would like to be alert when he does."

"Coffee it is, then. Let's head down now so we can get you back to Theo."

Margaret stands, wobbling for a moment before regaining her balance to walk to the door. When it's clear she has her footing, I breathe a sigh of relief and follow her out of the room, quickly typing Nik a message on my way out the door.

FOUR

SUNLIGHT FILTERS THROUGH THE CAR WINDOW AS Nik battles the congested Manhattan street, finding a rare opening to pull the car over to the curb. I look up at the steel and glass building we are idling in front of as Nik steps out of the car and walks around to open my door.

I much prefer to drive myself, but Nik was adamant about driving today. Along with Ben, he has been my saving grace these past months, so I find it difficult to argue with him. Besides, the drive over provided the perfect opportunity to update each other on the shit-show that was yesterday, since I slept the majority of the drive home from the hospital last night.

Nik explained that he arrived at the hospital shortly after I sent him the message letting him know the room was clear and the device was on a cart at the foot of Theo's bed. Luckily, he was able to grab the camera, which is currently with our tech team, before nurse Julie returned. The team hasn't been able to trace the source of the camera, but with a group of geniuses from MIT, I'm confident they will.

Nik opens my door. "I'll be here when you're finished."

Climbing out of the car, I surprise us both when I pull

him in for a hug. "Thank you for everything. I honestly don't know what I would do without you."

Nik pats my back as he clears his throat, absurdly uncomfortable with my show of affection. "Say nothing of it."

I squeeze harder in response. "Seriously, Nik, I know you could work anywhere with your background, and I realize your job has been far less exciting these past few months, but I'd be lost without you."

Nik releases the hug but keeps one hand on my shoulder. "When I started working for you and … uh, Mr. Tate," he adds delicately before continuing, "I promised to do everything in my power to protect you both, and that hasn't changed. If anything, that promise is truer today than when I made it six years ago."

Unbidden tears burn the back of my eyes. "Thank you, Nik. I hope you know we always considered you family, and that hasn't changed."

"Which is why I continue to work for you, even if it is boring."

I smile at Nik's attempt to mask that he cares. "Those may be the kindest words you've ever said to me, Nik. Be careful, I may start to think you care."

Nik smirks at my response. "Aren't you going to be late for your appointment?"

Giving him one last squeeze, I say, "Thank you, Nik. Truly. I'll be out in an hour," before I turn and begin to walk toward the building. I'm almost to the door when movement near the landscaped area in front of the building catches my eye.

I stop mid-step to watch a hummingbird dart from flower to flower, its movements so fast I can hardly follow with my eyes. I smile as the animated little bird brings forth a memory of my mother from so long ago.

I was around eight or nine years old and cherished the moments with my mom when it was just the two of us. It was a gorgeous day, the sun warming our bodies while a light breeze provided the ideal temperature. Not too hot, not too cold. The smell of honeysuckle was in the air as we snacked on dainty sandwiches and sipped sparkling lemonade. Our legs stretched out on a large blanket covering a portion of the lawn as we picnicked in the backyard.

We were laughing about something, though I don't recall what, when my mom excitedly pointed toward a swath of trees near where we were lounging. "Look, Eliana, right over there. Do you see the bird?"

I sat up as my eyes searched the area she was pointing toward. Sure enough, a colorful bird seemed to be floating in the air as it sucked from a flower. I was transfixed.

My mom's beautiful smile grew. "That's a hummingbird. It's incredibly rare to see this type of bird in New York."

I looked at her, eyes wide, fascinated we were witnessing something so special. "It's beautiful. Why is it here?" I had whispered in awe, not wanting to break the spell of the moment.

My mom smiled and lowered her voice, too, as if she were about to tell me a very important secret. "I think it's here as a sign."

My eyes widened in surprise, I was very much into Nancy Drew books at this age and loved any sort of mystery.

"What kind of sign?" I asked excitedly.

"Well," my mom started conspiratorially, "hummingbirds are a symbol of joy, love and healing, so I think this little friend is here to remind us of the joy we are experiencing in this moment and that we shouldn't take it for granted, the immense love I have for you—" I interrupted her to repeat a mantra we so often shared, "From here to eternity?"

My mother's warm smile grew. "From here to eternity, always."

We were silent for a moment as we watched the little bird dart about until my curiosity overtook my fascination with the tiny bird with invisible wings. "What about healing?"

My mom looked back at me, her expression sobering. "The most important of the three. Always remember to seek out the beauty in life, Eliana. Particularly when you feel as though there is none. Seek out the little hummingbirds, they will remind you that though you may be small, you are the strongest, most capable person I know. And no matter how badly you may be hurting, it will pass, and you will heal, and I will be with you. I will always be with you." My mom scooted over to me and placed her palm just under my collarbone, over my heart. "I'll be right here, always."

The gravity of my mother's words that day often come back to me when I need them most. That little girl had no idea what those words would come to mean over the years. She didn't know she would lean so heavily on that talisman, the omnipresent belief providing solace and comfort during her darkest hours. But she would quickly learn.

At the time, I felt pride and comfort at my mother's words, but also confusion. What did she mean she would be with me even when she's not? Why wouldn't she be with me? And why would I be hurting? Oh, to go back to that naïveté.

I look up at the clear, blue sky and smile before touching my palm to my chest. "From here to eternity," leaves my mouth on a breath before I drop my hand and continue into the building.

* * *

The elevator doors open on the thirty-sixth floor. I step out and walk the short distance down the hall, my heels sinking into the plush cream carpet with every step I take. How they are able keep the floor so clean is beyond me. Cream carpet in the hall of a public building is either risky, or a large middle finger to those paying the exorbitant fees to allow such foolishness, myself included.

I find myself in front of the familiar name placard and open the door to Dr. Wickham's office. I say hello to the receptionist before taking a seat in an uncomfortable leather chair to wait. I hate waiting rooms. The silent anticipation of your name being called while you're forced to sit and, well, wait. And wait. And wait some more. I don't think people are necessarily averse to being seen by a doctor, but rather suffering through the waiting room prior to their appointment. The requirement that you sit silently and wait for someone else to fix your problem, because that's your only option if you want your problem to be fixed. Whatever happened to house calls?

Dr. Wickham opens the door to his office, interrupting my internal monologue.

"Elle, please come in."

I jump up and am nearly through the doorway before he can finish his sentence. Walking to the arranged furniture in front of his desk I take my usual chair, which is thankfully far more comfortable than the furniture in the reception area.

Dr. Wickham sits opposite me, crossing one leg over the other. "Let's begin with what happened."

I lift my eyebrow. "What do you mean?"

He taps his iPad. "You phoned my cell at 6 a.m. this morning insisting I squeeze you in, which leads me to assume something happened. Am I incorrect?"

I take a deep breath; this is more difficult than I thought it would be. I brace myself for his reaction, knowing how crazy I'm about to sound. Eyeing the office door, I contemplate walking back to the car. The thought of ignoring this is quite appealing. It's not like I haven't become pretty good at the artful practice of denial.

Sighing, I remind myself that although the idea of ignoring my potential psychosis sounds appealing, the point of this appointment is to get help before I completely lose my grip on reality.

Squaring my shoulders, I take a cleansing breath and look the doctor in the eye. "I think I could be losing my mind."

To his credit, Dr. Wickham doesn't flinch. His expression remains inquisitive and without judgment. "Elle, I can assure you, you are not losing your mind."

"I'm being serious, something did happen and I'm …" I look toward the ceiling as I try to find the right words to express how I'm feeling. "I'm worried I may be on the verge of falling off the precipice I am currently balancing on."

Dr. Wickham maintains his composure when he responds. "I see. Let's start with what has you so worried."

I take another deep breath. "I know how this is going to sound, but …"

Ugh, just rip off the Band-Aid already! "I think I

smelled Alex last night." The sentence is a stream of consciousness, leaving my mouth as one jumbled word.

I wait for Dr. Wickham's reaction as he tilts his head considering what I just said. "Tell me what led up to this. Were you at home? Did something trigger you to remember his scent?"

I think back to yesterday—it already feels like ages ago. "No, I wasn't at home, and nothing could have triggered a memory beforehand because I was sleeping. In fact, it was his scent that woke me."

Dr. Wickham taps notes on his iPad before looking up. "You weren't at home, but you were sleeping?" He lifts one brow quizzically as if to say *this is getting interesting*.

Shaking my head, I reply, "It's a long story."

He smiles. "Well, we have an hour."

I describe the events from yesterday, explaining the meeting that led to Theo's health scare and the subsequent trip to the hospital.

Dr. Wickham continues tapping on his device. "Yesterday was stressful. How are you feeling now?"

Taking a moment to consider his question, I respond, "I feel better today. I spoke with Margaret this morning and Theo's health has improved. He may be able to go home today or tomorrow."

Dr. Wickham clears his throat and gives me a pointed look.

"Fine." I close my eyes and consciously assess how I'm feeling as I attempt to assign words to my emotions. This is an exercise the good doctor prescribes during each of our sessions. Not wanting to waste any more time, I open my eyes. "The predominant emotion is relief. But I also feel ..."

Dr. Wickham waits a full minute before prompting me, "You also feel what, Elle?"

"I'm anxious, nervous. Why am I smelling my dead husband in an empty hospital waiting room?" Damn waiting rooms, I wonder if it's possible to never enter one again.

I hesitate, knowing I need to voice my greatest fear, but not wanting to say it out loud. I lower my eyes, breaking eye contact with Dr. Wickham when I say, "I'm scared I'm breaking."

Dr. Wickham leans back in his chair. "I understand how smelling a scent you associate with Alexander would be disconcerting, but there could be a number of explanations. Perhaps someone entered the room wearing the same cologne he wore, subconsciously triggering a memory that woke you. Or perhaps you were still in a dream-like state when you first woke. The one thing I can tell you after meeting weekly for the past several months is you are mentally sound. The fact that you were concerned enough to contact me first thing this morning proves that."

His logic makes sense, but I know it couldn't have been someone else wearing the same cologne, because his scent was a mixture that didn't come from a Tom Ford bottle alone. But I suppose I could have been half-asleep, my subconscious creating a comforting scent after the stress of the day. I nod my head. "Thank you, Dr. Wickham. Upon consciously assessing my feelings in this moment, I can assure you that your professional opinion makes me feel much better."

Dr. Wickham smiles at my use of his favorite terms. "Fantastic, then I surmise the feeling for today is relief, both for Theo's improved health and for not losing your mind, as you put it."

I roll my eyes. The bulk of our sessions have focused on me accessing emotions to *feel* again. The death of Alex left me numb. My world disintegrated to muted black and white, leaving me apathetic to everyone and everything. I simply no longer cared. About anything. I was angry the three people I loved most deeply had been senselessly taken from me. First my parents, and then my husband. Therapy has helped to pull me out of my state of self-pity and has allowed me to begin to function again by focusing on what's important today: my firm, Tate, Inc., and all those who are still in my life.

Dr. Wickham leans forward and clears his throat before speaking. "Elle, you are making excellent progress. The fact that you are not only feeling emotions but are conscious of their source is leaps and bounds from where you were in September. As I said, I can assure you that you are not on the cusp of a psychotic break, but it appears you are facing a tremendous amount of stress and I don't want your progress to stall. You were right to call me, and I want you to do so whenever you feel things are just too much."

I nod my head in understanding.

"I also want you to make an effort where Ben and Nik are concerned. Do not allow yourself to push them away, you need them both right now."

Nodding again, I reply, "Now that I'm back to the land of the living, Ben is an annoyingly constant presence, and Nik has resumed his typical fretting. Even if I wanted to avoid them, it would be impossible."

Dr. Wickham fights a grin as the corner of his eyes wrinkle. "Good, I am pleased to hear that. You should also make an effort to spend time with the Murphys. As your only family, I know how much they mean to you."

Now it's my turn to fight a smile. "We have dinner plans as soon as Theo is back home and things return to normal for them."

Dr. Wickham stops fighting his smile. "Well then, my job here is done."

I barely contain my outburst of laughter … if only.

* * *

Feeling energized from my appointment now that I have expert confirmation that I don't need to be admitted to a psych ward, I exit the elevator and quicken my steps toward the lobby doors, anxious to get on with my day. My eyes are downcast in thought, causing me to nearly miss the sight of Nik, his back slightly turned as he talks on his phone. I check my watch to make sure I'm not late. I'm actually five minutes early since Dr. Wickham deemed me sane—at least for the day.

As I get closer to Nik, I hear his gruff voice end the call he's on. "I understand, sir. Consider it done." My feet freeze mid-step as my breath catches. I'm transported to nine months ago.

Rain was pouring down in sheets, causing us to jump over streams of water as we ran to a waiting SUV. I can still feel Nik's large hand at my back, his body shielding me as he held an umbrella over my head. Scott, one of Nik's employees, opened the car door and I threw myself into the backseat, sliding across to make room for Nik as he settled in beside me. I remember thinking it odd because Nik, the security control-freak that he is, normally drove. Scott took the front passenger seat. That's when I noticed the driver was someone I had never seen before. He put the SUV into drive and peeled away from the curb.

"What's going on, Nik?" I asked, my voice tight with anxiety.

Nik was looking down at his phone, the screen illuminated with an incoming call. He held up a finger. "I'll explain everything, but I have to take this first."

Nik answered with, "I'm here." Followed by a pause, "Yes, she's with me." And then a longer pause as the person on the other end of the line spoke.

"I understand, sir. Consider it done."

Nik turns, noticing me standing behind him. "Mrs. Tate, how was your appointment?"

I continue to stare, stunned into silence after revisiting the memory from the night I make a point to never think about. I can't bring myself to respond as everything plays out on repeat in my mind.

Nik puts his hand on my shoulder. "Mrs. Tate, are you well? You look quite pale."

I shake my head to dissipate my stupor. "Who was on the phone just now?"

Nik looks down, breaking eye contact, and begins to usher me toward the doors. I dig my heels in, not about to let him off the hook. "Nik?"

His voice lowers, "It was just someone on my team."

"And you now refer to members of your team as sir?" I ask incredulously.

"For this member, yes." Nik resumes his efforts to corral me to the door.

"Fine, play your games, but I don't buy it," I say as I quicken my steps, needing space from him.

Stepping out of the building and into the midday sun, I feel Nik close the distance between us. I narrow my eyes at him when I feel his body heat at my side, but he doesn't notice, his focus consumed with scanning the area around us as we walk to the car parked at a loading zone in front of the building. What the hell is going on?

"What's going on, Nik?"

"Nothing, I just saw someone loitering earlier who got my attention. I thought I would meet you inside instead of waiting in the car."

Nik opens the car door and all but pushes me into the backseat before snapping the door closed. What the ... I scan the area but I don't see anything out of the ordinary. I watch people walk in and out of the building we just left. No one looks suspicious, but I can't shake the feeling of being watched. I study the area once more, focusing on faces, as Nik starts the car and pulls into traffic.

There's an expression of incredulity on my face reflected from the rearview mirror as I stare at the back of Nik's head. He's obviously keeping something from me. I'm about to start asking questions when Nik interrupts my thoughts.

"We were able to trace the camera. It was sold by an online electronics store to someone named Sam Smith. It was mailed to a post office box nearly a year ago, but the P.O. box is now registered to a couple who, further research deduced, are in their eighties. We were able to locate the prior registered user, but it was a gentleman who died over twenty years ago."

This piques my interest enough to momentarily let Nik off the hook of my inquisition. Turning my focus back to more pressing issues, I look out the window, contemplating who would have gone through the trouble of planting a camera in Theo's room, and even more importantly, why.

"Where do we go from here?"

Nik makes eye contact with me in the rearview mirror. "We are pulling video surveillance from the post office for the days following delivery of the camera to see if we can get a visual of whoever picked up the package. We haven't had any leads from the hospital surveillance feed. The only people seen entering and exiting Theo's room, aside from you and Margaret, were two nurses, three medical assistants, and one cardiologist. All have been verified as hospital employees."

"Are you looking into the hospital employees?"

"Of course, they are all being vetted. The employees who have been assessed so far have been cleared."

A growl of frustration leaves my throat. "Any other good news you'd like to share? Have you found anything on Richard Dorn yet?"

"As far as I can tell, Richard doesn't have anything on you. He's just playing games, but I did learn that in addition to being arrested for breaking and entering five years ago, he has had two restraining orders placed on him."

My back presses against the seat as I process what Nik just told me. The breaking and entering charge was in his background check, but not the restraining orders.

Nik grabs an envelope sitting on the passenger seat and passes it back to me. "There's more—Richard is highly leveraged right now. If one card falls, his entire house will crumble."

I remove the financial documents from the envelope and start reading. "Shit, this could be a major blow to TA."

"Yes, and they unfortunately don't know it yet. Richard

has been injecting cash from an unknown source, so their losses aren't obvious."

An unknown source—that can't be a coincidence. "Immunotech."

Nik nods in agreement. "I believe so. I asked Genevieve to look through the documents while you were in your appointment. Forensic accounting found a revenue stream from a shell corporation. The amount matches the past three quarters of capital expenditures for Immunotech."

My original suspicions are further validated: Richard is bank-rolling TA's portfolio with Immunotech's profit. "We have to keep this from Theo until his health has improved. He won't take it well."

Nik begins to respond when he's forced to slam on the brakes as a bicycle messenger darts in front of the car. The documents I wasn't holding slide off the seat and scatter on the floor. My heart pounds against my chest as I try to catch my breath.

"That guy has a death wish! Thank God you were paying attention." I reach down to collect the documents that are now covering the floor of the car when a deafening noise reverberates against the car window. I remain hunched over as I cover my head, expecting glass to rain down on me. When it doesn't, I look up in time to see a hammer slam into the window closest to me. A second loud bang reverberates through the car as a dark-suited arm reaches out to open my door.

"What the hell!"

Before I have time to react, Nik goes from driving Miss Daisy to Indy 500 as he pulls the car into oncoming traffic. "STAY DOWN!" he yells before he brakes, swinging the front of the car in the opposite direction so we are now moving with the flow of traffic. He somehow manages to connect an incoming call to the car via Bluetooth, answering in his typical detached way with, "Yes."

Nik's employee's voice comes across the car speakers. "We are in pursuit of the individual now. Stephens and Braho are following you to ensure safe delivery."

"Keep me posted, Scott. Notify me the moment you have him."

"Yes, sir."

The call ends. I'm still bent sideways on the seat to keep away from the window that was just assaulted, although now that I look at it, the glass doesn't show any damage.

"Nik, what the fuck is going on?"

Nik continues to weave around traffic as he ignores my question.

"I am not an idiot, Nik. I'm fully aware you are keeping things from me, and I have been incredibly patient because I trust you. However, I believe the time has now passed for withholding information. Someone just tried to break my window with a hammer. In addition to everything else the past two days, this is clearly not a coincidence!" I am out of breath from yelling by the time I finish.

Nik continues to weave around cars, turning on multiple side streets. "I understand but allow me to focus on getting you to a safe place. I will provide an explanation once you are secure."

I sit up in time to see Nik flip around another corner, causing my hip to press against the door. "I would prefer you to keep your head down until we get to your building."

"My building? I need to get to work, Nik. I've already pushed three meetings this morning so I could see Dr. Wickham."

"I'm sorry, there really is no other option. Your building is the safest place for you."

My head of security is delusional. "Why do I need to be in a safe place, Nik? And how in the hell is my home more secure than my office? There is far more security at Tate, Inc. than at home."

Nik sounds uncomfortable when he replies, "That's not entirely true."

I shake my head, unbelievable. "Then I suppose you have quite a bit to explain."

Nik's voice is hesitant when he replies, "Yes, I believe I do."

FIVE

I'M SNUGGLED INTO THE CORNER OF MY SECTIONAL couch, my feet pulled under me, as Nik paces the living room, his leather soles tapping the hardwood floor every time he steps over the area rug. This must be his cue to turn and pace in the opposite direction, because I only hear this tap once on each side of the twenty-foot rug. Stephens and Braho have set up post in my foyer, and I just learned multiple members of Nik's security team are stationed throughout the building. Nik continues to assure me this is the safest place in the city, though he hasn't divulged why there is a need for safety. I look at the floor-to-ceiling glass windows that make up the exterior walls of my home and question his reasoning.

Nik stops pacing and sits in one of the two oversized, brown leather club chairs facing the couch. Alex and I found the chairs in a tiny secondhand store in Florence. We were exhausted after a day of dodging millions of tourists and climbing what felt like thousands of steps in the cramped and claustrophobic staircase of the Duomo of Florence. We were walking back to our hotel when we came across a shop nestled in a cobblestoned alley. Chairs and large antique mirrors spilled out of the storefront, piquing our curiosity.

We were sticky with sweat from the sun beating down on us, and it felt like heaven to enter the air-conditioned space. We sat in luxurious comfort for nearly an hour, soaking in the musty, overcrowded store filled with treasures. The shop owner, a small Italian man with a large personality, finally forced us to purchase or vacate. We ended up paying more for shipping and delivery to New York than what we paid for the chairs, but it was well worth it.

Nik leans forward, interrupting my thoughts, and rests his elbows on his knees. His shoulders are stiff, his eyes creased with tension, and a vein is protruding out of the side of his forehead. It's odd and a bit unnerving to see Nik this tense. Aside from Alex, he's one of the most self-contained people I've ever known.

Nik takes a breath and holds it for a moment before speaking. "This is going to come as a surprise, but we have had increased security in the building for over two years now."

My eyes widen. What the actual fuck?

Nik continues, "Mr. Tate felt it was a necessary precaution while he began working on IXB."

I feel a twinge of irrational jealousy that Alex shared something this important with Nik and not me. Even though it makes sense for him to do so; IXB was a classified project that I knew little about. I was only aware that the Office of the Director of National Intelligence, otherwise known as ODNI, and the U.S. counter-terrorism task force were involved, which led me to assume it may have been on the more dangerous side of his usual research. But I didn't realize it was dangerous enough to warrant increased security at home.

"He didn't want to worry you, so the team had,

and continues to have, explicit instructions to remain inconspicuous."

I shake my head in annoyance. "Well, they've done an excellent job. I had no idea we had undercover security in the building." Shit, what else don't I know about? I've been in such a despondent state these past months, I haven't considered Alex's work outside of Immunotech, or whether projects have continued. "Do you know what happened to the IXB project?"

Nik's body tenses and he looks down for a moment before meeting my eyes. "I believe the CDC continued the project. How are you feeling after the incident in the car?"

My eyes narrow at his horrible attempt at deflection. "That wasn't the most obvious change of subject." Nik doesn't react, so in keeping with our new normal, I let it slide and instead consider his question. How do I feel … the hammer to the car window and Nik's subsequent stunt driving were certainly startling but learning about the increased security has me more on edge than the attack on the window. "You don't think this was a random incident, do you?"

Nik manages to look even more uncomfortable when he replies, "I don't know."

I take a moment to study my head of security. He may be a master poker player, but I can tell there's more he isn't telling me. "Nik, if we were targeted, I need to know. A targeted attack has far more implications than if this was simply someone with a vendetta against capitalism or something."

Nik clears his throat before responding. "Mrs. Tate, please let me worry about what happened today. The team is gathering information now and we will know the motivation and implications soon enough. In the meantime, we will keep you safe. You have enough to worry about with Mr. Murphy's health and Tate, Inc."

My eyes move to the skyline view over Nik's shoulder as I contemplate his words. He's right, of course, there are far more pressing concerns. The last thing I need is to add psycho window attacker to the list. But that doesn't stop a thought from percolating.

"Fine, but I don't think this was random, and I don't think *you* think this was random. There have been too many strange situations lately for this to not be connected." Richard Dorn's behavior, the camera in Theo's hospital room, increased security I was unaware of—there's no way each variable is independent.

Nik's shoulders relax for the first time since the car ride home. "You are correct, I don't believe these are isolated incidents. We will get to the bottom of this, but in the meantime, we'll be increasing your security. From now on, when you leave the building, you will be traveling with myself or Scott, and two additional security personnel will tail you, just as they did today."

"That reminds me, why did you have security tailing us today? And why were you waiting for me in the lobby instead of the car?" I can see that he's about to brush off the question, so I continue before he can answer, "The real reason, Nik."

Nik grunts in annoyance. "Please let this go, Mrs. Tate. There's no need to be concerned." My gaze pins Nik to the chair he's sitting in, causing him to reluctantly continue. "I received a tip that security should be heightened. I complied, and it turns out to have been the right move. We will continue with the same security measures, but it will not impact your daily activities."

"You received a tip … What does that mean exactly? A tip from whom? The team member you were supposedly speaking to on the phone today?"

Nik rubs his eyes, his annoyance turning into frustration. "Mrs. Tate, I need you to let me do my job and trust that I will disclose all pertinent information. For now, all you need to know is you will have security detail on you when you leave this building."

I shake my head, reflecting Nik's annoyance back to him. Unbelievable. It makes absolutely no sense for Nik to keep me in the dark, but I am quickly running out of the energy to fight him on this. And I certainly can't argue with increased security; as annoying as it will be to have someone following me, there is obviously a need. The relief I felt today when I learned that Nik's team was able to go after the hammer-wielding suit makes me bite my tongue. I wonder how long Nik's men have been following me? I think back to the five miles I ran three days ago. "Did someone on your team follow me while I ran in Central Park the other morning?"

Nik nods. "I trailed you…it worked out well, actually, I was able to get in a run while keeping you under surveillance."

I huff out a breath of a laugh. How in the hell have I not noticed people following me? "Perhaps we should coordinate our schedules to make this easier on everyone. I would rather us run together than have you following me without my knowledge. I'm dealing with enough craziness at the moment."

Nik grins sheepishly. "That would be convenient, Mrs. Tate, thank you."

I level my eyes. "I can be understanding when I am

kept in the loop. I would appreciate increased communication moving forward. I'd much rather be aware of potential threats than blindsided by a hammer connecting with a window I'm sitting next to."

Nik's expression tightens. "That's understandable. I will make sure you are aware of all necessary information."

An alert pings on my phone. I look down to see I have ten minutes until my next meeting. "I'll work from home today. I need to jump on a conference call in a few minutes, please update me as soon as you learn anything."

Nik stands. "Of course, Mrs. Tate." He walks back to the foyer as I contemplate whether I can go back to being the recluse I was just a couple of weeks ago. Crawling under the covers and blocking out life is becoming more appealing by the day.

* * *

I'm sitting at my desk when the heavy oak pocket doors to my home office are thrown open. Ben stands in the entrance, a bottle of wine in each hand. "Wine night!" he declares in a sing-song voice. I smile at the welcome sight of my best friend holding my favorite beverage. "I heard you had another boring day. Really, Elle, you need to find adventure in your life."

I roll my eyes but can't help the laughter that bubbles up. "You are a welcome sight. Let me just finish this email and I'm all yours."

It's Ben's turn to roll his eyes. "Elle, it's 8 o'clock at night on a FRIDAY, not to mention you were almost ABDUCTED today. Get your skinny ass out here and drink with me!"

My laughter builds at Ben's theatrics, the tension from the day already beginning to melt away. "I was not almost abducted, but you're right, I need a break from this computer screen. Why don't you open one of those bottles and choose a movie, and I'll be out in five?"

Ben turns to leave as he throws out, "If you're not in the living room in five minutes, I'm stealing your computer for the night."

I quickly finish my response to Genevieve, outlining the next steps in *Project Take Back Immunotech* so she is prepared for our Monday morning meeting. I grab my cell and am pushing my chair back when I see I received a text message from Margaret. I open the message and read that Theo has been released from the hospital and is now resting at home. The wave of relief I feel catches me off guard. I'm able to breathe easily for the first time since the meeting with Theo and Richard. I check the time and see that the text was sent three hours ago. I consider calling but don't want to disturb them. I type a response instead, letting Margaret know I will call tomorrow. Hitting send, I leave my office in search of Ben.

I find him lounging on the couch, his feet resting on the coffee table along with two glasses of red wine. An action movie starring The Rock, Ben's Hollywood crush, is playing on the large TV. I pause and take in the normality of the scene. Warmth fills my chest and I realize with a smile that I am actually *feeling* something. I can't remember the last time I actually felt something other than the constant drop in my stomach, as if it's the dead of winter and I'm on a rollercoaster that never ends. The warmth is so abnormal I can't place the feeling, even after attempting Dr. Wickham's exercise. I don't think it's happiness, not quite, but perhaps contentment … maybe?

Ben notices me watching and pats the cushion beside him. I walk over and settle next to him, burrowing into his side as his arm drapes over my shoulder. I breathe in his clean linen scent and allow myself to relax farther into him. It has been such a long time since I've been held—nine months, to be exact. I've missed it, even if this particular arm over my shoulder is an entirely different experience than when I was last held by Alex. My mind takes me back to that glorious morning so many months ago.

I was awoken by sunlight streaming through the window and kisses pressed to my shoulder. Alex's sexy, graveled morning voice sent a bolt directly to my lower stomach when he said, "Good morning, beautiful. How did you sleep?"

I stretched as I soaked in the moment. "Not nearly as well as how I'm waking up." A deep chuckle vibrated against my back as Alex's hand leisurely stroked my side. I attempted to roll over, but his hand moved to my hip to stop me. It was my turn to laugh. This man's favorite game was to get me so turned on that I lost my mind. He continued with the kisses, trailing the area under my ear.

My smile widened as I pressed back into him, discovering my husband was ahead of me in the *who can make who lose control first* game. Or did that make me ahead of him?

He continued his leisurely exploration from my hipbone to my ribs, his fingers pausing to trace circles around the tiny hummingbird tattoo resting on the side of my rib. Alex was with me when I got the tattoo following the death of my parents. He always showed reverence to the tiny tattoo knowing the importance of its symbolism. He brought his lips to the hummingbird before moving his fingers to my nipple. My back arched, pressing against him once again. I felt his arousal against me as he squeezed, and the bite of pain followed by pleasure went straight to my core, causing me to clench my legs together and squirm. He chuckled once again. "Patience, my love."

He rubbed the offended nipple and I nearly detonated. The man knew exactly what he was doing. I moaned as he moved to the next nipple and repeated the sharp squeeze. I no longer had control over my body as it pressed against him, my back to his front. I bit my tongue to keep from begging as mewls and moans escaped my lips against my volition.

Alex moved his hand lower and I mentally rejoiced: finally. I needed him in that moment more than I needed my next breath. My legs parted as his fingers circled my center. I was so close. "Fuck, Elle, you're drenched. Do you know how hot that is? Always so ready for me," he had said. His finger circled again and then entered, immediately curling to press against that magical spot. I was gone. Incoherent words and sounds poured out of me as I unabashedly pressed against his hand. Without warning, he flipped me to my back, the look of a man who was about to have water after a week in the Sahara on his face, and supported his weight above me. My walls were still clenching when he thrust inside me, causing the climax to continue.

We devoured each other, the energy between us magnetic. I became so lightheaded, I thought I might pass out from the overwhelming pleasure—from the overwhelming intensity of it all.

After my second orgasm, the roll of Alex's hips increased to a frenetic pace before he stilled and poured himself into me. Both of us were spent and boneless as we collapsed onto the bed, him rolling to the side and holding me as we drifted back to sleep.

"You okay, Elle? You look flushed." I look up to see Ben staring at me, a look of speculation on his face. I feel the warmth of embarrassment spread across my own face. What the hell is my problem, reliving sex memories while sitting with my best friend?

I clear my throat. "Um, yeah. I was just thinking about a lazy Sunday with Alex before, well, before everything. That was the last time I was held. This feels nice." Ben squeezes me into him, and I close my eyes, relishing the contact.

"You want to talk about today?"

The warmth in my chest evaporates. "Not really, but I know you won't stop bothering me until I do."

I can hear Ben's smile when he says, "You're right, so you might as well start talking."

Looking up at Ben, I say, "I really don't know what to make of the car situation. To be honest, I'm reeling more from the revelations that followed."

Ben creases his forehead. "What do mean? What revelations?"

"It was odd. When I left my appointment with Dr. Wickham, I found Nik waiting for me in the lobby."

Ben interrupts with, "Why is that odd? I've been with you when he has met us inside a building instead of waiting in the car."

"If you would let me continue, I'll explain."

"By all means."

Rolling my eyes at Ben, I continue to explain. "Nik was on the phone with his back turned, so he didn't see me. The odd part was I overheard him call someone sir before hanging up. I've only ever heard him call Alex sir."

"Hmm, I guess that's unusual, but I'm sure it could be explained. I'm assuming there's more?"

"Of course, stop manterrupting me."

Ben lets out a belly laugh. "You did not just accuse me of manterrupting."

I wave his comment away. "After the window incident, Nik had us moving in the opposite direction with a tail of his own people within fifteen seconds. The reaction was too smooth, too orchestrated, for them not to have planned for something like this to happen. Nik admitted he has had increased security in this building for months."

Ben's eyes widen. "Months, why?"

"According to Nik, Alex felt extra security was necessary while he was working on a classified project for the government."

"And you didn't know."

It isn't a question; Ben can tell this is the crux of my unease. "Apparently he didn't want to worry me." I can't hide the hurt in my voice that he didn't tell me.

"Shiiiit…" Ben breathes out.

"Indeed."

We are both silent, each lost in our thoughts. Well, at least I am. Ben may be in a trance staring at The Rock, who is currently shirtless on the screen. Ben adjusts me as he leans forward to grab our wine glasses, handing one to me. "Cheers to overprotective husbands—at least I don't have to worry about you while you're at home."

I laugh and touch my glass to his. "And Jax won't have to worry about you when you visit." Ben winks and we settle back with our wine. In the mood to forget about everything for the night, I drain half the glass before resting my head against the couch cushion to watch the movie.

* * *

I wake with a kink in my neck and cotton in my mouth. The human pillow under my head is moving up and down in time with his breathing. Ben is leaning heavily to his left, his head at a precarious angle. I cringe when I think of the stiff neck he will be waking with. I move my head from one shoulder to the next to stretch my own neck and rise to take our empty wine glasses to the kitchen. Lumbering to the sink, I rinse the dark purple residue already staining the bottom of the glasses before stumbling back to the living room, still half-asleep, to adjust Ben's legs so they are now on the couch. I place a pillow under his head and cover him with a throw blanket. He looks so peaceful in sleep, I'm momentarily taken back to our sleepovers in middle school, when we would rent scary movies and load up on pizza, soda, and candy, bingeing on sugar and suspense. Our sleepovers became less frequent in high school, primarily reserved for those nights when Ben needed to get away from his family, but picked up again in college, becoming my saving grace when I was mourning my parents' deaths. Ben recently told me he stayed the night after Alex's death, but I don't remember. I was sequestered to my room and nearly dead myself. Looking at Ben now, I'm struck by how lucky I am to have him in my life. I lean down and kiss his forehead, whispering goodnight before shuffling to my room.

Eyeing my bed, every ounce of me wants to crawl under the covers and go back to sleep. I reluctantly continue to the bathroom to wash my face and brush my teeth, even if it is officially Saturday morning and I will be waking in a few hours. I complete my pre-bed ritual before finally—blessedly—melting into the covers. It's then I realize I thought of this bed as *my* bed and not *our* bed. My breaths become shallow as the weight of reality presses down on my chest. Too exhausted to participate in a grief spiral, I close my eyes and allow sleep to pull me under.

I dream about Alex. He's standing over the bed whispering something, but I can't make out the words. I can sense his face getting closer and try to talk, but I can't. I want to beg him not to leave me, but I'm unable to make a sound. Frustrated, I try to scream, but I'm mute as I feel his lips on my forehead. It's one of those dreams when you suspect you are dreaming but can't wake. Worse yet, you can't control the dream. My frustration mounts.

And then he's gone.

And my heart shatters into a million pieces.

How many times can one person's heart be pulverized? Tendrils of loss curl around my recently mended heart and rip the seams.

I need to wake up. I need to escape this nightmare. The weight on my chest gets heavier until I once again attempt to scream out in despair.

It's in this moment of helplessness that I feel an instant balm blanketing the terror. I turn my head to see Alex lying on his side of the bed. My prior hysteria dissipates as my nightmare becomes a dream I wish to never wake from.

All has righted itself in my world as the pressure on my chest lifts and I drift into a deeper sleep. No more dreams, just bliss as I reach for his hand. Our fingers twine together, and it's as if the nightmare never happened. Peace and contentment fill my soul and I bask in the moment. Dream Alex pulls me closer and I snuggle into him. Inhaling deeply, I take in the scent I'm most addicted to and pray I never wake from this dream.

* * *

My head shoots off my pillow as I gasp awake. My eyes squint against the sunlight streaming through the windows. I could have sworn I closed the blackout shades yesterday. I'm rubbing sleep from my eyes when I hear my cell phone vibrating on my bedside table. Grabbing my phone, I see *Margaret* on the screen.

I attempt to clear my throat before answering. "Margaret, good morning!"

"Elle, I'm so sorry, did I wake you?"

"No, no just a long night. Ben and I had one glass of wine too many."

Margaret chuckles in response before jumping to the point of her call, which is to invite Ben and me to dinner. She explains that Luca, a family friend who happens to be an amazing chef, will be in town and would like to treat us all to a meal.

"Luca will be preparing your favorite, so bring your appetite. You know there will be enough cacio e pepe to feed the entire neighborhood."

My stomach growls in response. "I'm looking forward to it.

"Okay, sweet girl, see you and Ben next Friday."

I hit end and lie back on my pillow, exhausted. What a horrible night of sleep. My stomach drops when I recall my nightmare—still so vivid. Rolling onto my side, I stare at the window on the opposite side of the room. I think about the turmoil of not being able to speak in my dream, of having everything my soul desires on a fundamental level so close, yet not being able to grasp it. I may have to start taking sleeping pills if this continues. My eyes move from the window to Alex's side of the bed. Empty, just like my heart.

My eyes fall to his pillow. What the hell? I shoot up in bed and stare. Not trusting my sight, I run a hand over the pillow. The cotton is cold to the touch as my hand dips down to follow the outline of an indentation. Why is there an imprint in the same pillow that was fluffed yesterday when the bed was made?

Jumping out of bed, I run down the hall, realizing too late that I'm in one of Alex's old T-shirts that barely covers my ass. Hopefully security isn't inside the condo yet. I enter the living room and find Ben in the exact same spot I left him last night. I check the other rooms on the main floor before running upstairs to check the gym and guest rooms. Nothing in the condo looks out of place. Returning to the living room, I shake Ben's shoulder. He moans and rolls over.

"Ben, wake up. I have to ask you something."

Ben opens one eye and looks at me, "What?"

"Did you sleep in my bed last night?"

Both eyes pop open at my question, and Ben looks at me like I've just asked him to explain the Pythagorean theorem.

I rush to fill the silence, "I know you are obviously on the couch now, but did you lie down next me at any point last night?"

"What's going on, Elle?" Ben's alarm is evident in his voice.

"Just answer the question."

Ben sits up and begins to rub his neck. "I slept here the entire night. I must have fallen asleep during the movie."

"Yeah, you did. How's the neck?"

He stretches his neck, moving his head from one shoulder to the next. "I need a massage, but don't change the subject. Why did you ask me if I slept in your bed?"

I begin to pace. "I know how this is going to sound, but there's an indentation on Alex's pillow that wasn't there when I went to sleep." I hesitate, suddenly unsure. At least, I'm pretty sure it wasn't there.

Pausing my pacing, I wait for Ben's response. To his credit, he masks his skepticism fairly well, but it's clear he thinks I'm losing it.

I slash the air with my hand as if I'm striking this entire conversation. "You know what, never mind. I must have rolled to that side of the bed last night," I respond in the most nonchalant tone I can conjure.

Ben continues to stare at me. Now that I've said it out loud, I realize how ridiculous I sound. I hear him clear his throat, the moment getting more uncomfortable by the minute.

"Honestly, Ben. Pretend I didn't ask, I just had a crazy night of sleep. First a nightmare I couldn't wake from, and then a dream I never wanted to wake from."

Ben chuckles and I narrow my eyes before adding, "Not that kind of dream, pervert." I look down at what I'm wearing. "I'm going to shower and change before Nik or his cronies show up." I begin walking toward my room.

"Elle?"

Pausing, I squeeze my eyes shut and pray Ben will let this go. I paste on my most congenial smile and turn around.

"Can you try to hurry, doll? The car leaves in an hour."

"The car? Where are we going? Is there an appointment I don't know about?"

Ben smiles and sings, "Spaaaaa daaaaay!"

When I start to protest, he cuts me off, "We are going. I don't care if it's with you over my shoulder kicking and screaming."

I smile at the visual. Yeah, I could see Ben acting on that threat.

"Fine, but you're going to the Murphys' with me for dinner next Friday. Margaret called a few minutes ago to invite us, I already accepted on your behalf."

"Deal."

"Oh, and Luca's in town," I add with a wink.

Ben flashes a mischievous grin. "Is that wink in reference to the make-out session you had with Luca while we were in Amalfi?"

I can't help but laugh. I met Luca while I was spending the summer before my sophomore year of college in Italy. My parents and Ben met me in Positano where we spent a month at the Murphys' cliffside home overlooking the sea. Ben and I met and lusted after the same beautiful twenty-two-year-old Italian. He was already an up-and-coming chef in Rome, but was spending the summer at the Amalfi coast to further develop his craft by immersing himself in different Italian regions. Fortunate for me, he also helped develop my kissing expertise. It was a win for us both. Luca stayed with the Murphys several summers after that and became a surrogate part of the family. "No, the wink is not in reference to Luca's kissing skills, it's in reference to his sinful pasta."

Ben returns my wink with one of his own. "Mm-hmm, orgasmic pasta, we'll see. Now get your skinny ass in the shower so we can go." He grabs a throw pillow from the couch and launches it in my direction.

"You're one to talk, I don't see you getting ready. You would still be sleeping if I hadn't woken you."

Ben raises his hands in a truce. "I'm going, I'm going. Right after I make us coffee."

"That's why I love you."

"Yes, you love me for my coffee-making skills, I know. Now scoot or we won't make our 10 o'clock appointments, and I need to stop by my place on our way to grab a change of clothes."

I stop my retreat and pivot to face Ben. "You already booked appointments? Isn't that a bit presumptuous?"

"Nope. I already told you my plan had you said no."

"Abduction is not a plan, Ben. Which reminds me, I have security stalking my every move. I'm not sure if a spa day is on the list of approved activities."

"Not a problem, I'm declaring it is. Besides, I arranged the car through Nik when I booked our massages yesterday, so we're covered. Your security detail can stalk you at the spa if they so choose. Now for the last time, go get ready."

I turn before Ben can see my smile and speed-walk to my bathroom.

SIX

Ben's voice filters in from the other room. I look at the clock next to my bed; quarter after six. Perfect, we won't be late. After the whirlwind week I've had, I'm looking forward to a relaxing dinner and spending quality time with Theo and Margaret.

I grab my clutch and make my way toward the voices drifting out of the front room. Ben and Nik are in the kitchen discussing security for the evening. Gone are the days of jumping into a car and driving wherever I damn well please.

"Is security really necessary? We're just going to Theo and Margaret's house."

Nik turns to address me. "As I continue to explain, security is non-negotiable. You just need to decide if you want to know about it or not."

I clench my teeth—this is the seventh or eighth time we have had this conversation in the past week. "Fine. Who will be tailing us this evening?"

"I am driving the two of you, and Scott will follow."

Ben turns to me and adds, "I had planned to drive, but Nik would rather we ride with him. It makes sense; it's not like I have a hammer-proof car."

Narrowing my eyes at Ben, I reply, "Very funny. I don't

care who drives as long as we leave in the next …" I look at my watch, "three minutes."

Nik grunts out a response as he walks toward the elevator. Ben and I share a conspiratorial smirk, knowing our antics are thoroughly annoying him. Ben loops his arm through mine, and we follow, stopping at my wine rack on the way out the door to grab a bottle of Barolo. The three of us enter the elevator and Nik presses the button for the lobby.

I raise a brow.

"Scott has the car waiting for us out front, there's no need for us to go to the garage."

Ben looks down at me and smirks as if to say *see, it's convenient to have security escort us everywhere.* I raise a brow in response. His joy at my expense is very quickly getting old.

As we walk through the lobby, I scan the faces we pass, wondering who is employed by the homeowners' association and who works for Nik. The concierge manager gives Nik a slight nod that wouldn't have been noticed had I not been looking for it. Okay, one identified. We make it to the car without incident, which I consider a success, all things considered. Ben and I settle into the backseat and are still trying to buckle our seat belts when Nik pulls into traffic, quickly moving to the inside lane.

"Nik, would you mind stopping at a Duane Reade on the way? I need to pick up something."

"Sure thing, Mrs. Tate. I'll have Scott run in to grab whatever you need."

I exhale my annoyance; this is becoming ridiculous. As much as I appreciate Nik's security efforts, I am not a child. "Great. I need an extra-large box of tampons—can he manage that?"

Nik touches his earpiece, listening intently, before

answering, "Yes, but she's just trying to make a point." Nik's eyes meet mine in the rearview mirror, "What is it you really need, Mrs. Tate?"

They really are no fun. "Fine, I need Toblerone chocolate bars," I answer haughtily as I lean back to sulk in my seat. If I must be babysat, I might as well act like a child. I add an eye roll to further demonstrate my adolescent behavior.

After a quick stop for Scott to run my errand, returning with chocolate and a giant box of tampons, proving he may have a sense of humor after all, we pull through the Murphys' gate. Ben has vastly improved my mood during the drive and I'm actually laughing by the time we park and make our way to the front door, Barolo and Toblerone in hand. I'm pleasantly surprised when both Margaret and Theo great us. Theo looks much better now that he's out of the hospital—his color has returned, and he almost looks like his usual self, not the frail form I visited last week.

The three of us hug as a group, and emotion constricts my throat as I take a moment to breathe the two of them in—to appreciate that Theo is standing in his home and not lying in a hospital bed. The stark realization that we so easily could have lost him, that this moment may not have been possible, is a punch to the stomach. I squeeze Theo and Margaret a little tighter.

Ben takes my place as we release our embrace and I blink back the moisture gathering in my eyes. Once everyone has hugged hello, I hand Margaret the wine we brought and give the Toblerone to Theo. His eyes light up and he lets out a boisterous laugh. He takes the chocolate and gives me a one-armed hug as we all walk into the house. Looking up at Theo, I can't help but smile; he looks like a boy on Christmas Day.

Ben slings an arm over my other shoulder and we all make our way from the foyer into the great room. My two favorite men on either side of me.

The delicious aroma of pasta sauce permeates the air, making my mouth water. A fire is lit in the large hearth, casting a warm glow throughout the room, and I feel a blanket of comfort settle over me. I love that there is almost always a fire burning in this room, even on this June evening. It somehow makes the expansive space homey. For the first time since I became a widow, I feel peace. The blunt edges of grief are dulled for the moment as a feeling of belonging settles over me. I pause to soak in the moment.

Theo has made his way to the couch and is sitting with one leg crossed over the other, his face relaxed and ... happy. His eyes crinkle at the corners as he laughs at whatever Ben is regaling him and Margaret with. Margaret has her hand on Ben's arm to brace herself as she is doubled over in laughter, and Ben is in his element, dutifully making everyone so damn happy with his commentary. I feel myself smile, warmth spreading from my chest to my stomach. Theo catches me watching the group and pats the space next to him. I walk over and sit, leaning my head on his shoulder as I try to follow Ben's story. Theo puts his arm around my shoulder, and I am taken back to college for the second time in one week, first with Margaret and now Theo.

"Ciao, bella!" interrupts my thoughts and I look up to see my college crush, at least for one summer, standing at the entry to the great room. I can't help but admit time has been in the man's favor. He looks like an Italian model with a 5 o'clock shadow. I jump up and we meet halfway, greeting each other with a strong hug—he was always a great hugger—and kisses for each cheek. He holds me at arm's length and mutters "Bellissima" under his breath.

I feel a blush rise to my cheeks. "Luca, you look wonderful." I step away to allow Ben room to greet him. After the two men hug, Luca announces that dinner is ready and places a hand on the small of my back as we follow the group to the dining room. I'm distracted by the heat from his hand, so it takes me a moment to notice he has moved into my personal space before he whispers, "I made cacio e pepe just for you," in my ear.

A shiver of unease travels up my spine at his too-close proximity. "Luca, it smells delicious. I've been waiting years to eat your pasta again." I don't disclose that aside from spending time with Theo and Margaret, Luca's cacio e pepe is the primary reason I agreed to dinner. True to the nature of a chef, Luca has a healthy ego; the last thing he needs is for me to inflate it further.

We enter the dining room, Theo making his way to his customary seat at the head of the table, his arm over Margaret's shoulder. I end up next to Luca with Margaret and Ben sitting across from us. The Murphys' staff immediately begin pouring wine and setting arugula salad in front of each plate.

Theo lifts his glass. "To old friends, aged wine, and most importantly, family." We echo with *salute* and quickly fall into pleasant conversation.

Luca immediately turns toward me. "How have you been, Eliana?" I can hear a twinge of concern but not pity, and for that I am grateful.

I turn toward Luca as I reply, "I've been managing, thank you for asking."

Luca smiles, the corner of his eyes creasing as he does.

"If anyone can manage life after the year you have had, it would be you."

I return Luca's smile and am about to respond when Theo interrupts the chatter by clearing his throat. "Eliana, there is something we need to discuss."

The table becomes silent at the gravity of Theo's tone. After a pregnant pause, he continues, "I have had a lot of time to think these past few days and, following our meeting last week, I believe it's imperative for you to regain control of Immunotech."

I inhale sharply, nearly choking on the wine I just sipped. To say Theo's words have taken me by surprise is an understatement. After all, it is TA Holdings, Theo's company, that I'm trying to regain control of Immunotech from.

Theo continues, "I don't trust Richard, and frankly, his behavior during our meeting was ... well, let's just say he is a liability. He's too desperate to keep Immunotech in his clutches, and desperation leads to poor choices."

Theo pauses as he looks into the distance, lost in thought, before continuing, "He either has a secondary motivation, outside of professional interest, or there is more going on than we know."

My eyes widen at Theo's admittance of what my team had already deduced. Ben wipes his mouth with his napkin before speaking. "I agree with you, Theo. Richard is oozing desperation, which is why we are in the middle of investigating him. I have to tell you, the more we uncover about this guy, the more I dislike him."

I make eye contact with Ben. Shooting darts with my eyes, I shake my head, silently communicating to drop the Richard Dorn conversation. Theo just got out of the hospital;

God forbid we put him back there! Ben leans back in his seat in reluctant acceptance.

I continue where Ben left off, channeling Nik's ability to provide information without *actually* providing information. "Theo, rest assured we are doing our due diligence. At this point, there is no reason to be concerned. We will let you know as soon as we know more."

Theo gives me a warm smile. "Eliana, I know you're deflecting this conversation, but there's no need. My health is fine." I raise an eyebrow, challenging his statement.

Theo gives me a mulish smile before adding, "Well, it's better than it was last week. Regardless, there are some things you need to hear." Margaret sets her hand on Theo's arm and I melt as he brings his hand up to caress it.

Theo clears his throat to speak and a jolt of unease hits my stomach. My eyes move from Theo to Margaret, the perfect picture of happiness, and I know I need to change the subject. Now. I refuse to be an accomplice to another cardiac event because of Richard fucking Dorn. I glance at Ben for help, but his expression screams *let Theo speak*. My eyes dart around the table as I search for a new topic of conversation before landing on Luca. I smile when I see his attention is ping-ponging from Theo to me, waiting for our cue. "Luca, how rude of me. It's been how many years since we've last seen you and I am monopolizing the conversation. Tell us, how long will you be in New York?"

Luca gives me a small wink. "My itinerary is open-ended at the moment."

Before I can ask what he means by open-ended, Theo interjects, "Eliana, I am not dropping this. I will remain perfectly relaxed if you would just listen to what I have to say."

My eyes return to Ben for help, but his expression hasn't

changed. My shoulders slump forward as my attempt to re-direct the conversation evaporates. Defeated, I pick up my wine glass. "By all means, Theo, please continue." I take a large, fortifying drink of wine before folding my hands in my lap and giving Theo my undivided attention.

Theo audibly exhales, as if he's purging all things Richard Dorn from his system. "Richard has produced an immediate return with the investments he is overseeing, which has resulted in the partners, myself included, becoming complacent. We've given him far too much autonomy." He shakes his head, as if he can't believe the partners had the wool pulled over their eyes.

"We shouldn't have trusted him so implicitly, but we allowed him to run with his investments, letting his financial performance cloud our judgment. As a result, we've had to buy him out of a couple of binds and launch an internal investigation to ascertain exactly how he is producing these returns."

I release a breath of relief that TA isn't completely in the dark with Richard's business practices. "Thank you for trusting us with this information, Theo. I can assure you we are doing everything we can to regain control of Immunotech."

Theo nods his head. "Perhaps I can help with that. I asked the board to reinstate you as Alex's proxy."

My jaw drops in shock. *Holy shit.* "Are you serious?" The question comes out broken and I hold my breath, waiting for Theo's response.

"Very much so. The board is becoming suspicious of Richard, and they realize you being involved would be best for Immunotech. However, they also want to make sure you are ready. They realize you have intrinsic motivation; but the group is concerned that, given the history, jumping in too soon carries risk for you, both personally and professionally."

Theo pauses as he assesses my reaction. When he sees I am calm and not screaming about the board having their heads up their collective asses, he continues. "I'm telling you this because I think it's important for you to know what you will be walking into. But you also need to know you have my support; I will back you all the way, kiddo."

I jump up and walk to Theo to envelop him in a side hug. "Theo, I can't possibly tell you how much this means to me." We both know this is the first step to me regaining control, and he is making it happen. I haven't felt this elated in months, maybe even years.

Theo chuckles. "Say nothing of it but remember this the next time you try to prevent an old man from speaking." There's a twinkle in his eye and a smile on his face as he gloats at his ability to prove me wrong. Theo continues, "I am perfectly capable of assessing my level of stress. Besides, the blood pressure medication they put me on is doing its job." Just as quickly as his jovial expression appeared, it turns to concern. "Now that I am on your good side, perhaps this is the time to discuss a second item with you."

I don't like the sound of this, but I straighten from hugging Theo and return to my chair. "What is it, Theo?"

"Margaret and I would like you to move in with us."

For the second time tonight, I can't keep the shocked expression off my face. "What, why?" I look from Theo to Margaret. "Do you need my help during your recuperation?"

Theo gives me an amused smile. "This request has nothing to do with me, my dear. We feel you would be safer here, at least for the short term."

Margaret nods her head. "Please consider staying with

us, sweetheart, at least until Nik is certain any threats have passed. We don't know everything that is happening, but there's a reason you have heightened security, and we can't stomach you facing this on your own."

Luca reaches over to put his hand on my back. "Perhaps this is a good idea. I will be here for at least a month. It will be like old times."

Oh my. I feel my face heat with embarrassment as I turn my attention back to Theo and Margaret to avoid eye contact with Ben. "Thank you both so much for the offer, I truly appreciate it. But I've been reassured my place is the safest location for me right now. Nik has the entire building teeming with security."

Theo shakes his head. "I don't like it."

"I agree, Theo. I don't like any of this, but the smartest option is for me to stay in the most secure place possible, and unbeknownst to me, Alex ensured Nik turned my building into a fortress months ago."

Theo and Margaret look at me in surprise and I feel Luca tense beside me. I'm not sure if they're more surprised I spoke Alex's name without falling apart, or that heightened security has been in place for months. I decide to go with the latter. "Alex arranged for increased security while he was working on a classified project for the government."

Margaret's eyes plead with me before she speaks, "I'm grateful to Alex for having the foresight to ensure your building is secure, Elle, but please consider our offer. We can happily place the same security precautions here, at our home."

I smile at Margaret and Theo. I am so lucky to have these amazing people in my life. They have their own issues to worry about at the moment, namely Theo's health. The last thing I want to do is disappoint either of them, but I refuse to bring any threat to their doorstep, and that is exactly what I would be doing by staying with them. I smile at the two of them as I respond, "I won't rule the option out, but I need to stay at my place for the time being. I promise to stay safe in the meantime, so please don't worry over this."

The Murphys' staff choose this moment to round the table, replacing our now-empty salad plates with Luca's delicious pasta, effectively interrupting the conversation. The tension in my shoulders relaxes with relief.

When the last plate of pasta is placed in front of Luca, he declares, "Buon appetito!" causing my mouth to water in anticipation. I look at the cacio e pepe and what looks like rigatoni with marinara and mozzarella artfully arranged on the plate in front of me. I start with the cacio e pepe, audibly moaning in pleasure as the first bite of the creamy toasted pepper and pecorino hit my taste buds. Heaven.

I feel Luca's eyes on me and straighten as he leans over to whisper, "You are magnificent when you eat. I can't take my eyes off you."

I jerk my head up and look at him, not knowing how to react. I feel so incredibly inept at handling this without making the situation any more awkward than it already is. "Luca, you say that to all the ladies. Your pasta is absolutely divine." He doesn't answer, and I can still feel his eyes on me after I return my attention to my plate.

Ben catches my eye and winks—he's clearly enjoying my level of discomfort. I shake my head at him. "Ben, is Jax enjoying London?"

Ben beams at the mention of his significant other as he begins to tell us about Jackson's meetings with art dealers. I sit back, my eyes not leaving Ben, even though I continue to feel Luca studying my profile. Well, this is going to be a long meal. I pretend to be engrossed in Ben's stories, intermittently taking bites of the pasta I can no longer enjoy as I studiously avoid Luca.

Luca leans over to me again. "Try the marinara, I used San Marzano tomatoes flown in from Italy."

I taste the rigatoni and can't help but close my eyes in appreciation. Holy shit, the bright flavor of the sauce explodes in my mouth. That's when I hear Luca moan next to me. My fork clangs against my plate when I drop it. The level of awkwardness becoming several degrees higher. Deciding it's best to give up on eating, I excuse myself to use the restroom.

The moment I'm out of the dining room, I can breathe freely. What a night. First learning that Theo is helping to reinstate me on the Immunotech board—I can't help but smile as I process Theo's proclamation—and then Luca's overly attentive ways that make me want to crawl out of my skin. I mean, his attention is flattering, and the man is gorgeous, but I don't want him to get the wrong impression. The reality is, I am a widow who is madly in love with her dead husband. I can't even bring myself to engage in harmless flirting. It all just feels so wrong. I have zero interest in Luca, and I don't want to lead him on. Shaking my head at my wayward thoughts, I finish washing my hands and step out of the powder room.

Shit.

As if conjured from my thoughts, Luca is leaning against the hallway wall, one foot casually crossed over the other, a devilish smile gracing his lips. "I wanted to make sure you were okay after the dinner conversation."

I don't know if he is referring to the discussion about increased security or his comments and attention, but I smile in appreciation. "I'm fine, Luca. Thank you for checking." I attempt to sidestep him to go back to the table when he grabs my wrist to stop me. My eyes snap to his in surprise, and the intensity of his expression causes me to take a step back.

"I'm here if you need a friend."

A moment passes with neither of us moving as we stand in the hall staring at each other. There is something in Luca's eyes I can't read, but that I don't like, and a chill runs down my spine. Shaking off the moment, I nod my head, giving him a small smile as I turn my back to him and return to the dining room.

A sense of levity returns once I'm back at the table, though it takes longer for the goosebumps raised on my arms to disappear. The remainder of the evening is filled with laughter. Not wanting Theo to overexert himself, we make our excuses to leave following dessert.

Margaret and Theo walk us to the foyer, where we wait for Nik and his team. I turn to Theo. "Thank you so much for your help with the board. You'll never know how much your support means to me."

Theo pulls me in for a hug. "No one is more suited or qualified, Eliana. You will do an exceptional job. I have no doubt."

Squeezing Theo, I feel Margaret's arms wrap around me as she joins our hug, ending the evening in the same way it began. Once Nik arrives to escort us to the car, I kiss Theo and Margaret's cheeks, promising to call tomorrow, before turning to leave.

Luca is standing next to the door. The awkward tension that has bounced between the two of us all evening snaps into place. A string strung too tightly. I paste on a smile. "Luca, it was wonderful to see you after so many years. Thank you for treating us to your delicious pasta."

Luca cradles each of my hands in his. "The pleasure is mine, truly. I would like the opportunity to treat you again, perhaps next weekend?"

I smile, with what I hope looks like graciousness. "I need to check my calendar. I'll be in touch to let you know." I turn toward Ben, who takes my arm in his to escort me to the car, effectively dislodging me from Luca and saving me from elaborating. It isn't until Ben and I are settled in the backseat of the car that the bondage of tension slowly releases its hold on my lungs. I suck in a breath of air and slowly let it out.

Ben looks at me in confusion. "What was that?"

I shake my head, not understanding. "What was what?

"Luca is more intense than I recall." I start laughing at the ridiculousness of Ben's comment. The man has no clue. Once I start laughing, I can't stop and it's not long before I'm doubled over, gasping for air because I'm unable to catch my breath. Ben looks at me in confusion. "I know I'm funny, doll, but not that funny."

After nearly a minute, my laughter subsides, and I'm spent. As if a balloon filled too full of air is now deflated, I feel my shoulders relax as I sag into the leather seat. "I apparently find irony hilarious. I would've given anything for Luca to have been interested in me that summer in college, but now his interest makes me want to run in the opposite direction."

Ben wraps his arm around my shoulders, pulling me over to him. "First of all, he *was* interested in you, just not so forward with his approach. Secondly, he was a bit much this evening. What do the kids say … extra? That's it, he was extra. Thirdly, you had a crush on him before you had met the love of your life, so it hardly counts."

I rest my head on Ben's shoulder, smiling at his ramblings that happen to make complete sense. "What would I do without your sound reasoning?" Ben chuckles in response. Still, I can't help but think about the absurdity of my current situation. Widow reconnects with Italian summer crush whom she can't be around because he makes her skin crawl. Yep, that sounds about right.

Ben leans to the side and reaches under him, interrupting my thoughts. The large box of tampons Scott had purchased earlier this evening is in his hand; he must have sat on them when we got in the car. He tosses the box over to me, and this time we are both laughing about the ridiculousness of the night.

SEVEN

THE CADENCE OF SHOES HITTING PAVEMENT LULLS ME into a meditative state. It's addicting, really. Being able to turn off my thoughts and live in the moment as I fly through the crisp morning air. The canopy of green leaves is in hyper-color and the early morning smell of freshly cut grass fills me with childlike joy. There is no better place to run than Central Park, even if I don't have complete privacy, I think as I look to my left.

Nik notices my sudden attention. "You haven't been sleeping, have you?" Nik sounds like he could be taking a brisk walk, not finishing our fifth mile.

"How are you not winded?" I manage to wheeze out between breaths.

Nik looks at me out of the corner of his eye, no words needed. I guess the man is the best for a reason. We near the park exit and begin to slow our pace to a jog as we head toward my building. Nik has been my running partner for the past two weeks, and though I miss the solace of running alone, I have to admit it's been nice to have someone to connect with. Especially someone who was so close to Alex. It's also given us the opportunity to work on our agreement of increased communication.

On Tuesday, I learned one of the medical assistants seen entering Theo's hospital room has disappeared. Apparently, this man took a loan from the wrong people to pay for his OxyContin addiction. Nik's team is attempting to ascertain whether the medical assistant disappeared as a result of this loan, or because he suddenly came into some cash. Regardless, the current assumption is this young man was paid to plant the camera in Theo's room.

Nik clears his throat expectantly, bringing me back to the present. "No, I haven't been sleeping well," I answer when I can speak without huffing.

"I … um … I've been having dreams. About Alex." I pause to gather my thoughts before continuing, "It's just that I feel like I'm missing something.

Nik slows to a walk. Instead of a response, he touches his earpiece to speak to his team. "Move ahead and scan the front of the building."

I huff out a short laugh. "Which poor soul did you make tail us today?"

Nik ignores my question, instead responding to my prior comment. "Is there anything I can do? Are you not sleeping because you don't feel safe?"

Of course that would be his first thought, taking the blame for my lack of sleep. I consider his question before answering honestly, "No, I believed you when you said home is the safest place for me. I'm sure the dreams are because I keep thinking about the days leading up to *that* day. Well, that and the weird things that have been happening," I add under my breath.

This gets Nik's attention. "What weird things?"

"How did you hear me?" Nik doesn't respond, so I continue, "It started when I was at the hospital—

"Last week?" Nik interrupts.

"No, when Theo was first brought in. This is going to sound crazy, in fact this was the reason I saw Dr. Wickham the following day, but I fell asleep in the hospital waiting room and was awoken by a scent." I hesitate to continue, knowing I'm most likely about to lose all credibility with my head of security.

To Nik's credit he simply waits, his expression unchanged. Nearly a minute passes and I begin to think I may have gotten out of further explanation when he motions for me to continue. So much for that plan.

I glance at Nik and respond with, "The scent was distinctly Alex." I watch Nik closely to gauge his reaction. The man is good … he somehow manages to maintain his stony expression.

"Anyhow, after discussing this with Dr. Wickham, he surmised this was most likely caused by stress. Or someone wearing the same cologne as Alex may have entered the room shortly before I woke up, which I suppose makes sense." Except Alex had a distinctly delicious scent that was unique to him, I think to myself. Instead, I continue, "The problem is, I can't shake the feeling that I'm missing something."

I watch as Nik's expression closes, morphing into a stoic mask as he positions his body closer to mine—his right hand moves to my back, his body shielding the majority of my left side. He touches his earpiece with his free hand. "Copy, we're two-hundred feet from the front entrance."

I'm instantly on alert as I feel the zap of adrenaline surge through my body. The beat of my heart thrums in my ears as I hold my breath, scanning the area around us.

Nothing stands out as suspicious, but that doesn't ease the fight or flight response my body is currently experiencing. I focus on the left side of the road since that's where Nik appears to be shielding me from. It's then that I notice movement. I squint against the sun to see Scott running after someone in a dark jacket and hat. My feet stop as I focus on what appears to be a foot pursuit, my brain trying to make sense of the situation. Nik pushes me forward, causing me to stumble. The hand that was on my back circles my waist and I'm nearly lifted off the ground as we speed walk toward my building. My now-weightless legs attempt to keep up with Nik's pace.

Movement in my periphery causes me to whip my head to the right before my arm is gripped in a vise. I yelp out in surprise, but instead of being ripped away from Nik, as I anticipate, I am lifted off the ground completely, and our pace to the front door quickens to a sprint. Braho takes point in front of us. Oh, thank God. I look to the new arrival on my right and recognition allows me to breathe for the first time in nearly a minute. Stephens. The gang's all here.

The back of my neck prickles as we near the front door. Instinctively, my head turns to look across the street again and my muscles lock. There's a shadow of a person, a man based on the size. I can't make out his features with the sun blinding me, but I feel electricity pulse through me. An urgency to see who this man is overrides all other thoughts.

I struggle against Nik and Stephens, but their hold is too tight. I glower at Nik. "Put me down!" He ignores me and ushers the three of us through the front door of the building. I strain my neck for one more glimpse of the tree across the street. I can't reconcile the unexplainable feeling of loss that grips me, making my throat thick with emotion, when I see the shadow is gone.

Nik and Stephens carry me to the elevator and enter the code for the penthouse. I vaguely notice staff taking position around the lobby door as the elevator doors close. When the natural light of the lobby is shut out, the men finally let me go. I sag against the elevator wall; placing my shaking hands on my knees, my eyes are on the floor as I try to slow my breathing.

I feel a hand on my back. "Mrs. Tate, are you okay?"

I shake my head and look up. "What the fuck was that?"

Nik and Stephens mutely stare at me for what seems like an eternity. My frustration grows with every second they don't speak, until I hear the elevator ding, announcing our arrival. I am a pressure cooker, ready to burst, as I push my way into the foyer before the two men attempt to help me further. I rush through the kitchen, not bothering to grab my customary post-workout bottle of water, sprint down the hall, and enter my bedroom, slamming the door behind me. I strip the sweaty Lycra pants and tank off as I walk to the shower and turn the water to near scalding. Stepping under the shower heads, I let the water run over my body, turning my skin a shade of bright pink.

The hot water doesn't alleviate the muscle spasms making my entire body shake. I haven't felt this alone and lost in months. I lean against the shower wall for support, but it's not enough to keep me upright. I stop trying and succumb to the gravity pressing down on me. Sliding down the tiled wall, I hug my legs as the punishing water rains down on me.

I've lost track of time, but I'm lobster-red and my fingers look like prunes when I finally stop shaking. I turn off the water, wrap myself in a bath towel, and look around, not knowing what to do next. Wanting to stay in the warm steam, I walk to my vanity and sit to comb out my hair.

Wiping the film of condensation from the mirror, I can't tear my eyes away from the woman staring back at me. She looks nothing like the woman from a year ago. She looks hollow, broken, a husk of her former self.

Absently, I stare for long minutes that stretch into an hour until, finally, a sense of resolve solidifies.

I will not break.

I may never again be the woman I once was. I may never have the carefree air of someone who hasn't lost a piece of their essence, a piece of their soul—but I am a hell of a lot stronger than the person I've become. This is not the woman who scraped and clawed to start her own private equity firm. This is not the same woman who went without meals so she could make payroll the first year following the launch of Tate, Inc. because she refused to accept financial help from anyone. I may not be able to change the past, but I can certainly change how I respond to it. And it's then, while staring at the broken woman in the mirror, I resolve to take control of the things I do have control over. I will no longer be a victim of circumstance.

The bathroom has long-since cooled when I finally exchange my towel for a robe and open the door to my bedroom. There's an unopened bottle of water on my bedside table. I smile at Nik's kind gesture as I close the distance and drain half the bottle. A knock on my bedroom door interrupts me mid-gulp. I take a fortifying breath: I suppose it's time to face reality. I repeat my new mantra, *I will not be a victim of circumstance,* before responding. "I'll be out in a minute."

* * *

After throwing on jeans and a fitted T-shirt, I grab the water bottle and leave my room in search of Nik. I hesitate before entering the living room when I hear low voices, but my eavesdropping is thwarted when all I can make out is the low mumble of garbled words. Rounding the corner, I see Scott and Nik speaking with a man and woman I've never seen before.

Nik's eyes meet mine. "Mrs. Tate, Detectives Rodriguez and Price are here to speak with you about the events from this morning."

My attention moves back to the detectives. A woman in her mid- to late-thirties, resembling Eva Mendez sans makeup, walks up to me. With her dark hair and chestnut eyes, I have the feeling she's one of those women who tries to downplay their natural beauty. The woman stretches her hand out to shake mine and introduces herself as Detective Rodriguez. Her partner, a man in his mid-forties with salt and pepper hair and deeply indented smile lines introduces himself as Detective Price. Both are wearing tailored suits.

Rodriguez is the first to speak following introductions. "Do you mind if we ask you some questions?"

This snaps me out of my contemplative trance, and I respond with, "Of course. Can I get you something to drink?"

Rodriguez smiles. "No, thank you, Mrs. Tate."

I still at her words. The only person who continues to call me Mrs. Instead of Ms., out of fear that I'll break down on the spot, is Nik. Noticing my reaction, the detective raises a brow. I smile, affecting nonchalance, and motion toward the living room. "Feel free to sit wherever you would like."

Nik and I sit on the couch as Rodriguez and Price choose the leather club chairs. Scott continues to move in and out of the room, dealing with the fallout from today, I'm sure.

Rodriguez leans forward in her chair. "Mrs. Tate, Detective Price and I won't take too much of your time. We only have a few questions."

I look at Price and then Rodriguez for direction, "Where should I begin?"

Rodriguez, clearly the primary, speaks up. "Why don't you run us through the sequence of events this morning?"

I nod in agreement. "I doubt there's anything of value I can add, but I started my morning run shortly after 5 AM. Nik and I had just finished our run through Central Park and were walking back to my building when I noticed Scott chasing someone. Nik and Stephens had me off the sidewalk and into the elevator before I could fully grasp what was happening." Rodriguez nods, clearly already aware of what I just said.

"I see. Can you tell us anything about the individual Scott was chasing?" Price asks with warm eyes.

I sigh in frustration before answering, "Only that he, at least I think it was a man based on size, was wearing dark clothes and a hat." A feeling of impotence at the lack of information I'm able to provide fills me. "Have you spoken with Scott? He may have gotten a better look."

Price smiles, making the corner of his eyes squint. "We have, thank you. We just wanted to hear your point of view. Was this the first time you or your security have noticed someone suspicious hanging around the building? Have there been any other abnormal situations?"

I look at Nik, not sure how to answer. Did Nik tell them

about the incident in the car? I decide to hedge, "Nik noticed someone suspicious while I was leaving an appointment last week. Nik, did you have a chance to cover this with the detectives?"

Nik answers with a simple, "Yes, I gave the detectives a description of the man I saw."

Ooo-kay, glad I hedged. I nod my head at Nik in acknowledgment before looking back to Price. "That's the only thing that stands out to me."

The two detectives share a look before Rodriguez continues, "What about people who may be angry with you. Do you have any enemies? Anyone who may be holding a grudge?"

I smile at the detective. "I am the founder of a successful private equity firm. I suspect there are many people who dislike me, but I can't think of anyone who particularly stands out."

Rodriguez and Price exchange another look. What the—what am I missing here?

Rodriguez clears her throat, "Mrs. Tate, there's no one from your past who would want to scare you? Perhaps someone with a grudge who slipped your mind?"

The detective's persistence makes the hair on the back of my neck stand for the second time today. I lean back into the couch and cross my arms protectively over me as I take a moment to think. Richard is the first person to come to mind, but Nik has been monitoring him since the meeting that sent Theo to the hospital. All reports have indicated a rather boring routine of work, CrossFit training, the occasional dinner outing and sleep. If it's not Richard, who on earth would be harassing me? I sort through past memories, trying to recall arguments or people who may be out to get me. Aside from a handful of disgruntled employees who were let go for legitimate reasons, and competitors who dislike me for sweeping up investments they were going after, no one comes to mind.

I uncross my arms and look each of the officers in the eye before answering. "Aside from four employees who were fired, I would say only competitors, but I don't see any of them trying to attack me. That takes friendly competition to a new level."

Price eyes Rodriguez before responding, "Maybe so, but we would still like you to create a list of all the people you just mentioned."

This is absurd. I internally roll my eyes as I smile at the officers. "Absolutely, whatever I can do to help." Even if it's a complete waste of time, I think to myself.

Rodriguez looks momentarily mollified by my response until she continues her questions. "How often do you run in the park?"

Well, that's a change in direction. "I've been running nearly every morning for the past couple of weeks."

"And you always take the same route?"

"Yes, with small deviations, but always in the park and always the same general route."

Rodriguez nods her head, as if I just confirmed something. "I suggest you stop running outside, at least for the time being."

The inexplicable urge to lash out overtakes me. Running is the only solace I've had these past weeks. "Is that really necessary? I haven't been running alone, Nik has been with me." I cringe at my pleading tone. I know I sound like a spoiled child, but running has been my therapy. My escape.

The officers exchange yet another look before Price adds, "Yes, it is necessary, at least for the short term. You don't want to keep a predictable schedule if someone is following you."

I look past the officers to stare out the window as the burn of tears stings my eyes. Claustrophobia builds as I mentally resign to my new normal … house arrest. Reciting my new mantra, *I will not be a victim of circumstance,* there's only one thing that makes me feel better. I silently vow that once I figure out who is behind this, I'll kick their ass myself.

The detectives stand and Rodriguez hands me a card, interrupting my pity party for one. "Feel free to email me the list of people who come to mind once it's completed." Taking the card, I mumble my thanks as Nik and I walk them to the elevator. Scott already has the elevator doors open and waiting. *Thank you, Scott.*

Rodriguez pauses before stepping onto the elevator. "Call us if you happen to remember anything else."

"I will, thank you."

As the elevator doors close, Scott absently takes off his hat to run his fingers through his hair, showcasing a large bump above his right eye.

"Scott, what happened!" Pinching his chin, I turn his head to get a better look.

Scott looks down sheepishly. "It's nothing, Ms. Tate."

My wide eyes fly to Nik as I await an explanation. His eyes are pinched as he rubs his temples. "Mrs. Tate, let's go back into the living room so we can properly brief you. Scott, will you make us some tea?"

"Don't be ridiculous. Scott, you need to have your head examined. I can make the damn tea."

Scott smiles. "Thank you, Ms. Tate. I was examined

while you were in the shower. According to the fancy test the doc ran, I don't need a scan."

I look back at Nik with a raised eyebrow. Nik's patience is stretched as he grinds out, "The physician ran a biomarker test, which indicated Scott is not concussed."

His explanation provides a small level of relief. "Even so, Scott, please have a seat at the island while I make us all some tea."

The men climb onto the island stools as I fill a kettle with water and toss an assortment of tea packets and pain relievers onto the marble surface of the island.

Once seated, Nik begins to explain. "The team was alerted that a suspicious person was loitering in front of the building as we were walking up. The person started walking toward us at the exact moment we rounded the corner, so it appears the man knew when you would be approaching." Nik raises his brows and narrows his eyes at me before continuing. "Scott called out to redirect his attention, and the suspect took off. Scott gave chase."

Nik pauses long enough to pass Scott a bottle of painkillers. We watch Scott shake out three and swallow them dry just as the kettle emits a piercing whistle. I jump up to remove the boiling water, silencing the incessant, high-pitched wail.

Scott shuffles through the tea options and then picks up the story without missing a beat. "I chased the target for about two blocks, when out of nowhere, something hit me."

My hand stills as I slide two mugs of hot water across the island. "Something hit you?"

Scott nods. "I have no idea what it was. One minute I'm running after the guy, and the next I'm lying on my back staring at the sky. By the time I got back to my feet, the target was gone." Scott averts his eyes and shakes his head slowly as his shoulders go limp. "I can't believe I let him get away."

"Scott, it's not your fault he got away. I'm just glad you aren't seriously injured."

Nik, always the hard-ass, doesn't look like he agrees with me as he looks at Scott with contempt. I certainly don't care to witness the showdown these two are sure to have once we are finished here. Nik looks up abruptly, catching me studying him. "The detectives were right."

My eyebrows raise in question. "What on earth about?"

Nik grunts as he continues to rub his temples before responding. "No more running through Central Park. It was too much of a risk before today, and now it's just idiotic."

Every fiber of my being wants to rebel against Nik's decree, yet the logical part of me prevails. "Fine, I'll work out here. I can use the tread and bike in the gym upstairs for cardio." Mint tea sloshes over the side of my mug as I set it down a bit too hard.

Nik looks at me with utter shock, and then suspicion, as he exhales the air he must have been holding in preparation of an impending argument over my lack of freedom.

I raise my hands in surrender. "Nik, I'm being serious. I don't want to put others in unnecessary danger just so I can enjoy a morning run."

He continues to look at me with suspicion as he studies my face until, finally, he relaxes, satisfied I'm telling the truth. He then addresses Scott. "Scott, will you go downstairs to debrief Andy and the others?"

Scott stands to leave. "Of course, boss. Call if you need me." He pauses to look back at me, I'm glad you're okay, Ms. Tate."

The corners of my mouth lift in a small smile. "Take

care of that bump. You really should put some ice on it."
Scott nods as he leaves the room. I turn my attention back
to Nik and raise a questioning eyebrow. "Andy?"

Nik looks abashed as he shakes his head. "You haven't
met him, he's on my team."

"And he's downstairs?"

Nik's discomfort turns up a notch as he rubs his eyes
for the fifth time. "Yes, the team works out of my unit
downstairs."

What the—? "You live downstairs? How did I not know
this?" I always assumed he lived nearby, but had no idea we
lived in the same building.

Nik relaxes marginally. "I moved in a year ago and, well,
you've been busy. Now, can we get back to today?"

What the hell? "No, we can't get back to today."

Nik's shoulders drop in resignation at the bite in my
tone. "I suppose the subject of where I live never came up,
that's all." Nik's eyes showcase confusion and a touch of vulnerability as he continues. "Why? Does it bother you that
I live in the building?"

Now it's my turn to deflate. "No, of course not, but it's
helpful information to know after today."

Nik nods his agreement and I continue, "Speaking of
today. it's obvious you perceive these events as serious, or
you wouldn't have involved …" I grab the card I placed on
the island and scrunch my face in confusion. I turn the nondescript card over to see a blank back. "That's odd." I look
up at Nik. "The card Detective Rodriguez gave me only has
her name, phone number, and personal email. It doesn't in-
dicate who she is with. I mean, I assumed NYPD, but the
card doesn't say."

Ignoring my question about Detective Rodriguez,

Nik's face becomes granite as he looks me in the eye. "These threats are now beyond serious. We know, without a doubt, you are being targeted."

I give Nik a look of exasperation. "You don't say?"

He ignores my comment. "Additionally, we haven't ascertained what this is connected to or who may be behind the threats."

I lean against the counter as anxiety curls in my stomach. "You really don't have any leads?"

Nik shakes his head. "Nothing substantial, which is why it was time to involve Detectives Rodriguez and Price."

Nik has a pretty solid poker face, but his eyes tell a different story. There are still things he isn't telling me, and I am willing to bet one of those things is the reason he suspects I am being targeted.

Nik closes his eyes in frustration. Not having control over the situation is taking its toll on him. Even though I'm still annoyed that he's keeping things from me, my heart goes out to him. He has done such a remarkable job keeping everyone safe in my corner, but I wonder if anyone is taking care of him. I've only ever seen him with his team, and he's never mentioned anyone else in his life. My heart goes out to the guy. Everyone needs their someone, that one person you can be yourself with, avoiding the pretense of what the rest of the world expects of you.

"Nik, what do you do when you're not saving me from mysterious lunatics and babysitting Tate, Inc.'s security team? Do you have any hobbies?"

Nik's wide eyes meet mine before he deadpans, "Saving you is my full-time job AND my hobby."

Tea sprays out of my mouth as I choke-laugh at his

retort. It takes a full minute before I am able to breathe properly. "Nik, did you just make a joke?"

Nik fights a smile, but his eyes crinkle at the corners, warming me more than the tea. I rest my hand over his. "We really need to find you a new hobby." This gets his smile to break through, and the moment feels monumental.

The moment is short-lived though when I think about the amount of work that will go into planning next week. I straighten my spine. "Next week will be a big week for Tate. I'll need to attend several meetings in person and won't be able to remain sequestered to this building. The Immunotech board is meeting, and if I'm not there, the vote to reinstate my seat will not be in my favor. I need to prove I'm back in the game."

Nik nods in agreement. "I'm aware. We have already begun working with Darcy to set up the necessary precautions for your appointments next week. You will be able to work from the Tate office but know there will be increased security presence while you are there, and that's nonnegotiable."

I breathe a sigh of relief. "That's more than fair, thank you."

Nik stands and pauses as he stares down at me, a look of resolute determination radiating from his eyes. "I need to get downstairs to regroup with the team."

"I have no doubt you'll get this figured out, Nik. In the meantime, I have work to do." He begins to object but I raise my hand to stop him. "From home. I'll be in my office if you need me."

Nik nods and exits the kitchen without speaking another word. It isn't until I hear the ding of the elevator arriving a few moments later that I place our mugs in the dishwasher and walk down the hall to my office.

The primal, delicious scent of my husband is the first thing to greet me when I enter the room. My eyes flit across the objects in office—everything appears to be in its place. The room becomes black as my eyelids lower and my lungs fill with air. It's faint, but the heady scent of leather, spice and a hint of vanilla envelops me.

Every muscle in my body freezes, terrified that if I move, like a mirage, the scent will disappear. Opening my eyes once again to search the room, my mind cobbles together the puzzle of how Alex's scent could possibly be lingering in this space. I pinch myself and my brain catalogs what I know to be true: I'm awake and lucid, fact number one. No one would have access to this office without Nik knowing, so I am not smelling someone else's cologne, fact number two.

Scanning the office again, my eyes focus on an ice-blue sweater draped over the arm of the leather couch. I walk over to pick it up. Tears spring to my eyes before my brain can process what I am holding. Alex's clothes have been hanging untouched in his area of our closet these past nine-and-a-half months. So, the sight of what was my favorite sweater on him does something to me I couldn't articulate if I tried. This is different than the college T-shirt under my bed, which ended up being just as much mine as his since I always stole it to sleep in.

I gave Alex this sweater, knowing that it would look phenomenal on him. The cashmere hugging his biceps and abs like a glove. The light blue of the sweater bringing out the blue in his ever-changing blue-gray eyes. I bring the sweater to my nose and inhale the delicious masculine scent.

The scent so well-preserved, the notes so crisp, it's as if he had been wearing the sweater today. Not even his college T-shirt, the one I keep in a Ziploc bag for emotional emergencies, has maintained his scent as well as this sweater.

I can't help myself. I pull the sweater over my shirt and snuggle into the cashmere. The sting from my frayed nerves lessens as I sit on the couch. Pulling my legs up, I rest my chin on my knees and proceed to fall apart.

It's a cathartic cry that sheds my uncertainty over all the unknowns, my fear bleeding out in every tear running down my face. The warm sweater hugs my body, providing a level of comfort I would be far too embarrassed to ever admit to out loud.

It's not until I am wrung dry, with no tears left to shed, that there's a moment when I feel more like myself than I have since Alex's death. It's in this moment that I reaffirm my new mantra. I will not let a crazy person targeting me for some unknown reason win. I'm done playing defense, relying on Nik to save the day if and when this person decides to make their move. I need to rely on myself. That's the only way I can maintain my sanity. Control the controllable.

With my resolve bolstered, I move to my desk and begin to compile the list of people who could potentially be targeting me.

1) Richard Dorn

EIGHT

Butterflies flutter in my stomach as Nik fights the morning Manhattan traffic. The stop and go of the car echoes with the rhythmic beat of the city as we cut through an intangible, pulsing energy. An energy that is punctuated by the white noise of engines revving and the clang of never-ending construction. I soak in the familiar comfort of the city I love as I try to shake the foreboding feeling that has been sabotaging my thoughts all morning.

In need of a distraction, I scroll through the screen on my phone until I find my news alerts. The first alert causes all noise to mute and my limbs to go numb.

"Oh my God," escapes my lips in a whisper.

I click on the alert and watch as *The Wall Street Journal* loads. I read the headline four times to be sure I'm not seeing things.

Any pre-meeting anxiety I felt a moment ago is replaced with outrage.

"Motherfucker."

Nik's eyes fly up to meet mine in the rearview mirror. "Mrs. Tate?"

"I'm assuming you haven't read the *Journal* this morning."

Nik shakes his head. "No, I haven't had the chance."

"Well, our friend Richard Dorn continues to fuck with my company." I shake my head in disbelief. "He raised the price of PD-23 by 700%. This will make it nearly impossible for patients to access the immunotherapy. There's no way insurance companies will pay for this!" I feel my shoulders tighten as fire incinerates the butterflies that were in my stomach. "This will quite literally kill patients the immunotherapy was meant to save."

Tossing my phone aside, I stare out the window in a daze as my breakfast churns in my stomach. What the hell is Dorn thinking? This move not only highlights his complete lack of humanity, but it shows he's a novice in biotech. He doesn't realize this will inevitably decrease revenue due to the lack of access this price hike will create once insurance companies stop covering the immunotherapy. Not to mention this will force patients to undergo chemotherapy instead, which is predominately ineffective.

The audacity of this parasite is unbelievable.

I need to get this company out of Dorn's clutches as soon as possible. How can that monster sleep at night knowing he is effectively preventing patients from a medication that could save their lives? He's diabolical.

We stop at a red light, and I watch absentmindedly as pedestrians rush to wherever it is they need to be, women in dresses wearing flats or running shoes, their heels in their oversized designer bags; men in the standard Manhattan uniform of dark suit, starched white shirt and tie.

My phone vibrates on the seat beside me. Expecting to see a message from my team notifying me of Richard Dorn's price hike, my eyebrows raise when I flip my phone over to see a text from Luca. As annoying as he has become,

I can't help but admire his persistence. Luca started texting the day after the Murphys' dinner, and calling the day after that. I told him I would be busy preparing for this meeting and we could regroup after, but I didn't mean at 7 o'clock in the morning.

Ignoring Luca's text, I quickly compose a message to my team with a link to the article I just read. Time to play hard ball. I pull up Theo's latest email. He will be attending the board meeting this morning—his first meeting since leaving the hospital. I am grateful he will be there, but I'm also nervous this will cause him undue stress.

"Are you feeling well, Mrs. Tate?"

A knowing smile lifts the corners of my lips when I realize I've been rubbing my temples as a tension headache builds. I force myself to return both hands to my phone. "I'm fine, thank you."

There's unease in Nik's eyes. "And do you feel prepared for today's meeting?"

My stomach clenches. What the hell, is Nik doubting me? I eye him from the rearview mirror. "Nik, I will get Immunotech back. There is simply no other option." The conviction in my voice brokers no argument.

The corners of Nik's eyes crinkle as he smiles. "I have no doubt about that, Mrs. Tate. I just feel bad for anyone who tries to get in your way." I slump back in my seat at Nik's words. At least he hasn't completely lost faith, but that won't help me get Alex's company back.

A dark sludge coats my insides when I think about Dorn's actions. "Any person who would willingly prevent others from accessing lifesaving medication is a sociopath." I look out the window, lost in thought, before adding, "I suppose the same could be said about insurance companies."

Nik grunts in agreement and I continue, "Dorn should never have been in the position to make such a vital decision."

I return my attention to the specs of people in drab colors outside my hammer-proof window and swear a personal oath. I will make up for deserting this company, starting today.

Feeling Nik's eyes on me, I return my gaze to the rear-view mirror. "Mrs. Tate, you chose the best option at the time and assumed, rightfully so, Mr. Murphy would make sure the company remained healthy. You never would have agreed to allow TA Holdings to take controlling interest if you had known Dorn was in the picture."

I can't help but smile. "Nik, how is it you can always read my mind?"

Nik chuckles as he responds, "With all due respect, Mrs. Tate, your thoughts are written all over your face." My eyes narrow at his response. "Thank God you don't play poker, you would lose your shirt."

As much as I would like to contradict him, Nik isn't wrong. Returning my attention to the window, the series of events from months ago filter through my mind. Nausea engulfs the fire in my stomach as I think back to the utter despair of making the impossible decision of stepping down from the Immunotech board, while knowing it was the only logical option at the time. It would have been beyond difficult to navigate the company while simultaneously wading through a suffocating sea of grief. But there's no way I would have allowed TA to take controlling interest had I known Dorn would be running point. I should have listened to my gut and held on. I could have made it work. I didn't give myself enough credit at the time because I simply wasn't in my right mind to do so, but I could have continued if necessary. The other companies in the Tate portfolio continued to run smoothly—though they all had capable CEOs who were still alive.

Nik pulls into the parking garage, interrupting my thoughts. Butterflies once again take flight in my stomach, and I allow the excitement to build as the pre-game familiarity settles over me, easing my nauseous stomach. My phone vibrates in my hand, and I look down to see a text from Ben: *Fucking kill it, doll.* The adrenaline-inducing moment sears away every negative thought, centering me in the present. I forgot how much I loved the anticipation of an impending win.

"The team has already cleared our route to the TA Holdings office," Nik informs me as we move from the parked car to the parking garage elevator.

We check in at the reception desk in the lobby and are on an elevator shooting to the twenty-seventh floor within two minutes of arrival. Nik clears his throat to get my attention. "I'll be right outside if you need anything at all." My response is to smile up at Nik in gratitude.

The elevator doors open, and we are greeted by an expansive reception desk made of polished black marble. A gorgeous blonde wearing Prada eyeglasses, I suspect for the effect, sits primly behind the desk. Her pink lips spread into a welcoming smile, showcasing her extremely white teeth as she stands. "Ms. Tate, right this way, please." We follow executive assistant Barbie as she escorts us to a conference room.

When I enter the room, I'm relieved to see Theo is already seated. He winks at me and tilts his head to the empty seat beside him. I greet the four other men already in the room as I make my way over to him, pleased to see Dorn isn't in the mix.

Theo stands and kisses my cheek in greeting. "I prepared the group, and they're aware of my concerns with Dorn. You have my support, but now it's up to you, Eliana." I have to strain to hear the last few words, they're spoken so softly, but that doesn't diminish the electric zing of anticipation elicited by Theo's words. I squeeze Theo's hand and whisper a thank-you in his ear.

Hearing several voices, I look toward the door to see the remaining board members enter the room. Plastering on a confident smile, I straighten to my full height, plus a few inches thanks to my Louboutins, and survey the group. Four of the eight board members helped Alex launch Immunotech and have been part of this journey from the beginning. Two scientists and two former venture capitalists who provided seed funding; all have skin in the game by way of equity. The other four were brought on after TA took control, but after a week of research, I now know everything there is to know about each of them. There are two, in particular, who may make this difficult: the man who took Alex's role as chair, Edward Dooling, and his sidekick, Elizabeth Sanders.

After several greetings and introductions, we take our seats so Edward can begin the meeting, his deep voice capturing the room's attention with the first word he speaks. "As you are all aware, we are here today to assess and vote on Eliana Tate returning to the board following her absence this past year." He pauses and clears his throat before continuing. "I am of the opinion we should not disrupt the current Immunotech leadership team when we restructured just nine months ago. Immunotech is in its infancy, a vulnerable time for a biotech company. It is absolutely necessary for the focus to be on quickly gaining market share if we want to see a profit. Additionally, if we want to see a return, it's imperative to have solid leadership in place. With change comes disruption, and Immunotech cannot be disrupted right now, particularly when the company is currently syphoning capital." He fixes his eyes on me. "Eliana, you did wonderful things while you were the proxy chair, but that time has passed. Immunotech needs a seasoned board for the company to succeed. Individuals who have experience with early-stage life science companies. Surely you see that."

The word *asshole* screams through my mind as I smile at Edward. I'm about to respond when a deep chuckle fills the room. As a group, our heads turn toward the doorway to see the devil leaning against the entrance.

Richard Dorn straightens from the doorway to give the room a swarthy smile. "I couldn't have said it better myself, Edward."

My blood turns to ice as I feel my pulse accelerate. I'm about to speak when Theo beats me to it.

"Richard, as you know, the board felt it best for one member from TA and one member from Tate to be present today. This requirement is satisfied with Eliana and me in attendance. Please step out of the room and I will brief you when we are finished."

Richard's sinister smile morphs into something dark and, frankly, somewhat frightening. "Yes, Theo, I'm aware you tried to keep me out of this meeting, but as the interim CEO of Immunotech, I have as much, if not more, of a right to be here than either of you."

Hearing him declare interim CEO feels like a punch to the stomach, but his absurd belief he has any right in regard to Immuntech makes me nauseous for the second time in the span of thirty minutes. The wind is knocked out of me as I scan the faces around the table. Pinched expressions and downcast eyes telegraph their unease with Dick's interruption. I need to take control of the interruption before the board decides to postpone the meeting.

My muscles tighten in preparation of stepping into the lion's den. "If I may." Seconds tick by, each bringing another ounce of tension, until every eye is on me. Anxiety buzzes through me, causing my voice to wobble as I say, "I don't object to Richard attending the meeting. In fact, this may save us the hassle of scheduling an additional meeting in the future."

The board members look at one another, clearly at a loss for what to say. Theo studies me out of the corner of his eye for several long seconds. Finally, he adds, "If Eliana doesn't object to Richard's attendance, far be it for me to have an opinion."

Edward sits back in his chair and studies me before turning his gaze to Dick. "So be it. Mr. Dorn, please take a seat."

Richard chooses the only open seat, which thankfully is near the end of the long, mahogany conference table, putting him a safe distance from me. The room is thick with anticipation as Edward continues, "Now, where were we?"

Unable to keep his mouth shut, Dorn jumps in, "I believe you were saying Eliana's involvement with Immunotech is unwarranted."

My usual annoyance of Dick's use of my full name is replaced by white-hot fire racing through my veins as he attempts to mold Edward's words into a knife he can wield in my direction. I notice several members of the group look down in either shame or awkwardness as the charge in the room amplifies.

My eyes meet the pale blue eyes of Calvin Sweeney, one of the two brilliant scientists Alex spent countless hours with during the development of Immunotech's checkpoint inhibitor, PD-23. He gives me a sympathetic smile from across the table, which elicits a pang of discomfort deep in my belly. He thinks Dick has already won. I look at Giulia next, the second scientist who had become family to Alex and me. She gives me a warm smile of encouragement.

Returning her smile, I turn my focus to Edward, fully ignoring Dick's comment. "I appreciate your candor, Edward. I understand your hesitation to disrupt the current process after only nine months, but if I may be frank, I believe it is imperative to make this change for Immunotech to survive."

The room echoes with the sound of a snort from Richard.

Ignoring him, I take a deep breath before continuing, "We have reason to believe funds from Immunotech are being mismanaged."

Murmurings from the group replace the nasal-produced noises coming from Richard. A loud thwack makes every head turn toward the end of the table. Richard's face is an alarming shade of red as he shouts, "This accusation is preposterous!"

I sit back and watch as the board members turn to one another in surprise, silently assessing whether anyone else at the table has insight into the accusation I just made. Hushed voices create a buzz as the group realizes this is news to all of them. I look at Theo sitting beside me, who, like me, is silently observing the group's reaction to my accusation.

Edward stands, placing both hands on the conference table as he leans forward in an attempt to regain control of the meeting. "Ladies and gentlemen, if you would please cease the side conversations so we may continue." He turns his attention to me, "Eliana, I assume you have basis for these claims?"

The corners of my mouth lift as I respond with, "Of course." I look each board member in the eye before continuing, "As you are all aware, PD-23 volume has reached an all-time high. In fact, quarter over quarter volume has tripled. However, profit has decreased at the same rate."

Dick slaps the table again. "Really, Eliana, this is your reasoning for slinging accusations? The loss is easily explained by increased costs. If you had half a brain for business, you would know this. Growth phase products often have a large burn rate. The fact that you would even attempt to tie this to mismanagement of funds further substantiates the need for you to step back and let TA continue to run things."

I feel a heightened level of awareness as adrenaline floods my system. A slow smile spreads across my lips. "Thank you for the business 101 lesson, Dick. I can assure you Columbia did a fine job covering the financial needs of capturing market share. In fact, we also had a lesson or two on Ponzi schemes. It was fascinating to study the complex web of shell companies that allowed Enron to fool the most respected people in finance."

Dick rolls his eyes. "Stop wasting our time, Eliana. State your point."

My smile widens. "I am simply trying to shed light on the fact that although Immunotech's income statement shows a decrease in COGS," and I can't help but add,

"Otherwise known as cost of goods sold, which makes sense due to scale, cash burn is at an all-time high."

Reaching down to grab a folder out of my bag, my eyes meet Theo's. He gives me a small nod of support before I straighten, pursing my lips in an attempt not to smile as I return my attention to Edward and Elizabeth. "We uncovered that capital expenditures are now more than ten times what they were a year ago. I toss the folder between the two. "According to these statements, Immunotech profits are being poured into three shell companies, all of which are owned and operated by none other than Richard Dorn."

All conversation stops as the room absorbs this new information. The silence blanketing the room stretches until it feels as though it will snap. I wait for the tension to peak before driving home my message. "Immunotech has been funding Richard's portfolio of companies for the past nine months. In fact, without Immunotech, he would no longer have a portfolio to manage. This explains the PD-23 price hike. Richard is nearing the end of his runway, and he needs more capital to continue the charade."

The table erupts in a cacophony of noise as Edward and Elizabeth study the contents of the folder, ignoring the outbursts of the members sitting around them. I watch as Edward stops shuffling through the papers, a look of surprise stretches his face as he pauses to read. His accusation-filled eyes shoot to Richard. "Mr. Dorn, would you care to explain these statements? Why are Immunotech profits being poured into Capital Expenditures?"

It takes a moment for Richard to register the question. I notice with satisfaction that his face has gone from blazing red to ghostly white. His unfocused eyes dart from side to side as if he is trying to solve a difficult puzzle or, more likely, figure out an escape route. He takes a sip of water and finally looks at Edward. There's defeat in his voice when he replies, "This is slander. These allegations are blatant lies."

I shake my head in disappointment. I thought Dick might have it in him to be a worthy adversary, but his response is predictably unoriginal.

It's evident that Edward is also disappointed by Richard's response as he narrows his eyes and says, "Let's try this again, Mr. Dorn. Why don't you start by explaining why millions of Immunotech dollars have been funneled into three separate entities since you have been at the helm?"

Richard leans back in his chair before responding. "Edward, there is a simple explanation for this. Two of the companies are suppliers, and the increase in payables is directly related to volume. The third company is a firm we hired to consult on strategy during this growth phase."

Edward shifts through the papers until he uncovers the page he's looking for. "Can you explain why *you* are the majority shareholder for each of these companies?"

"Of course. I own interest in a number of companies because I prefer to do business with entities I'm familiar with."

It takes everything for me to hold my tongue. The never-ending absurdity of this asshole is astounding.

Edward must agree because his fist hits the table, making several of us jump. The stoic mask he wore at the beginning of the meeting has been replaced with impatience and anger, which is all I need to see to remain silent and let this scene play out. "That *would* be a simple explanation, Mr. Dorn, except for one glaring problem. As Ms. Tate already explained, an explanation evidenced by these documents—"

Edward jabs at the folders with his sausage-shaped index finger, "these companies are shell companies!"

The tension in the room continues to thicken as everyone looks from Edward to Dorn.

Edward draws in a breath, followed by a long exhale, before continuing, "I would understand the consultancy not having a brick-and-mortar location, but I don't understand how two suppliers are running a legitimate business without physical space or assets. Furthermore, the fact that you own these entities, and you didn't question the ethical concerns surrounding their use, even if these companies were legitimate, is highly concerning!"

The room is silent following Edward's words, all of us nervous we might breathe too loudly and wind up being the center of Edward's rage. Theo reaches for a silver pitcher of water sitting in front of us. The sound of water pouring into a glass provides a small reprieve from the heavy fog of tension suffocating the room.

Theo looks at Edward. "TA was notified of these financial documents yesterday. Since then, we have enlisted IMG to perform an external audit on all of Dorn's holdings. We will have a preliminary report within two weeks. As the representative for TA Holdings, I propose Ms. Tate be named interim CEO and Ms. Genevieve Wesley, the woman who uncovered this issue, be named Immunotech's CFO immediately. We can reconvene following the audit to discuss a permanent solution moving forward."

As badly as I want to, I don't dare sneak a glance at Richard. I maintain a mask of impassivity while keeping my focus on Edward, who sits back in his chair and steeples his fingers while contemplating Theo's proposal. His eyebrows pull together in thought. "I agree this suggestion would make the most sense, but I am hesitant to make any changes until we can validate our assumptions. I propose Mr. Dorn remain the interim CEO, but he will cease all CFO responsibilities. Additionally, we will place a freeze on all spending until we are able to reconvene and vote on whether to name Ms. Tate interim CEO while we are searching for Mr. Dorn's replacement.

I pull my shoulders back, straighten my spine, and look Edward in the eye. "If I may address the room, Mr. Dooling?"

Edward extends his upturned hand in my direction and replies, "By all means."

"As previously mentioned, I understand the importance of not disrupting the current operational process at Immunotech. However, the company is experiencing hockey stick growth, and I believe freezing all spending would have grave consequences. Having said that, it's clear we cannot allow Mr. Dorn access to the coffers. I propose a vote to reinstate my place on the board but keep Immunotech leadership as is for the time being, with the exception of placing Ms. Genevieve Wesley as acting CFO. I believe not ensuring the books are accurate is too great of a financial threat if we wait for the external audit to be completed."

Edward and Elizabeth look at each other in silent communication before Elizabeth speaks. "I believe Ms. Tate's proposal may be our best course of action. This would eliminate our concern of disruption, while adding a strong CFO to Immunotech's leadership team. Additionally, I believe this company will achieve growth forecasts only if Eliana is involved. She, along with Giulia and Calvin, provide the backbone of this company. As Immunotech pioneers, their early involvement provides motivation that is beyond what any of us can provide."

Edward nods his head in agreement. "Very well, all in favor of offering Ms. Wesley the CFO position and reinstating Ms. Tate's role on the board?"

Elizabeth begins with her declaration, "Aye."

Edward rounds the table, skipping over Dick, and one by one, the board members agree. I can't help but smile as Calvin Sweeney, smiling ear to ear, nearly shouts, "Aye." Giulia is next, casting me an almost maternal gaze, with misty eyes, as she declares, "Aye."

I have the inexplicable urge to laugh. This is actually going to happen. I'm about to reclaim my seat at the table. The vote skips me and goes to Theo. I can't help but smile as the anticipation of saving Immunotech crescendos.

Theo clears his throat, and the floor drops out from under me when a clear "no" leaves his mouth.

NINE

BLINK STUPIDLY AT THEO. THIS MUST BE A JOKE; DID I hear him correctly? The ever-present fog of tension that has been suffocating the room is now a thick sludge that might very well drown me.

Edward and Elizabeth look at Theo in confusion before resuming the vote. The remaining members vote in my favor, but I am hardly paying attention as I try to make sense of why Theo would vote against me after declaring that I should be the CEO.

I vaguely hear Edward talking, but I don't register what he's saying until I hear my name. "Congratulations, Elle. Welcome back to the board."

The room comes back into focus as I look around the table, making eye contact with every person except Richard, because he's not worth a millisecond of my time, and Theo, because I need to keep my emotions in check. "Thank you all for your vote of confidence. As you are aware, I have personal interest in ensuring Immunotech flourishes, which is why I would like my first act back on the board to be issuing a vote to reinstate the previous list price of PD-23. The price hike is an unethical public relations nightmare that will result in unintended consequences, one of which will be revenue loss as there is no way insurance companies will pay for PD-23 at the increased rate."

Edward nods his head. "I agree, in fact, this was the next topic on our agenda. Let's move to it now, shall we? All in favor of reinstating the original list price for PD-23?"

The board members collectively agree. I glance at Richard to see his scowling face emanating pure rage.

"With that settled, are there any other items we need to address?" The room is silent. "Well then, I move to adjourn this meeting and reconvene when we have the report from the external audit."

Theo and Edward are discussing a three-week window before the next meeting to ensure the group has time to review the report when Richard stands abruptly. With one last parting glare directed my way, he spins and marches out of the room, making his dramatic exit before Edward dismisses the group. Good riddance, Dick.

Once the meeting is adjourned, I stand to say my goodbyes to the others, thanking them again for their support, which is apparently more than I can say for my own family. I hazard a glance at Theo, who is smiling as he speaks with Giulia, not an ounce of guilt present.

One by one the room clears until I am left with Theo and Edward. Edward walks to the door and then stops and turns to look at me. His eyes are warm and his expression relaxed when he speaks, "You did well, Elle. Thank you for taking the initiative where Immunotech is concerned. If your allegations are confirmed, which I regrettably believe they will be …" He pauses to take a deep breath, as if even he can't believe they allowed Richard Dorn to almost impale the company, "then you very well saved Immunotech from certain failure. We look forward to having your leadership and expertise back on the board." With that, he walks out the door.

I turn to Theo, confusion and hurt swirl to create a cyclone of doubt. Theo's expression falls: he is fully aware how much his vote cut me as he takes my hand. "I had to do it, Eliana."

A sharp pain clenches my heart and I pull my hand away. "Why?"

"You made the right play with your counterproposal, especially after Edward showed his hand. But I'm playing the long game, darling, and now, not only am I on record proposing you run Immunotech, but I am demonstrating that I, and TA by association, won't settle for anything less. As a senior partner of TA, I needed to place a stake in the ground. The deck is stacked to get rid of Richard and return Immunotech to its rightful owner. Me stating that you should be named CEO and then voting against anything less shouts of TA's confidence in you. Defaulting to the next best option would have been a mere whisper. My intentions are now on record should we need to garner shareholder support to make this happen."

Understanding strips away my fog of self-pity and I can't help but smile at this wonderfully manipulating, brilliant man. "I still have so much to learn, but why didn't you explain this during the vote?"

Theo's eyes warm. "For two reasons: the first—because it doesn't matter. The vote was binary. Even if I were to provide an explanation, my commentary wouldn't be on record, only my vote. The second reason is Dorn— the likelihood of TA uncovering his transgressions will be greater if he doesn't view me as an enemy. If he believes I am putting TA employees, specifically him, first, he may be more forthcoming."

Nodding in understanding, I process Theo's explanation. "I suppose that makes sense, though I don't think Dorn is stupid enough to believe you are on his side. Especially after today."

Theo's eyes crinkle at the corners as he smiles. "I don't disagree. I am merely attempting to keep the peace until we have a better understanding of Dorn's reach at TA. I'll set the record straight when I push for you to be interim CEO at the next meeting."

Theo places his hand on my upper back. "Now, let's get out of here. Can you spare some time for an old man?"

Smiling up at Theo, we say, "Stella's," in unison.

I loop my arm through his. "Lead the way."

* * *

Theo and I meet Nik in the lobby and, after waiting fifteen minutes for Nik's team to secure the location, the three of us walk the short distance to the coffee shop we once frequented far too often.

The aroma of coffee and pastries greets us when we open the door. The space is crowded, but Nik steers us to a table near a rear exit and we settle in.

"Oh, my heavens, if it isn't my two favorite people!" I hear Stella's familiar, smooth-as-honey voice behind me before she wraps her arms around my shoulders. I stand to return her hug and she envelops me. "Let me look at you, it's been nearly a year since I last saw you. You need to eat, you're withering away."

Laughing at Stella's words, I answer with a smirk, "It has been too long, yet your greeting remains the same."

Stella responds with a laugh of her own. "Sugar, you know I'll take any chance I get to put some meat on those bones." I feel a warmth in my core. Stella is one of those rare people whose presence alone provides a salve for your soul. My smile amps up a notch. Stella is basically *Chicken Soup for the Soul* personified. Who needs the book when you have this wonderful woman around?

"You have no idea how much I've missed you and your coffee, Stella."

She winks, "Speaking of, I'll be back in a jiffy. Ya'll want your usual?"

Theo and I nod to confirm, and Nik orders tea. I take my seat as I watch Stella walk away to get our drinks, her tight jeans and black sweater showcasing her subtle curves and bright blond curls. If I didn't know better, I would assume she was a long-lost relative of Marilyn Monroe. The woman makes mid-forties look like a welcome place to be.

Stella disappears around the corner, and I sit back in my chair to take in the room, the familiar scent of coffee and wood polish taking me back to simpler times.

I catch Theo studying me. "It's been a while since you've been here."

I nod as I continue to take in the café. Everything is exactly the same, as if the place had been frozen in time. The dark polished wood of the long coffee bar gleams from the pendant lights overhead. Nearly every seat is taken, the crowd a mixture of college students and professionals. Stella's youth spent in Alabama and her love for Paris shines through in the bizarre, mismatched décor that is somehow perfect for this quaint little café. A feeling of home washes over me.

"I didn't realize how much I missed this place," I say absentmindedly as nostalgia begins to work away the ever-present edge of grief pressing into my heart. I think back to when Theo and Margaret would meet me for coffee every Friday when I first invested in my first two portfolio companies. I suspect the coffee dates began because they were aware I barely had a penny to my name; they did always send me off with a bag full of pastries that lasted through the following week.

I had a small inheritance from my parents, and savings from working at TA, but after paying for grad school and pouring everything I had into the business that is now Tate, I was living on Top Ramen and dreams. Our Friday coffee meetings and dinner dates with Alex were often my sustenance for the week.

The coffee date tradition continued until, like everything else, life was placed on a perpetual hold when I went into hibernation following Alex's death. "Theo, what would you say to resuming our Friday coffee dates? Do you think Margaret could spare the time?"

Theo smiles. "That's an excellent idea, and I don't need to ask to know Margaret will make time. She would cancel tea with the Queen to have coffee with you." I smirk at Theo's response, knowing Margaret loves her tea but detests coffee.

A Parisian bowl filled with espresso and steamed milk is placed in front of me. "Speaking of …" I look up to see one of Stella's baristas set another bowl in front of Theo and a cup of tea in front of Nik. Nik doesn't move from his position, a mask of passive observation on his face. I would love to know what runs through his head. I assume he is constantly playing out worst-case scenarios and strategies for getting out of them. He reminds me of a duck, calm on the surface, but frantically kicking his legs under the water.

"All right, Nik, I know you are impatiently trying to remain patient. Go ahead and ask."

Nik narrows his gaze at my taunting. "How did it go?"

"The meeting was …" I trail off as I try to find the proper adjective. "Eventful?"

Theo chuckles before elaborating, "Our Eliana put the boys through their paces."

Nik looks at me with pride, a ghost of a small smile breaking through. We fill Nik in on the meeting as we drink our coffee and eat the delicious pastries Stella continues to deliver to our table.

Taking his final bite of chocolate croissant, the only indulgence I've ever known Nik to enjoy, he responds with, "So, you *are* back on the board?"

"Yes, I am back on the board. And with Genevieve's help, we now have control of the books."

Nik beams and I'm once again filled with a sense of accomplishment. We are stitching Immunotech back together, one piece at a time. I can't help but think Alex would be proud. Perhaps he's cheering me on from the other side. The thought makes me feel the connection we always shared, even as my stomach clenches, my feelings forever on a rollercoaster. God, I miss him so much.

"And the price hike?"

Returning my attention to Nik, I raise an eyebrow. He is far more interested in this than I would expect him to be. I study his expression before replying, "We are reinstating the previous price. I will work with the public relations team to have a statement released this afternoon."

Nik absentmindedly nods his head. "Good, this is all very good, Mrs. Tate."

I continue to study Nik. His support is touching, but his level of interest is odd. Maybe he's worried I'll once again turn into a recluse if this goes south, which is a fair assumption.

I drink the last of my café crème and look at my watch as Theo stands. "I'll pay the bill and we can be on our way."

We say our goodbyes to Stella, who makes us promise to be back soon with Margaret, before she and Nik share a lingering look that makes Nik duck his head and walk to the door. Interesting, I don't think I've ever seen Nik embarrassed. Hugging Stella goodbye, I sigh into her embrace; she gives the best hugs. I shoot her one last knowing smile before following Nik out the door.

"This was lovely, Eliana. I know you have a lot on your plate today, so thank you for taking the time to grab coffee."

Looping my arm through Theo's once again, I reply, "Thank you, for your support *and* for the coffee."

We walk down the street in companionable silence as Nik trails behind us. After entering the lobby, we say our goodbyes. Nik and I take the garage elevator to our awaiting car as Theo heads back to his office. I don't envy him the political acrobatics required to deal with golden-boy Richard Dorn. I can't help but cringe at the thought.

The elevator doors open to the parking garage, and I see Braho as we step out. "All is quiet here, sir."

Nik doesn't pause as he replies, "Good. Tail us back to Tate, Inc. and then join Scott."

"You got it."

I shake my head at Nik as we walk toward the car. "What?"

"Have you ever considered being cordial to your employees?"

Nik's eyebrows raise in surprise, as if he has no clue what I'm referring to. "What about that interaction wasn't cordial?"

"Oh, Nik. Forever the stoic."

He shakes his head in exasperation, not understanding my comment. "Come on, I'll get you back to the office so you can work on the press release."

I pause as I'm opening the car door. "Nik, if I didn't know better, I would assume you had as much interest in Immunotech as me."

Nik slides into the car without answering, and I climb into the backseat. I'm about to press him on his odd behavior when my bag vibrates next to me. I fish through its contents trying to locate my phone, finally finding it under my wallet after the fifth vibration. *Genevieve* is illuminated on the screen. "Gen, I'm glad you called, I have news."

Gen's response is a sarcastic laugh. "If by news you're referring to shipping me off like a misfit bound for boarding school, then I would say you most definitely have news."

Shit. "Gen, it isn't like that at all. And how the hell have you already heard about this…I left the meeting an hour ago?"

"Oh, you can thank your best friend for that. Richard Dorn sent an email to a blind list of recipients accusing you of, and I quote, 'Wielding your relationships and family pedigree in a desperate and underhanded attempt to steal his position at Immunotech.'"

I close my eyes in exasperation. "You have got to be kidding me?"

"Afraid not, boss. What happened?"

Dumbfounded, I turn to Nik, who is watching me in the rearview mirror, and shake my head. How can one person cause so many migraines?

"Gen, listen, I don't know the specifics of Dorn's email, but the meeting went well, and we are not shipping you off like a ..." I draw a blank trying to remember the ridiculous analogy she used.

Gen sighs in annoyance. "Misfit. Like a misfit who is sent away to boarding school."

"Got it, I think we should revisit the boarding school comment another time, perhaps over some wine. But please know we are not shipping you off. Look, I'm ten minutes from the office. Are you free? I'll give you the play-by-play."

"I suppose I can make that work."

I try to stifle the chuckle that leaves my lips at Gen's attempt to act like she's angry. "See you in ten." Ending the call, I pull up my emails. Fifty-six unread emails in the past two hours. Fantastic. I scroll through the inbox, but there aren't any emails from Dorn.

"Nik, do you have plans this afternoon?"

"Just making sure you remain in one piece."

"Right, well, would you mind if I took advantage of your IT sleuthing skills?"

Nik's eyebrows raise in question. "What's going on?"

I shake my head at Dorn's audacity. "Dorn is unable to comprehend that he needs to cut his losses. He sent an email in what I surmise is a last-ditch effort for him to remain as interim CEO. He's probably trying to get key shareholders to voice support in an attempt to sway the board. I need to know who the recipients were. Apparently, everyone was on blind copy."

"Consider it done."

* * *

The funny thing about an impending storm is we know, on a cellular level, something inclement is brewing, whether it be the feel of energy shifting as air is pulled into an invisible storm system, or the atmosphere projecting a warning by way of a low-pressure vacuum. Or perhaps it's simply primal intuition, something embedded in our DNA, passed down from generation to generation. A result of the .001% Neanderthal heritage represented in our 23andMe genetic test reports. Whatever the cause, the electricity in the air is tangible as I sit in my office reading a brief outlining the virtues of Feme, a start-up we are considering investing in that provides direct-to-consumer diagnosis of HPV, and consequently cervical cancer. The company uses machine learning and DNA analysis to provide results from samples sent directly from a consumer's house via FDA-cleared kits. I re-read the line I had just skimmed, *over 90% of cervical cancers are caused by HPV and 80% of the U.S. population has HPV.* Eighty percent, wow. I think of the people I've spoken to in the past two hours and try to deduce which of them are walking around with HPV. Richard Dorn, without a doubt.

A cyclone of commotion enters my office as Genevieve takes purposeful strides toward my desk. There's a small hiccup in her glide as her left foot is unable to keep up with her momentum. She plants her feet in front of my desk, bending at the waist, her fingers pressing into the glass of my desk as she stares me down. The silence stretches as I gather my thoughts. I swivel my chair and square my shoulders, giving her my full attention.

Gen's left eyebrow raises. "Spill it."

Exhaling the breath I was holding, I proceed to explain that regardless of whether or not Tate manages to retake controlling interest in Immunotech, we can still save the company by planting ourselves among leadership. We need to replace the bad apples with our people, and there is no better person to ensure the books are restored to their previous, spotless glory than her.

Being the steadfast and loyal employee she is, Genevieve's eyes take on a look of laser focus as she straightens. I watch in fascination as she transforms, her inner bull emerging. She begins pacing in front of my desk as I wait for her response. After what feels like an eternity, she faces me. "I'm in. I mean, who else will be able to fix the financial cluster Dorn created?"

Smiling in relief as another small piece falls into place, the remnants of my shattered life continuing to be stitched back together. I stand and walk around my desk to hug Genevieve, my gratitude overflowing. I'm barefoot and five inches shorter than normal, so I wrap my arms around her middle in what would be an awkward embrace had Gen been anyone else. The hug stretches a moment until we both drop our arms. Leaning my hip against my desk, I cross my arms as I contemplate our next steps. "Will you forward me the email Dorn sent? I need to assess whether damage control is necessary."

Genevieve lets out a hybrid snort-laugh. "Of course." She starts typing on her phone. "But let me save you the time, Dorn is digging his own grave with this shit."

I nod my head. "I agree. Still, I need to read the email

so I know what I'm up against when I figure out who was blind copied."

"Done."

My computer dings, alerting me to a new email. I walk behind the desk and lean over my chair to click the bolded subject line. As I read, the corner of my lip twitches in a half-smile at Dorn's impudence. Pulling my chair out, I sit and lean forward, as if Dorn's email will start to make sense the closer I get to the screen. "This guy is certifiable."

Genevieve snickers. "He's definitely crazy. I actually hope he did send this to the Immunotech board so they can see how off the rails he is."

I'm about to answer when Darcy's frantic voice comes through the intercom. "Ms. Tate, Mr. Thompson is ..."

There's a knock on my office door as Ben enters, shaking his head. "Richard Dorn is doing our work for us."

I press the phone intercom button to respond, "It's fine, Darcy. Thank you."

I look up at Ben as he gives Gen a one-armed side hug. "No kidding, I almost feel like I'm missing something. Surely he can't be this stupid. I assume you were blind copied on the email he sent today?"

Ben pulls his phone from the inside of his jacket as he nods his head.

"I need to know who else the email went to."

Ben begins to tap his screen as he responds, "Yeah, Nik sent the two of us a list of recipients a minute ago. Let's see, it looks like the Immunotech leadership team, names I'm unfamiliar with and the board—minus you, of course."

The level of annoyance one person can cause would be impressive if it wasn't at my expense. "I'll schedule a meeting with the Immunotech team to update them. It's important we're transparent about the state of business and our strategy to preserve Immunotech."

Ben and Genevieve nod in agreement before Ben adds, "You know that team is nearly as passionate about Immunotech and Alex's work as you. They'll see through Dorn's bullshit."

I nod in agreement; I certainly hope that's the case. "What are the names you don't recognize?"

Ben reads three names, and I don't need to hear more. "The bastard emailed key investors." Another ounce of frustration is added to the metaphorical pot that is quickly turning into a pressure cooker. I punch the intercom button on my phone. "Darcy, can you please schedule an hour with the Immunotech team, Ben, Genevieve, and me for later today, or tomorrow morning, at the latest?"

Darcy agrees and tells me I have another visitor.

"Who is it, Darcy?"

"He said his name is Luca…he didn't give a last name."

Yet another ounce of annoyance is added. "Give me five minutes and then send him in."

Ben laughs. "That's our cue to get lost."

My eyes widen as I respond, "Absolutely not. The only reason I agreed to see him is because the two of you are here."

Gen's eyebrow lifts once again. "What am I missing? Who's Luca?"

I shake my head indicating he's no one important. "He's just an old family friend who is incredibly persistent."

Tapping the floor with my foot until it hits my discarded heels, I slide my shoes back on. "We have a few minutes before Darcy shows him in…let's discuss next steps."

Ben sighs in resignation as he sits in his favorite chair.

"In addition to scheduling a meeting with the Immunotech team, we need to capitalize on Dorn's recent antics to ensure the board has no other option than to oust him. I'll schedule a meeting with Elizabeth—she's the key to getting rid of Dorn and smoothing things over with any investors who may have been included on that email."

Ben nods. "Edward relies on her counsel for everything. It probably wouldn't hurt to loop in Theo either. He can set the process in motion with Edward while you convince Elizabeth."

The knock on my office door interrupts Ben as Luca enters. "Buongiorno!"

I can't help but smile at his enthusiasm. Italians certainly have flair.

"Buongiorno, Luca," I reply as he walks to me and kisses both cheeks.

I introduce him to Gen, whom he also graces with *il bacetto*, and then he and Ben do the handshake and back-pat move every guy seems to know.

"To what do I owe the pleasure of your company? I wasn't expecting you."

Luca grabs one of my hands, gently holding it between his own. "Bella, you know I couldn't stay away. I am hoping you will join me for an early lunch, I would like your opinion on a restaurant I am interested in acquiring."

Well, shit, how can I say no to that? "I'm flattered you would care for my opinion, Luca. Unfortunately, I've been out all morning and now have emergency damage control to attend to. Rain check?"

"Of course. We will instead have dinner."

My eyes widen in surprise as I try to think of a way to dodge dinner. Luca starts heading toward the door before

I can think of an acceptable excuse. "It was a pleasure meeting you, Genevieve," he calls over his shoulder.

Gen gives him her signature crooked smile that looks more like a smirk. "The pleasure is mine, Luca. Please, stop by whenever you would like."

I elbow her in the ribs.

Luca turns back to face us when he reaches the door, his eyes skate past Gen to bore into mine "Ciao, Bella. I will pick you up tomorrow at eight." With that, he turns and is out the door before I can reply.

What the hell was that? Why do I feel as though this entire interaction was orchestrated?

Genevieve and Ben erupt in fits of laughter as I rub my temples. "I hate you both right now."

Ben stands to put his arm around my shoulder and Gen heads for the door. Turning before she exits, Gen replies, "You may hate me, but you need to let loose, and who better to do that with than a gorgeous Italian?"

Ben squeezes my shoulder. "She's right, doll. Dinner with Luca will be good for you."

I shift from under his arm and round my desk. Reclaiming my chair as if it's my throne, I look up at Ben. "As amusing as it is that the two of you think you know what's in my best interest, I have to disagree with your judgment. Having said that, it appears I won't have a say in the matter since Luca will be picking me up tomorrow evening. Now, did you need anything else? Because I need to get back to work."

Ben lets out a loud belly laugh. "I just wanted to make sure you were aware of Dorn's email and, more importantly, ask how the meeting went?"

Shit. "You're right, I still need to update you."

Ben retakes his spot in his favorite chair, crossing his ankle over his knee in his signature *let's get down to business* pose.

"You'll never guess who showed up to the meeting."

Ben quirks an eyebrow before replying, "He didn't."

Laughter is my response. "He very much did." I proceed to give Ben the play-by-play of the board meeting. When I'm finally finished explaining Theo's strategic move to vote against me, Ben's eyes are wide in disbelief. "What are you planning to do?"

The corners of my lips slowly stretch into a smile. "I plan to sit back and watch the show, my friend."

Ben's face lights up as he stands, his eyes reflecting his anticipation. "Get him, Tyson."

I roll my eyes, but secretly, or maybe it's not such a secret judging by Ben's smirk, I love his response. If there is one thing I'm certain about, it's that this asshole will regret ever knowing my name.

TEN

"**A**RE YOU CERTAIN YOU WANT TO MOVE FORWARD with this?" Nik's disgruntled voice makes me lift my head from an email I'm replying to on my phone. His expression is almost scornful.

"Frankly, no, I don't want to waste time with this dinner, but Luca is an old friend. I felt an obligation to accept. Besides, this is a business meeting. He wants my feedback on a potential acquisition, how could I say no? You know that would be the equivalent of either of us turning down one of Stella's chocolate croissants."

Nik grunts his disapproval as he pulls up to the curb. After several long minutes of negotiating, I was able to convince Luca that I would meet him at the restaurant in lieu of him picking me up. He finally agreed after I explained security won't let me out of their sight. That led to several follow-up questions, for which I dodged answers. Deflating, I reluctantly remove my seat belt and grab my clutch. Nik interrupts my departure by saying, "I'm not able to park here long term. Text me ten minutes before you're ready to leave and I'll meet you here."

"Thank you, Nik. I don't anticipate this dinner taking long. If I have my way, I'll be out in an hour, but I'll text ten minutes ahead of time." Nik gets out of the SUV and walks around to open my door. I step out and hear the door shutting behind me. When I turn to thank Nik, his back is already to me as he rounds the car, shoulders tense. I stare at Nik in surprise—this hostility is so unlike him.

Nik opens the driver's side door, the interior light illuminating his face, which is set in the same scowl he wore on the drive over. Whatever. I shake my head and turn to make my way to the entrance of the restaurant. Nik can be pissy if he wants, I won't let his attitude further dampen my already negative attitude toward this dinner.

Shaking off Nik's behavior, I step through the restaurant door and take in the opulence. Wow, the space is gorgeous. Low lighting and candles appropriately set the mood, giant eighteenth-century mercury mirrors are hung along the far wall, and crystal chandeliers glint, casting a low, warm glow from above. The bar area straight ahead contains a wall of liquor. The bottles rest on shelves from counter to ceiling, with a sliding library ladder attached. The tall bar chairs are a deep emerald green with brass legs, one of which supports Luca as he casually leans against it while sipping a drink. I make my way over and stand on the opposite side of the chair. Luca is discussing the restaurant scene with the bartender, who turns his attention to me and smiles. I return my own polite smile. "I'll have whatever he's having." The bartender nods his head as something I can't quite place flashes in his eyes.

"Bella, you're here!" Luca moves the chair and takes my hands in his own pressing a kiss to each cheek.

I draw my attention away from the bartender and chuckle at Luca's enthusiasm. "Yes, Luca, I am here."

He laughs self-consciously and I feel like a jerk for my response.

Luca smiles, appearing to brush of his unease. "I wasn't sure if you would show. You are very good at avoiding me."

"I haven't been avoiding you, Luca." He narrows his eyes at my response, his expression telegraphing that I'm not fooling him. I soften my eyes and try again. "Okay, I admit, I may have been postponing time alone with you, but only because my life is an absolute mess right now. I don't know how to add you to the compartmentalization of it all." A Negroni is slid in front of me, allowing me to break eye contact with Luca to thank the bartender, who nods his head, an odd, knowing glint in his eyes. What the hell, what's this guy's deal?

I take a small sip to taste the drink and then a second, much larger, sip for courage before returning my attention to Luca to see his eyes boring into me. "Luca, we've been friends for so many years. As you know, I've been dealing with quite a bit these past months and I'm just trying to keep my head above water, which is still a daily struggle. The truth is, I'm not the same person you knew all those years ago. I don't want to give you the impression that this," I point from myself to him, "can be anything other than friendship. I hope that works for you."

Luca smiles and responds with, "Of course, bella. All I want is your friendship."

What? Did I misinterpret Luca's intentions?

I look down at my drink as I fold the corners of the cocktail napkin against the glass. Luca places a hand over mine, halting the napkin folding. "Bella, I know this has been a trying year. Let me be your friend."

I smile at Luca, feeling relieved that he appears to be

okay with remaining in the friend zone. "Thank you, I'm relieved our friendship can continue. I know we've lost touch the last few years, but now that you are spending more time in New York, we'll have time to reconnect."

Luca's smile widens as he replies, "Yes, perfecto." Before he sweeps his hand around the bar with dramatic flair. "Now tell me, what do you think?"

I look around. "What do I think about what?"

"The restaurant, of course! What do you think?"

"Well, the ambience is divine, and my drink is delicious. I'm looking forward to eating. Hopefully the food is as good as it smells."

Luca has a twinkle in his eye as he lowers his voice, "The food is good, but it will be even better when I take over."

I jerk my head back in surprise. "Oh my goodness, Luca! This is the restaurant you are considering? Wow, it's gorgeous." I look toward the restaurant section of the space. "And so busy! I'm shocked the current owners would consider selling."

An unsettled look flits across Luca's face, disappearing into a smile before I can analyze it further. He looks toward the reception desk and waves his hand, smiling. "I believe our table is ready, shall we?"

Luca ushers me to the host station, where three beautiful women are busily working. A striking woman with radiant mocha skin turns our way giving Luca a dazzling smile. "Luca, I see your guest has arrived." She glances at me before returning her attention to Luca. "Let me show you to your table."

I roll my eyes when I see the table is nestled in a secluded back corner. Friends, my ass. Luca pulls my chair out before sitting across from me. We mull over the menu, both of us periodically commenting on the creativity of the dishes. My mouth waters as I continue to read—everything sounds delicious.

When the waiter arrives to fill our water glasses, we order several plates to share and a bottle of Volnay. The moment the waiter leaves our table, I get to the point of the dinner. "It appears you are excited about this opportunity, so what can I help you with, Luca?"

Luca chuckles. "Right to it, I see."

I answer by raising my eyebrows and shrugging one shoulder. I mean, give me a break, at least I waited until we ordered. Luca runs his fingers through his hair before looking up at me. "You assumed correctly; the owners don't want to sell."

There's a beat of silence as Luca waits for my response. He sighs in frustration and continues when I remain silent. "This restaurant is heavily leveraged, and I happen to know the person who provided the financial backing. He assured me that I could take possession within ninety days."

I sit back in my chair, my face falling in disappointment. Far be it for me to judge Luca's business dealings, but this feels wrong. "But the owners don't want to sell?" Luca notices my reaction and cages the excitement he exuded a moment ago.

I attempt a less-accusatory tone. "What do you know about the owners?"

"It's a husband-and-wife team. They opened Bec four years ago, the name is a play on the wife's name and the location, since the restaurant is in Tribeca."

"A husband-and-wife team? Interesting."

Luca's expression shifts before his mask is back in place. "That's my understanding, yes."

"Have you met with them? You're certain they aren't interested in selling?"

Luca pinches his lips in agitation. "I'm certain. They don't want to sell. In fact, they are doing everything possible to pay back the investor to prevent a sale."

My eyes widen in surprise. That was more forthcoming than I anticipated. "Luca, why does it have to be this restaurant? Why not focus on the restaurant you are already planning to open, or find owners willing to sell?"

Pinched eyebrows accompany Luca's pinched lips and I know I've reached his limit of patience. A fierce determination emanates from his dark eyes. His voice is steel when he says, "It has to be this restaurant, that's all there is to say."

Uhhh—"Well … you clearly have your own ideas of what you want to do, so what can I do for you? What did you want my opinion on?"

Luca's eyes clear and his smile returns, back to the charismatic man who can easily captivate a room. This Jekyll and Hyde act has my head spinning. Perhaps I don't know Luca as well as I thought I did.

"I would like to know what you think of Bec." He gestures with his hand to the opulent room we are sitting in.

"Right, well, as I said, the ambience is inviting, and the menu is impressive. It appears to be a great restaurant, Luca. That's obvious even before tasting the food." I lean forward to drive home my next point. "I may not understand why you want this restaurant so badly and frankly, I'm uneasy that you are working with an investor to usurp the owners, but that's your business. Having said that, I doubt you needed me to tell you I think this restaurant is pretty…so what is this really about?"

Luca drops his eyes to the table for a moment before looking up, his eyes softening while his mask remains firmly in place. "I brought you here because I want to ask if you would consider backing me?"

I feel myself deflate in disappointment. How did I not see this coming? Luca is too proud to ask for my professional opinion. Apparently, he's not too proud to ask for my money.

Not noticing my unease, Luca continues, "I realize you will need more information before making a decision. I'll send you the financials tomorrow. The investor has agreed to let me buy the owners out, but I will need financial backing to do so."

I stare at Luca as I contemplate my response. It's obvious his investor friend is going to call the loan, which will require the owners to pay it off by a deadline. A deadline that appears to be in the next couple months if the investor told Luca he could have the restaurant within ninety days.

Luca obviously doesn't know me if he thinks I would help him with this ridiculous scheme. I want to tell him as much, but I'm intrigued to learn more about the current owners and their situation. I absentmindedly trace the condensation on my water glass. My eyes zeroing in on a small drop of water that begins to slide down the glass, somewhat symbolic of where this evening is headed.

Luca grasps my hand away from my glass, casually running his finger over my engagement and wedding rings, drawing my attention to my one weakness. The ever-present pain in my heart flares at the subtle reminder.

"Bella, this is a smart investment. If you think this restaurant is busy now, just wait until I am in the kitchen."

I pull my hand out of Luca's grip and plaster a fake smile on my face. "Send me the financials and any other information you have. I'll review what you send and get back to you."

Appeased, Luca smiles. And I'm suddenly feeling claustrophobic. "If you'll excuse me, I need to use the restroom." Luca stands as I do, ever the consummate gentleman I think as I cringe internally.

The restroom is blessedly empty, allowing me to take my time at the sink. I study myself in the mirror. The faint purple smudges under my eyes are almost invisible thanks to my concealer, but makeup can't fix the empty look in my eyes. After several minutes, I take a cleansing breath to gear up for this charade we are calling dinner and push away from the sink, feeling marginally better now that I've regained my equilibrium. I look at my watch as I exit the restroom—only thirty more minutes before I can leave, I can handle that...

"Umph!" Large hands grip my shoulders, preventing me from falling on my ass. I look up at the flesh wall I just ran into "I'm so sor—" My words die on my lips. "Richard? What the hell?" I attempt to step out of his reach, but he digs his fingers into my shoulders and brings me closer to his sweaty, sneering face.

"I saw you when I was in the dining room and thought the two of us should have a little chat."

"Richard, you are the last person I care to *chat* with." I attempt to pull a shoulder out of his hold by twisting my torso, but his grip tightens, sure to leave bruises.

Richard's red, swollen face gets closer to mine as he

growls in my ear, "You have no idea who you are fucking with, Eliana." Malevolence shines through his eyes. "If you are half as smart as you think you are, you will fix what you broke yesterday."

My throat tightens as indignation consumes me. I narrow my eyes, mentally shooting daggers at Richard's bloated face as I straighten my spine. "Remove your hands or I will scream."

Richard finally lowers his hands, giving me a little shove as he does. His anger is becoming less restrained by the second. When I attempt to sidestep him, he blocks my exit a second time. "Move. Someone is waiting for me," I growl under my breath, making sure he's aware I'm not alone.

Richard's face smooths and the malevolent smile returns. "By all means," He stretches his arm out toward Luca. "Return to your meeting. Just remember to do the right thing, Eliana. The smart thing."

I laugh at his dramatic performance. This guy is truly next-level crazy.

Brushing past him, I take my phone out of my clutch and text Nik as I make my way back to Luca. He stands as I approach the table, but I don't sit. "Luca, I apologize, but I need to get going, something came up." Luca's face falls and, as irrational as it is, I feel a smidge of guilt for leaving before we eat—guilt that I squash when I remember that the purpose of this dinner was for Luca to ask me for money. "Send me the financial statements, I'll review them and let you know what I think."

This brings the first genuine smile to Luca's face all night. "Perfecto! I'll send you everything tomorrow. Do you have a car, or can I give you a ride home?"

"Thank you for the offer, Luca, but Nik is waiting for me outside."

Luca nods his head. "Let me walk you out."

We are interrupted by a waiter delivering our meal, the plates of food look and smell delicious, causing my mouth to water. "Excuse me, may I get these to-go?" I point to the chicory salad and branzino with saffron cauliflower sauce. The waiter complies and disappears with the dishes. "Luca, please sit. Enjoy your meal, I'll grab mine on the way out." Luca reluctantly nods before kissing both cheeks goodbye. I scan the restaurant as I make my way back toward the reception stand, but there is no sign of Richard. Thank God.

I wait at the mouth of a hallway entrance near double swinging doors separating the restaurant from the kitchen so that I can intercept the waiter. Two minutes later, the waiter exits in a flourish and hands me a paper bag with Bec printed on the side. After thanking him, I make my way to the sidewalk in front of the restaurant, which does not have a black SUV idling at the curb. That's odd. Digging my phone out of my clutch, I see there are two missed calls from Nik. I press his name and he answers on the first ring. "I'm two minutes away, I had to park five blocks from the restaurant and traffic is a mess."

"No problem, Nik. I just stepped out of the restaurant."

"You what?" I pull the phone away from my ear. "Stay inside, Mrs. Tate!" Nik bellows into the phone.

Sheesh. "Okay, okay. I'm walking back in now. I'll see you in two minutes." I disconnect the phone as I step back inside the restaurant. There's an alcove to my right that is out of the way and has a clear line of sight to the street. Perfect.

Leaning against the wall, I process the last half hour. What a waste of a night. Luca inviting me to dinner just to ask for money. Richard Dorn magically appearing like the cockroach he is. Why the hell is he here? I don't believe in coincidences, but how would he have known I would be here tonight? My thoughts are running wild with probable and improbable scenarios when I hear a familiar Italian accent. I peek around the wall of the alcove obscuring my view. The pieces of this mess of an evening are picked up, shaken, and thrown into the air.

"Ah, Richard!" Luca shakes Dick's hand.

My eyes are saucers as I watch my nemesis and Luca together. *What the hell?* It's obvious they are friendly with each other, and that this isn't the first time they have met. I tilt my head as I strain to hear what they are saying, but their voices are too low. Like an obscene car accident, I don't want to watch, but I can't take my eyes away as their large smiles and back slaps cause my stomach to roil.

My clutch vibrates, interrupting the trance I'm under. Retrieving my phone, I see a text from Nik letting me know he's out front. I look back at Luca and Richard as they walk toward the main dining area, most likely to the table I just vacated.

I can't bring myself to move as I continue to watch the two men until they turn a corner and are out of sight. Shaking my head in disbelief, I push away from the wall and stumble out of the restaurant. I climb into the backseat of the waiting SUV before Nik has a chance to walk around to open my door.

Nik looks over his shoulder. "You're earlier than I expected, everything okay?"

I look back at the restaurant, still stunned. "I'm pretty sure I just saw Dorn take my place as Luca's dinner companion."

Nik's eyes snap to the restaurant. "Dorn's in there now?"

Absentmindedly nodding my head, I reply with a simple "Yes."

Nik rubs the back of his neck, clearly affected by this news. "Did he approach you?"

Before I can reply, Nick pulls out his phone and taps a contact. I hear two rings and then a muffled voice on the other end but can't make out the words. Nik sits and listens, grunting a couple of times, until his patience is depleted. "You had one task and you failed." There's a beat of silence and then more muffled talking until Nik ends the call, cutting off the stream of chatter.

I raise my eyebrows in question. "Who was that?"

"We are hiring additional field personnel and I am currently interviewing a few people. One of the candidates was supposed to play point tonight. He failed his job and won't be hired." I feel my eyebrows manage to raise another degree. I'm going to need Botox in my forehead at this rate. Nik looks up as if he's asking for divine intervention before answering the question that's clearly written on my face. "The bartender."

For the first time since my ride home with Ben after dinner at the Murphys', I find myself laughing. Slaphappy, punch-drunk laughter at the ridiculousness of it all.

Of course, the bartender would be a covert recruit to Nik's team, totally normal. After a couple of minutes, I finally manage to dampen my laughter when I see Nik looking at me with concern. I take a moment to catch my breath as I look out the window. "I actually sensed something was off with the bartender. Good to know I can still trust my instincts."

Nik grunts something indiscernible as he pulls away from the curb, clearly not as impressed with my killer instincts as me. I relax into the leather seat and stare absently out the window as I contemplate why I have been ignoring my instincts about Luca. I've felt something was off ever since the Murphys' dinner, and now, knowing he is friendly with Dorn, it's obvious I need to proceed with caution.

ELEVEN

MY FIRST YEAR OUT OF BUSINESS SCHOOL, I LEARNED several invaluable lessons that have guided me through my time in corporate America. Of these lessons, the first was particularly poignant.

Prior to launching Tate, Inc., I worked at TA holdings. Theo and my father started the firm when they were in their thirties, so it made sense that I would cut my teeth in the family business. I was being fast-tracked, which resulted in some colleagues feeling that nepotism over merit was behind my expedited success. Looking back objectively, I would agree I was hired because of Theo and my father, even though I graduated top of my class, but once employed, my work spoke for itself.

I was vying for a promotion to director of acquisitions. I knew without a doubt this role was made for me. I was obsessed with finding the next investment that would yield a 10X return, and I was good at it. But above all, this role would give me the experience I needed to eventually start my own firm.

I had been working under the current director and had found and negotiated the terms for the last six companies we had acquired, all of which had produced the highest returns in the shortest amount of time in the history of TA Holdings. I was working on what would be my biggest deal at TA and was provided a team that included two analysts to perform due diligence. One of the analysts, Fred, was not my biggest fan. He believed I was in my position because my father's name, Andrew, was the A in TA. Theo representing the T was most likely another strike against me.

We spent hundreds of hours working through this deal. It was a diamond in the rough, a sound investment that was synergistic to TA's portfolio of businesses. Fred was cordial during the due diligence process, with periodic moments of kindness to my face, but he was also secretly talking to leadership. Feeling he was passed over, Fred told management I was in over my head and that the deal would be lost if he wasn't leading the team. Luckily, management was fully aware of what was happening under their noses, including who was and wasn't contributing. Fred's antics got back to me, and I gave him the benefit of the doubt. I reasoned this was a difficult situation for him to be in since he had more experience. It was obvious he felt he should be promoted and belittling my abilities would shine a spotlight on him.

Negotiations were proceeding beautifully when Fred decided he could get the deal closed for three million dollars less than what we originally planned to pay. He believed if he closed the deal for less than what we were approved to spend, management would have no other option than to promote him instead of me. He scheduled a meeting with the target company behind our backs and pitched them on the decreased rate. The company, furious we would renege, called me demanding to know why I didn't have the decency to low-ball them face to face. I removed Fred from the project and immediately met with the target company's leadership team to grovel in person. I explained that we had no intention of reducing the price we had already discussed, and Fred was off the project. But we had lost face at that point and the target lost their confidence in TA. We inevitably lost the deal.

I was devastated. I'd poured everything into this deal and believed down to my marrow TA Holdings was the best option for the target company's growth. The situation taught me an important lesson: second chances should not be given freely; they should be reserved for the very few people worthy of them. I should have removed Fred from the project the moment I learned he was attempting to undermine me to management.

It's this lesson that comes to mind as I sit at my desk reviewing the Bec prospectus Luca sent me this morning. I see why Luca wants this restaurant; it's incredibly profitable. The owners are making monthly payments on one large loan from a private investor, and all have been on time. But something's off. There's a reason the restaurant is still heavily leveraged when it's so profitable. The owners could be mismanaging their money, but I don't think that's the case. Not when the books are spotless and, aside from the debt payments, profits have been reinvested into the business.

I massage my temples as I contemplate possible scenarios and the reasons behind Luca's involvement. Needing a logic check, I grab my cell to text Ben.

Twenty minutes later, Darcy's voice is shrill over the intercom as she frantically attempts to warn me that Ben has once again bypassed her request to wait. I can't help but laugh as he saunters to my desk, leaning down to kiss my cheek before sitting in his usual chair. He snickers as I pick up the phone. "Thank you for letting me know, Darcy.

It's fine." I narrow my eyes at Ben before continuing, "Trust me, I know how difficult it is to get him to do anything he doesn't want to do. Even if it's simply to wait for thirty seconds."

Ben arches an eyebrow. "Did you ask me to come in here to tell me about your date?"

My eyes widen—that's one way to change the subject. "Not exactly." I run Ben through Luca's request for capital to pay off the lead investor of Bec, explaining that the restaurant has solid financials and that I suspect Luca isn't disclosing everything. The memory of Luca and Dorn laughing as they walked toward the dining room makes my stomach clench as if I'm once again peeking around the wall of the alcove. *Second chances should be reserved for the very few who deserve them.*

Ben sits back as he takes a moment to think. We stare at each other contemplatively until he finally speaks. "You think there's more to this than an over-leveraged restaurant."

It's a statement, not a question, but I nod my head. "Yes, I do. And I can't shake the feeling there's a story behind Bec's owners. Why are they leveraged and only making the minimum payments when the restaurant is turning enough profit to pay off their primary investor if that's what's needed to keep it?" My gaze drifts over Ben's shoulder as I think through the potential scenarios and next steps.

"The restaurant is a great investment on paper, but I'm not giving Luca a penny; I don't trust a word out of his mouth."

Ben looks at me in surprise. "So, I take it the date didn't go well?"

"First of all, it was not a date. Luca just wanted to ask

me for money. And the evening ended rather abruptly when Richard Dorn accosted me outside the restroom."

Ben sucks in a breath. "What? Why in the hell was he there?"

I shake my head in frustration at the memory. "If only that was the worst of it. I had to wait for Nik since dinner ended earlier than anticipated. I was near the front of the restaurant when I saw Luca and Dorn together, acting like long-lost friends. So, no, the evening did not go well, and I have no idea why Dorn was there, though it appears it had something to do with Luca."

Ben gapes at me. "Are you serious?"

"Entirely. But that's not why I wanted to speak with you. I need your help figuring out the story behind Bec."

Ben's eyes light with the impending challenge as he claps his hands. "What do you need?" I can't help but smile at Ben's enthusiasm. He would have made a fantastic investigator.

"I need everything you can find on the owners and anything you can find on the investor the owners are trying to pay off." I flip through the prospectus and slide a page in front of Ben, pointing to the debt payment. "Payments are currently being made to Capri, Inc., which is registered to a Henry Sullivan. I haven't been able to find anything on Mr. Sullivan."

I see the excitement of the chase electrify the blue of Ben's eyes as he taps the prospectus. "Mind if I borrow this for a couple of hours?"

I motion for him to take it. "It's all yours."

Ben jumps out of the chair. "I'll be back."

I can't help but chuckle as I reply, "I'll be here."

* * *

"You do realize I've been waiting for you to look up for the past three minutes, don't you?"

I shriek as my spine snaps straight and my body freezes in surprise. "Ben, you scared the shit out of me!" I look at my phone, wondering why I didn't receive a frantic warning from Darcy.

"My welcoming committee is grabbing coffee." Ben sits in his customary chair. "Sorry to startle you, did you really not know I was here?" He looks at me skeptically.

I take another deep breath in an attempt to calm my racing heart. "I had no idea. I've been going over reports for three of our investments, two of which I suspect will go public next year. I've been so engrossed in modeling various scenarios, time just slipped away from me."

Ben grins knowingly. "Ah, I see. Make sure you get every possible penny."

"You bet, and I'm questioning whether the rate of growth can continue for one investment. I think the IPO will be a bust if not. We may have to sell to another private equity firm."

I set the papers aside and look at my watch. "Were you stopping by to creepily stare at me, or for another reason?"

Ben is nearly vibrating with excitement when he responds with, "I came by to tell you we are going to a party!"

I raise my eyebrows as I begin to collect the papers strewn across my desk. "A party? What kind of party?"

"An opening for a new club."

"Mmm, thanks for the invite, but I don't think so."

Ben's eyes twinkle as he smirks at me. "What if the opening is for a club with backing from Capri, Inc.?" I pause as I'm about to shove the reports into my bag so I can finish reviewing later tonight. Ben takes my pause as his cue to continue. "And what if I told you everyone who's anyone in the culinary scene will be in attendance, including the owners of Bec?"

Well damn, the potential of having Bec's owners and investor in the same place at the same time is too perfect to pass up. I stand, grab my bag and roll my eyes at Ben's expectant expression as he waits for my reply. "Fine. When and where?"

The room is blinded by Ben's signature megawatt smile. "This Friday in Tribeca, near Bec, actually. The party starts at ten, but the restaurateurs probably won't arrive until after twelve, so I suggest we shoot for a midnight entrance, Cinderella."

I nod my head and point toward the door. "I'm heading out. I still need to clear this with Nik." The thought causes me to grimace—it won't be a pleasant conversation. "But that should work. Will Jax be there?"

Ben stands to walk me out. "Jackson will be in London." His lips turn down in a pout. "I swear, London is Jax's mistress at this point. He's there more than he's home."

I know he's kidding but I feel a pang for Ben. I remember how much I missed Alex when he had long stretches of travel. At the time I missed the little things, like waking up next to him and sharing coffee in the morning. I took so many moments for granted; I even took the ability to miss a spouse because they are away for a few days for granted. I would happily take missing Alex for weeks on end if I knew I would see him again.

Ben interrupts my melancholic thoughts. "I'll meet

you at your place around eleven for a glass of champagne before we head to the opening."

"Perfect, I'll let you know if anything changes."

"It wo-oon't," Ben singsongs as we exit my office and he turns to wink at Darcy.

I tell Darcy goodnight and text Nik to let him know I'm on my way to the car. Ben nudges my shoulder as we make our way down the hall to the elevator. "What are you getting into this evening, another date with Luca?" Ben wags his eyebrows, and I can't help but laugh.

"That is definitely not on the agenda."

"Then what is on the agenda?"

Lowering my phone, I stare at the elevator doors, not really seeing them. "I would love nothing more than to throw on my running shoes and disappear for an hour or two, but that's not in my cards." I hear the dejection in my voice.

Ben puts his arm over my shoulder and squeezes. "This too shall pass, doll. Nik and the team will figure out who has been harassing you, and you'll be able to have your freedom again." Ben means well, but I don't think I'll have much freedom for a while. There are no new leads, and Nik's team is as frustrated as I am at this point, but I paste on an agreeable smile as I look up at him.

The elevator dings announcing its arrival.

"Well, I can't wait—omph!"

My bag is knocked out of my hand as I'm thrown into Ben.

"I'm so sorry, I wasn't paying attention." A deep voice raises from our feet. I look down to see broad shoulders belonging to the man who just body-checked me. He's collecting the contents from my bag now scattered on the floor.

Ben's arm, the only reason I'm still standing, has me glued to his chest.

The man stands and holds out my bag, the contents replaced, before I have time to catch my breath.

"Again, I apologize. I'm running late and I wasn't paying attention."

I shake my head clear as I take my bag from the man. "No harm done, thank you for picking up my things."

The man's eyes shift wildly over my shoulder, as if he's looking for someone. Before I can say anything else, he rushes past us calling out, "It's the least I can do," as he speed-walks away.

I give Ben a "what the hell" look as he releases me, and we step onto the elevator.

Ben leans down to look me in the eye. "Are you okay?"

I raise a shaky hand to push a piece of hair out of my face. "I'm fine, I just wasn't expecting to be run over while waiting for the elevator."

Ben continues to search my face when I'm saved by the ding announcing our third-floor arrival. We step from the elevator into the parking garage, and Ben's focus is re-directed to Nik, who is standing near the elevator bank.

"Nik, perfect timing. Elle and I were just discussing an opening we will be attending this Friday; you don't suppose that will be a problem, do you?"

My eyes widen as I gape at Ben. What the hell, way to pull the Band-Aid off with this one, Ben. Sheesh.

Nik narrows his eyes. "An opening? Where?" Suspicion is heavy in his tone, and I know this will be more of a nego-tiation than a conversation.

I start walking toward the car not having the energy

to hash this out now. "I'll send you the details later this evening.

"See you tomorrow, *Benjamin*," I add, with just enough venom for Ben to know I'm not happy with his little game. I look back to see him smiling as he winks and turns to walk to his car. I lift my eyes to the concrete ceiling as I fight a smile at his mic-drop exit. I guess that's one way of making sure I don't use Nik as an excuse to get out of this party. Little does he know I'm much too interested in meeting the owners of Bec to back out now. This could be the break I've been looking for to figuring out Luca's motivation to purchase Bec, and possibly even his involvement with Dorn. Solving at least one of the mysteries circling me is too appealing to back down from.

* * *

Scanning the row of dresses in front of me, I contemplate what the hell I'm going to wear. I impatiently flick through my cocktail dresses for the sixth time, but no new items have magically appeared. I pause the shuffling to run a hand over a black draped silk Armani I bought a couple of years ago for some event that I can't recall. Pulling the dress from the rack, I hold it in front of me and look in the mirror. The image causes an onslaught of memories to assault me. Like a picture book, I recall Alex's face when I stepped out of our room wearing this dress. First awe, and then hunger filled his eyes before he prowled to me, caging me between him and the hall wall. His pupil-black eyes stared into me, not at me, as one finger trailed down the side of my cheek to my neck and then collarbone. His deep voice, pitched even deeper, had hit me in all the right places, when he said, "*You are quite literally breathtaking,"* right before we devoured one another, volleying each other for every demanding kiss and caress.

I give my head a little shake to blink the memory away. My gaze returns to my reflection in the mirror. The sharp stab of ice-cold pain that always follows the warmth of a memory from my former life hits right on cue. I watch as the dress slips from my fingers, the light fabric floating to the floor, before I brace myself on the closet island.

Deep breaths, Elle. Just breathe.

I inhale through my nose and exhale through my mouth in an attempt to rein in the wave of devastation before it crests, wishing I could return to the glorious warmth I felt just a moment ago. The memory of both of us sweaty, my back against the wall, my dress around my stomach and my legs around Alex. A breath of a laugh leaves my lips as I recall we were late to the event and didn't have time to freshen up before Nik was summoning us to the car. We were disheveled and couldn't keep our hands off one another throughout the night. It was indecently sublime.

I straighten in surprise. *Holy shit, it worked.* Well, how about that, thank God for memories of hot sex to prevent a meltdown.

"Are you about ready, doll?" Ben's voice filters in from my bedroom.

I look down at the puddle of black silk on the floor. "Be out in a minute."

I wrangle my way into the dress, needing but lacking the skills of a contortionist, and buckle gunmetal metallic stilettos to my feet. A quick look in the mirror tells me the outfit may be a bit much, so I grab a leather jacket to dress the ensemble down and step out of my closet.

"Damn, doll!" Ben's megawatt smile holds an extra watt or two.

I can't help but smile at his exaggerated excitement. "It's a bit much, but I'm bringing this to tone it down." I raise the arm with my jacket draped over it.

Ben scowls. "Don't you dare. Do you know how long it has been since I've seen you dressed to impress?"

"Are you suggesting my work attire isn't impressive?"

Ben smiles, unconcerned he just insulted me. "You know that's not what I meant. Your work attire is entirely impressive for work, not for a night out." Ben's eyes roam up and down my body. "Now *this* is impressive for a night out. So where are the bubbles?"

Laughing, I walk to the kitchen and grab a bottle of champagne out of the wine fridge. Ben leans against the island as I uncork the bottle and pour two glasses, passing one to him. "Santé."

He touches his glass to mine. "To health, finding answers, *and* having a little fun tonight." He raises his index finger to stop the objection I'm about to make as he takes a sip from his glass. "Just a smidge of fun, I promise."

I lean against the counter opposite the island. "I'll make you a deal." Ben quirks his head to the side and purses his lips in interest before taking another healthy drink. "If we are able to get to the bottom of Luca's interest in Bec, I'll have a couple of drinks and may even dance."

Ben's eyes light in surprise. "Whaaat?"

"You heard me, but we have to find information first."

"Oh, doll, do you not know me? I'll have your information within thirty minutes of walking through the club doors."

I feel myself smirk at Ben's proclamation. "Okay,

hotshot, then I suppose we might find a little fun. Let me grab a clutch and we can be on our way."

I set my glass down as Ben refills his and walk back to my room to grab a clutch. Ben is finishing his second glass of bubbles when I return to the kitchen. I eye the empty glass. "You do realize this is a champagne flute, not a shot glass, right?" When Ben doesn't respond, I turn my attention from him to locating my wallet. I look around the kitchen as I try to remember where I dumped my bag when I got home.

"Entry table."

"Ah, what would I do without you? Can you let Nik know we're ready?"

Ben chuckles. "Speaking of …" He raises his voice to be heard as I walk to the entry. "I can only imagine the amount of years Nik has aged this week preparing for tonight. I'm actually shocked he's letting you go."

"You have no idea. I wouldn't be surprised if the cocktail servers are on his payroll," I yell back in response.

My bag is exactly where Ben said it would be, on a side table in the foyer. I dig for my wallet, finding it under files, lotion, and a protein bar. Ben walks up to me while typing on his phone as I transfer my license, credit cards, and lip gloss to my clutch. "Nik is on his way up."

Ben looks up from his phone and his expression warms. "You really do look fantastic, Elle."

"Well, thank you, Benjamin. You look very dapper yourself."

I watch as Ben continues to study my dress. "Is that the dress you wore to the Blackwell's engagement party?"

A guffaw of laughter leaves my mouth—leave it to Ben to remember where I last wore this dress. I take a deep breath to regain my composure only to start laughing again when Ben looks at me like he's waiting to catch up with the joke. "I'm sorry, it's been a long day and this champagne is going to my head."

Ben narrows his eyes. "No, you're not getting out of this that easily, what's so funny? Spill."

"It's really nothing, I just … well, when I chose this dress, I remembered wearing it a couple of years ago but couldn't remember where. It's fitting you remembered when I could only remember other moments from the evening."

Ben smirks. "Ah, you remembered *other* moments from the evening, huh?"

I feel my face burn with embarrassment as I return Ben's smirk with one of my own. "Yes, there are a few I remember fondly, but I couldn't recall the event, so thanks for the reminder."

Ben laughs in response. "That sounds about right. If I remember correctly, it was evident you had been thoroughly ravaged prior to you and Alex arriving to the party."

"Benjamin!" I add a slap to his arm for good measure as I feel my face heat a few more degrees.

We are both doubled over in laughter, the contagious kind that makes your stomach muscles ache and tears leak from your eyes, when the elevator dings announcing its arrival. The doors open and Nik steps out looking like a Jason Statham-James Bond mashup in his suit, interrupting our delirium. When I'm able to regain enough composure to speak, I look from Nik to Ben. "I'm certainly a lucky lady tonight, being escorted by what are sure to be the two most handsome men in the club."

Nik looks down, uncomfortable with my compliment. "Shall we?"

Ben and I chuckle at Nik's expense as the three of us

file onto the elevator. I lean against Ben's arm. "Well, this evening is already off to a great start."

Ben smirks before replying, "Is that a result of your hot sex memories with Alex?"

Nik coughs, choking on the air he's breathing.

I just laugh because Ben's right. Being able to not only think about Alex but talk about him without completely melting down is miles from where I was just weeks ago. Maybe tonight really will be a good night.

TWELVE

LIGHTS PULSE IN TIME WITH THE BEAT OF THE MUSIC. The heady scent of jasmine, ambergris, and champagne creates an expectant atmosphere that has bodies swaying and grinding to the deep thrum of the music filling the space.

Relaxed into a velvet, crescent-shaped booth, I watch Genevieve, who just arrived, down her second glass of champagne. Not hiding my smirk, I shift my eyes to Ben; his relaxed pose makes him look like he should be on the cover of *Vogue* instead of in a booth at a club. I follow his gaze to see beautiful, scantily clad women swarming the cavernous space. The dance floor directly in front of us is a sea of undulating bodies, and large crowds of smiling patrons mill at the bars lining the perimeter of the open space as they wait in haphazard lines for refreshed drinks.

Scanning the other booths, there's still no sign of the three people we are here to see. My eyes meet Nik's and I raise my eyebrows, silently asking if he has spotted Bec's owners or the founder of Capri, Inc. Nik gives his head a sharp shake.

Returning my attention to Ben and Genevieve, I sip my champagne while surreptitiously looking for anyone resembling the photos Nik sent earlier today when the music changes. The deep bass of a Beyonce song vibrates through the space. "This is my song!" Genevieve jumps up and grabs my hand, managing to slide my body to the edge of the seat. "Come on, Elle, we have to dance!"

I can't help but laugh at Gen's enthusiasm. "Okay, okay. Stop pulling me, I'll end up on the floor." I follow Gen to the center of the dance floor and push my prior declaration that I wouldn't have fun until we found Bec's owners from my mind.

For a glorious frame of time, Gen and I become lost to the music, dancing to one song after another. I feel free and lighthearted in a way I haven't since Alex was taken from me. I try to appreciate this moment. To hold onto it with a steel grip, memorizing this feeling so I can draw from it days and weeks from now. Until then, I close my eyes and move, falling deeper into the music.

We are both sweaty and high on endorphins when an attractive guy Gen had been eyeing breaks away from his friends and starts dancing with her. I give Gen the universal *do you want me to save you* look. She shakes her head no, and returns my look with her own, which screams for me to get lost.

Chuckling, I mouth and mime for Gen to meet me back at the table when she's finished. She beams and nods her head before returning her attention to her new dance partner, who strangely resembles a Ken doll.

Smiling, I wink at her before turning to fight my way through the crowd. I lose count of the number of swaying bodies I dodge as one person after another interrupts my path to the table. Finally, I see a very alert Nik laser-focused on me through a clearing in the sea of bodies. I dart to the table before the clearing is once again blocked, and immediately grab my champagne, swallowing the bubbly liquid in one drink. "Where's Ben?"

Nik continues to scan the room as he answers, "He left for the restroom about five minutes ago."

I take inventory of our now-empty table before shouting over the music. "Why don't we mingle? Bec's owners may be in the lounge section we walked by when we arrived."

Nik nods in agreement, and we make our way past the bars along the perimeter of the club into a second space on the opposite side of the largest bar separating the two areas. The space has a sophisticated feel, with stately chaise lounges and plush chairs arranged around small, mirrored tables that reflect dim light from the chandeliers above. The lounge area is decidedly cozy yet sexy, and I immediately decide to spend the remainder of the evening here instead of on the club side.

We walk around, looking at the faces clustered together in groups, but still no sign of Bec's owners. "Do we need to let Gen and Ben know we've moved to the lounge section?"

Nik shakes his head. "No, Scott is watching Genevieve; he can direct her to us when she's finished dancing, and Stephens is waiting for Ben."

Nik's fingers fly over his phone screen as he's talking. "They'll meet us here," he confirms.

I nod toward an open-seating arrangement, and the two of us make our way over. I sit toward one end of the chaise, but Nik remains standing. "Nik, will you please sit down, you don't need to hover." He purses his lips in objection but sits in the chair opposite the couch. His head remains on a swivel as he scans the room.

A waitress greets us and asks for our drink order. I order glasses of champagne, which Nik amends with an unopened bottle of champagne and bottled waters. To her credit, the waitress doesn't falter at the request for all items to be delivered unopened, and she's off to the next table before I have time to be embarrassed that we are implying we don't trust her.

Shaking my head at Nik, I sit back and take in the room. The familiar silhouette of Ben catches my eye as he and Stephens enter the lounge. I raise my hand to wave them over, but pause when a loud, boisterous laugh diverts my attention. I look toward the corner nearest us and see a middle-aged man with a barrel chest, blond-gray hair gelled back, rosy swollen cheeks, and a red nose holding court for a small group of men in suits and woman in strips of fabric attempting to pass for dresses. I make eye contact with Nik and nod my head toward the group. Nik's eyes narrow as he surveys the group.

"Did you enjoy your cardio session?" I look up to see Ben and Stephens. Ben sits next to me and I nod my head toward the man in the corner. Ben's eyes alight in anticipation when he realizes who it is. "What's our next move?"

Nik interrupts before I can respond. "The next move is for you both to sit here and ..." he looks over my shoulder, "enjoy the champagne."

I turn to see our waitress approaching the table with a bottle of champagne in a bucket and several glass bottles of unopened water. The waitress opens the champagne and pours two glasses, at Nik's instruction, prior to leaving.

Sipping the pink bubbles, I pretend to be engaged in conversation as I keep an eye on the table in the corner. Finally, after nearly an hour, the red-faced man stands and begins walking toward the restrooms.

Anticipating my move, Nik places a hand on my shoulder.

"Please stay here and wait for the man to return, Mrs. Tate." Ignoring Nik, I jump up and follow the man as he exits the lounge area and walks down the main hallway to a small lobby outside the restrooms. I catch up to him just as he enters a door with a stick-figured man on the front. I have to wait nearly ten minutes, my time spent texting Gen, who is not responding, before the restroom door is flung open and the man saunters out, not a care in the world. I place my phone in my clutch and pretend to be walking toward the restroom. I see his sleazy appreciation of my dress as his eyes rake up, and then down, my body. I pause just before he passes. "Excuse me," I say, and his eyes flip up to my own. "Do I know you?"

The man's startled expression, most likely because he was expecting to be called out for gawking, morphs into a slimy smile he must think is charming.

"No, sugar," he responds in a syrupy voice with a thick southern drawl, "I would have remembered meeting a girl like you." I grind my teeth at being called sugar *and* girl in the same sentence and force my lips to smile as I pretend to be flattered.

"Hmm, are you sure? You look so familiar." I cock my head to the side and study his face, tiny beads of sweat line his forehead and cheeks, and I absently wonder if he always walks around with sweat dripping from his face, before I snap my fingers as if his identity just came to me. "Wait, are you by chance affiliated with Capri, Inc.?"

His slimy expression turns a bit suspicious. "What do you know about Capri?"

I go with honesty. "Well, I was asked to invest in a small business I believe Capri has a stake in."

His suspicion turns to curiosity as he considers what I just said before asking, "Which business?"

"Are you familiar with a restaurant called Bec?"

His expression goes blank, a mask of indifference sliding into place. "Possibly."

I lift my eyebrows. Really, buddy, you can't put two and two together?

"Welllll … "I say, drawing out the l, "this is the business I was asked to invest in. I'm just trying to better understand why there is a need for additional funding?"

The man's expression transitions from blank to surprise before he releases a boisterous laugh similar to the one that originally drew my attention. He looks into the distance before the words "that motherfucker" leave his mouth.

My eyebrows raise in surprise at his reaction. "And who is this motherfucker you're referring to?"

His eyes snap back to mine and he lets out another surprised laugh before stretching out his large paw of a hand. "Well, you're a surprising little thing now, aren't ya. I'm Henry, pleased to meet ya."

I shake his meaty hand and introduce myself before repeating my question. "So, who exactly is the motherfucker you referred to?"

Henry grins and shakes his head. "You're a live wire."

I give Henry a placating smile. "I've been called worse."

He brings his face closer to mine and lowers his voice. I try not to back away from the smell of gingivitis mixed with bourbon as Henry murmurs, "The *motherfucker* is my so-called partner." He pauses and looks down in thought as if he's trying to work out a difficult equation before looking up and again shaking his head. "I think my partner is trying to slip the rug out from under me on this deal."

"The individual who asked me to invest is definitely not your partner, he's a chef from Italy."

Henry gives me a condescending smile. "The chef may be the one asking for money, but I guarantee Richard is behind this."

Now it's my turn to snap to attention. "Wait, you aren't referring to Richard Dorn, are you?"

The side of Henry's lip turns up in disgust at the mention of Dorn. "That's the one. He's becoming more trouble than I bargained for."

Holy shit, Dorn is this guy's partner. "With all due respect, why is he your partner if you clearly don't like him?"

Henry looks at me as if I just called him an idiot to his face, which I suppose is partially true from the tone of my question. I mean, who would ever go into business with an obvious snake like Richard Dorn? Henry's expression turns from insulted to suspicious. "How do you know Richard?"

I cringe at the mention of his name. "Are you from the south, Henry?"

Henry nods his head once before replying, "Kentucky, born and raised."

Perfect. "Well, Henry from Kentucky, let's just say that Richard is the Hatfield to my McCoy."

Suspicion becomes anger as Henry nods his head. His expression opens as he pats my shoulder, our mutual distaste of Richard forming an unspoken camaraderie between us. Henry lowers his hand and leans in so that I can hear his lowered voice. "The only reason I agreed to the partnership was because he had a funding source that practically printed money." He raises his shoulders in a shrug. "But the source dried up, and now he's apparently scrambling to buy our prime investments out from under me; I reckon he plans to dissolve the partnership once he has some of our investments locked up."

"But why Bec? Sure, it's a profitable business, but you don't have stake in the restaurant, right? You are just collecting interest on the loan you provided, which I assume can't be lucrative enough for Dorn to go through all this trouble."

Henry looks disappointed that I wasn't able to draw a conclusion on my own, which I assume is the only reason he's forthcoming when he replies, "It's not the interest we're after. It's the lien on the restaurant and the gamble that the owners will default once their medical bills pile up. When that happens, we will take ownership of a successful business with opportunity for expansion."

What the hell?

Henry pats my shoulder. "Thank ya kindly for the intel, I need to get back to my friends."

He starts to walk away as I stand speechless but pauses and takes his wallet out of the interior pocket of his jacket. "Here's my card, give me a call if y'all find out anything else."

I stare at his retreating back. "Yeah, don't hold your breath."

* * *

I am frozen in place, piecing together this new information, when Nik steps out of the shadows. "Did you hear any of that?"

Nik looks to where Henry departed. "Some."

"Dorn is obviously using Luca to get the funds to buy Bec, but why when he already had a plan in place with Capri?"

Nik scratches his chin contemplatively. "Perhaps they

don't actually want to buy the restaurant. Luca and Dorn could be planning to convince the owners to use their funds to pay off the current loan, moving their investment to the primary lien position."

"You may be right. From what Henry said, it appears the restaurant was used as collateral. If they take over the loan and the owner's default, the restaurant would be theirs."

Nik nods as he takes my elbow. "Let's get back to the table." We walk back into the lounge in silence as I think through the implications of what I just learned. Nik's reasoning makes sense, especially if the owners don't want to sell and they are feeling pressured for a buyout. If Luca pays off Capri, making him the primary investor, the restaurant would be his if the owners default on the loan. My thoughts are interrupted as we round the bar and I see Ben and Stephens sitting at the same table I left. I begin to walk toward them when an ear-shattering alarm screams throughout the building.

The entire room appears to freeze in place as stunned expressions look around, trying to figure out if we should vacate or if this is merely an accidental fire alarm. An automated voice, with a British accent, interrupts the repeated blare of the alarm, "The fire detection system has been activated, please calmly make your way to the nearest exit."

Nik moves his hand from my elbow to my back as he tucks me into his side. I look back to where Ben was sitting, but the room is now a chaotic mass of people moving in different directions and I can't find him in the crowd.

My heart is in my throat as I strain my neck to try to see over the heads rushing by. "Where's Ben?"

Nik's one free hand is cupped to his ear, trying to hear something in his earpiece over the shriek of the alarm and panicked voices. "Stephens is moving Ben to the exit," Nik shouts over the cacophony of noise.

We continue past the large bar dividing the club from the lounge but turn left instead of following the crowd to the front entrance to our right. "What about Gen?" I scream to be heard over the chaos.

"Just keep moving, we'll see everyone when we get outside." Nik continues to shepherd me toward what I assume is a back exit, his arm around my shoulders providing a buffer for the shoulder checks I would otherwise be taking from the river of people rushing to the front of the club. My gaze jumps from one panicked face to another as people run from the dance floor. Shit, where the hell is Gen?

We continue to fight the crowd, a disorienting kaleidoscope of faces flashing by as we work our way up the stream of people. Everything becomes a blur of color until my eyes lock onto a familiar face, a face I studied from the photos Nik provided to prepare for this very moment. Without thinking, I reach out and grab the muscled arm of Bec's owner as he passes. He looks affronted that I interrupted his escape before I point in the opposite direction. "Follow us!"

His head turns toward where he was heading before I interrupted and then back to us, indecision in his eyes until he takes in Nik. He must be appeased by what he sees because he nods his head in agreement and turns to follow us.

As we near the back of the club, the crowd begins to thin until it's only the three of us. We follow Nik through a nondescript door in a back corner and then down a dark hallway. Nik's steps are sure; it's obvious he knows exactly where he is going.

After several turns, we come to a heavy exterior door that Nik pushes open. Fresh air hits my face and it feels like

I'm diving into cool water on a hot summer day. I close my eyes and soak in the respite. After being in the sweaty club, followed by the claustrophobia-inducing sprint down the dark, narrow hallway, the cool air is a balm against my overheated skin.

Nik continues to lead me through a small crowd of people, who also managed to use the back exit, until we find Ben and Stephens. Ben scoops me under his arm. "You good, doll?"

Snuggling into him, I nod my head. "Where's Gen?"

Stephens steps forward to respond, "She's in front of the building with Scott."

I breathe out a sigh of relief. "Thank God."

"Hey, thanks for redirecting me. It was getting crazy in there."

I look up at the unfamiliar voice to see Bec's owner offer his hand in introduction. "I'm James."

I take the offered hand. "Nice to meet you, I'm Elle. Sorry about grabbing you in there, I just thought you would rather avoid a mass stampede." We share a smile as I try to think through the best way to tell James I attended this event to meet him without sounding like a stalker. "Actually, I was hoping I might run into you and your wife tonight."

James's head jerks back in surprise. Right, maybe a bit too forward. My words quicken in an attempt to explain. "It's a long story, but I ate at Bec a few days ago, and let's just say I was impressed."

James smiles at the compliment but his expression remains guarded. "Umm, thanks."

"I realize this isn't an ideal time to discuss business, but I wanted to pose the possibility of me investing in Bec to you and your wife."

James's face becomes granite as I scramble to back-pedal. Raising my voice to be heard over the sirens that are closing in on us in the background, I continue. "Like I said, this isn't the time or place." I open my clutch to retrieve a card and hand it to James. "Why don't you call me next week and we can discuss further."

James looks down at the card. The disgust in his eyes when he looks up causes me to take a step back.

His jaw tightens as he leans forward, "You tell that worthless piece of shit I will never sell." He shakes his head. "If I had known who you were in the club, I would have taken my chances with the front entrance."

My head is spinning as I raise my hands in a placating gesture. "James, I honestly have no idea who or what you are talking about?"

James releases a sarcastic laugh before continuing, "You expect me to believe you aren't pulling strings in an attempt to take our restaurant?"

I take another step back at the wrath directed my way.

James's fury is a flame thrower pointed at me. "There's a special place in hell for people who try to capitalize on someone else's weakness for their own gain."

What the actual fuck? "Listen, we need to pause, I don't know what the hell you are talking about, but you are completely off-base with your assumption of who I am."

James doesn't react, which I take as an invitation to continue. "A family friend, who is a chef from Italy, asked me if I was interested in investing in your restaurant. I have been trying to figure out why you may need additional capital—the restaurant is clearly profitable. My team did some research and discovered you have a loan from a company called Capri, Inc. I happened to run into a partner of Capri,

Inc. tonight, and I now believe his partner is trying to take over the lien with the hope that you will default so he can take your restaurant. I happen to loathe this asshole and would like to help you."

Before James can respond, Nik is at my elbow. "We need to leave. Now." My eyes snap to Nik's at the hard edge in his voice. I see it in his eyes before the words leave his lips.

"Genevieve's missing."

* * *

My body turns to ice as panic seizes my lungs. Before I can consider what I'm doing, I find myself running toward the flashing red and blue lights on the other side of the building. I only make it a few feet when I am bear-hugged from behind and hoisted into the air. On autopilot, I shoot my head back in an attempt to head butt whoever is holding me, but I'm immediately placed on my feet and spun to face the person who stopped my run. Nik is crouched so that we are eye level. "Elle, stop. Stephens and the crew are looking for her now. You running into the mess out front will take our focus away from finding Genevieve."

I suck in air as I try to piece together what Nik is telling me. "I thought she was out front! Stephens said Scott had her, what the hell happened, Nik!" My voice is as shrill as the sirens filling the night sky by the time I stop screaming long enough to suck in another breath.

Nik doesn't answer, but takes my arm and leads me to a black SUV idling at the curb. Ben is holding the back door open, motioning for me to hurry.

Nik doesn't speak until Ben and I are deposited in the backseat. "You two will be driven to your place, Mrs. Tate, where you will both stay until I return." Nik stops and looks me in the eye. "And I will return with Genevieve." The conviction in his tone and resolve in his eyes provides a modicum of reassurance.

He straightens, ready to shut the door when panic grips my stomach. "Nik, wait!"

He pauses to look back at me.

"Please—please be safe."

Nik averts his eyes and says, "Always," before closing the car door.

I spend the drive home calling and texting Gen, my hands shaking the entire time. The calls continue to go to voicemail and my texts go unanswered. Come on, Gen, answer, damn it.

Ben places his hand on my bouncing knee. "They will find her. You need to calm down."

Those are his words of wisdom? Unbelievable. "I was told she made it out of the club and was safe. What the fuck happened between then and her disappearing?"

Ben turns his body toward me. "I don't know, doll, but I do know they will find her. I mean, come on, it's Nik. When has he ever failed at something?" My mind goes back to that rainy night months ago when Nik stayed with me instead of going with Alex.

The metal garage gate rolls up and our SUV enters. I shake off my previous thoughts as the car stops in front of the elevator bank where two of Nik's security detail are waiting. The four of us are whisked up to the fortieth floor, and it isn't until Nik's men search every room in my home that they finally leave.

I pace in the kitchen, looking down at the phone in my hand every few seconds as if that will cause Gen to respond.

I just don't understand, how can she be out of the chaos and accounted for one moment, and gone the next? Ben stops my pacing by placing his hands on my shoulders. "Why don't you change and we can see if there's anything on the news."

My eyes widen—the news, of course.

I shuck off my heels and rush to the living room to turn on the TV. I only have to flip through a few channels before I see the front of the club we just left, now bathed in red strobe lights from the emergency response vehicles. The crowd is still fairly large, with people huddled together in multiple groups. A pretty brunette with perfectly coiffed hair is explaining there is no evidence of a fire, and authorities are actively investigating the cause of the alarm.

I listen intently as the news correspondent speaks. "Four people have been taken to the hospital after being trampled by the large crowd as they tried to exit the venue and, as you can see, many more are being treated behind me."

Frozen in front of the TV, I anxiously scan the crowd, looking for anyone I may know. A stretcher is loaded into an ambulance, police officers talk to three men in suits near the entrance, and there are indeed several people being treated by EMTs. The reporter finishes and the screen goes back to the anchors at the station.

Feeling lost, I look around the room for answers. Not finding any, I toss the remote next to Ben, who is now sitting on the couch. "I'm going to change." Ben nods and I walk out of the living room to clear my head.

Once I'm in my closet, I throw on yoga pants and a tank top. I'm sorting through my sweaters when my phone vibrates in my hand. I look down to see *Gen* on the screen. "Gen! Oh my God, where are you, I've been going crazy!"

A deep voice chuckles. "Do not say a word. Calmly

walk away from whoever is near you, or you will not see your friend again."

My throat constricts as cortisol floods my system. "Who is this? Where's Gen?"

The dark chuckle echoes in my ear, causing goosebumps to rise on my arms. "You are not in a position to ask questions. Now, do as I say, or you won't like the consequences."

"I'm not around anyone, asshole. Now, Where. The. Fuck. Is. My. Friend!"

There is a long pause followed by, "I am really going to enjoy teaching you a lesson on manners." The voice is too deep, too dark, and I realize it's somehow being altered.

I should hold my tongue, I know I should, but I am physically unable to when I respond with, "Really, did you get that line from a *bad guy for dummies* book? Let me guess, next you'll tell me I have two hours to meet you at a creepy abandoned warehouse where I can try to save my friend?"

The goosebump-inducing chuckle returns. "Close, but you have one hour, and we aren't meeting at a warehouse. I'll text you the address. If you try anything stupid, Genevieve will be in a highly compromised position when you see her next. Arrive alone or you will not see your friend again." He pauses before adding, "Alive, anyhow."

"Wait! Don't hang up, I need to hear her voice or I'm not going anywhere."

There's another long pause and then a growl of annoyance. "Well, aren't you surprising?"

I hear a godawful scream in the background followed by, "Don't listen to him, Elle, stay away!"

My vision blurs. No, no, no, no. This isn't happening. Oh my God. I hold my hand over my mouth to stifle a cry that escapes my throat. "Don't you fucking touch her!"

Silence. I look at the screen to see he ended the call. "FUCK!" My hand covers my mouth again as I run to the toilet and vomit every last drop of champagne I've consumed this evening. I'm sitting in front of the toilet, my forehead resting on my folded arms as I process my next move, when I hear footsteps.

"Elle, what the—are you okay?" Ben kneels next to me and runs his hand in soothing motions over my back.

I turn my head to look at him. "I'll be fine, a migraine hit me out of nowhere. I just need to take medication and lie down."

Ben nods. "I'll get your pill, you get into bed."

I place my forehead back on my folded arms and mumble, "Thank you."

I've just finished brushing my teeth when Ben returns with a pill and glass of water. "Thanks." I offer a weak smile and walk past him as I pretend to take the pill before sliding into bed and slipping it under my pillow.

Ben stands a few feet away with his arms crossed. "Do you still feel nauseous?"

I answer truthfully. "A little, but I'll be fine after resting."

Ben studies me, a crease between his eyes. "I'll let you know if I hear anything about Gen?"

It's a question, not a statement, and my stomach roils. Ben knows I would never lie down with Gen still missing, even with a migraine. "Yes, of course, I'm just going to rest my eyes for a few minutes so I can be somewhat coherent when Nik finds her. I'm sure I'll be up before we hear anything else."

Ben doesn't move as he continues to study me. Shit, he suspects something, and I don't have time to convince him I don't have a crazy plan up my sleeve. I feign exhaustion from the migraine pill. Closing my eyes, I sink farther into my pillow and focus on evening out my breaths as I pretend to be nearing sleep.

After what feels like an eternity, I finally hear a noise from outside the bedroom. Peeking one eye open I see I'm alone. Finally.

* * *

Not able to waste another second, I jump out of bed and run to the bathroom. My phone is still sitting on the counter next to the sink. I slide the text alert icon to see an unfamiliar address. I copy the address and paste it into my maps app as I grab a sweater and slide my feet into flats. Shit, the address is to a warehouse near the High Line. I roll my eyes—not a warehouse, my ass, this guy is so cliché.

I look at the time of our call and see that fifteen minutes have already passed. I'll need to drive to save time, and Nik has the keys to the cars. I tap the phone against my leg as I think through next steps. Find keys, sneak out of my own home, meet an insane man and manage to get both Gen and me out of this, all within the next forty-five minutes.

First step, keys. Where would Nik keep the spare keys? In the control room he mentioned after Scott was attacked? No, too many people have access to that room. Perhaps his office? My eyes widen and I release a silent laugh as I remember what should be nestled in the desk drawer of my own office.

Cracking my bedroom door open enough to see the hallway is clear, I take a deep breath, slip out of my room, and silently make my way down the hall. Once inside my office, I slide the door closed and run to my desk. Holding my breath, I slowly slide open the top desk drawer, careful not to make a noise. I delicately lift stationery and stamps to see a key fob shaped like a car with the Porsche emblem on the hood resting underneath. A small silver bow is still tied around the roof of the car-shaped key. I run my finger over the silhouette as the memory of receiving the key plays out in my mind.

Alex had just returned from a trip to find me working in our home office. I had been counting down the minutes until his return so we could celebrate the FDA approval of Immunotech. I recall being engrossed in spreadsheets, preparing for the IPO of one of the companies in Tate's portfolio, when the delicious scent that was uniquely Alex filled the room. Strong arms circled my shoulders as he kissed my temple. I raised my eyes, no words needed as we looked at one another, our souls sighing in contentment at being reunited.

Alex brushed a swath of hair from my eye with his pinky and I noticed something dark in his hand. I turned my head to see a car-shaped key fob. I looked back at him, my eyes wide in surprise. "You didn't?"

He answered with his signature panty-dropping smile. "I most certainly did. Congratulations on your first IPO, my love."

I jumped up and wrapped my arms around him as he picked me up and walked us to the front of my desk. He sat me down on an area clear of papers and rained kisses down my neck and body until he was kneeling in front of me. "Do you have any idea how much I missed you?"

I smiled before cheekily responding with, "I'm getting an idea."

He looked up, his expression strangely intense for my

teasing response, and as was always the case, I became lost in his hypnotizing eyes. That is, until his hands began making the slow, tortuous journey up my legs, pushing my dress up to expose my lace panties. His deft fingers slowly lowered the lace until it was around my ankles, and then dropped them to the floor. He traced the track his fingers had just made with his lips, moving higher and higher until he grabbed my ass, scooting me to the edge of the desk.

"You are so beautiful. I've been dreaming about this for the past five days."

I had laughed and said, "But you've only been gone for four."

He smirked. "Yes, but you worked late the day before I left. You were exhausted so we went straight to bed, remember? And that means it's been five days since I've tasted you."

The intensity of this moment magnified everything else. As if we had carved out our own section of the universe for just the two of us. Alex followed his words with a lick before wrapping his arms around my thighs and uninhibitedly feasting on me. I was never into oral sex before Alex, but this man was magic. And I came in record time. He scooped me up before I collapsed backward onto my laptop docking station and kissed me like I was the sustenance he wouldn't survive without. I could have come again from that kiss alone. I began writhing against him, and as was always the case, Alex knew exactly what I needed. He helped me off the desk and turned me around. He placed his hand on my upper back, signaling for me to bend over my desk, and all I could think was hell, yes.

My dress was still bunched around my waist and Alex took full advantage as he massaged my ass with one hand and inserted one, and then two fingers into my slick entrance with his other. I was dripping for him as disjointed mono-syllables and noises streamed from my mouth. He inserted a third finger and I nearly combusted. It wasn't until I told him I needed him that he withdrew his fingers, and I finally felt that glorious steel at my entrance. He thrust forward, filling me. The feeling so perfect, so right, it brought tears to my eyes.

We were beyond passionate, our love manifesting it-self in the physical sense. So intense, both of us pushing and pulling in sync. Needing more, needing to be embedded within the other, our souls forever entwined. One of his hands braced his body weight as his chest grazed my back. The other hand reached down and around to do magical things to my body, causing me to see stars as I came a sec-ond time. Alex's orgasm followed mine, shattering us both.

Breathing heavily, we continued to lean over my desk until Alex took me in his arms and lowered us to the floor. The chill of the room cooled our sweat-glistened bodies as we tried to catch our breath. I had looked up at Alex's sex-tousled hair and the glassy look of contentment in his eyes and couldn't hold back the *holy shit* sentiment that left my mouth. My head bounced on his chest in time with his deep laughter. He answered with, "Holy shit, indeed," a smile in his voice. We rested in silence for some time, Alex running his finger up and down my back and me soaking in his warmth.

I was beginning to drift to sleep when Alex reminded me I still had something important to do. "Do you want to see your gift?"

I propped my torso up to look at him, my excitement clearly evident. Alex had chuckled in amusement and cupped the side of my face to bring me in for a kiss. I jumped up and pulled the hem of my dress back over my hips as I looked around the room for my panties. Alex held the black lace up. "Looking for these?"

I smiled. "I was."

He gave me his sexy smirk as he pocketed the lace. I shrugged a shoulder in response. "Keep them, easier access after I see my car."

His gaze snapped from playful to fire in an instant—the man was insatiable. I gave him a smirk of my own and walked around the desk to retrieve my heels from where I had kicked them off earlier. When I looked up, Alex was fully clothed and waiting, not a hair out of place. Rolling my eyes, I reached for the key, but Alex held up another set. "You can keep those as a spare."

Anxious to see the car I had lusted over for years, I tossed the key with the silver bow in my desk drawer and followed Alex out of the office.

* * *

I look down at the car-shaped key my fingers are clutching and send a silent thank you to Alex. It suddenly feels like he is with me. Like he is by my side, and I feel as though I really can do this.

With renewed confidence, coupled with a mixture of residual melancholy following my trip down memory lane, I mentally slap myself. I need to get it together and focus on Gen. I illuminate my phone to see the time—shit, I need to move. My license, credit cards, and cash are in the clutch I used tonight, which I left in the kitchen. Phone and keys will have to do.

Peeking my head out of the office, I see that the hall is

still clear. With my heart beating in my ears, I slip out and backtrack to a secondary staircase in the rear of the condo. As silently as possible, I take the steps two at a time and breathe another sigh of relief when I see the second floor is dark and there aren't lingering security personnel around.

I rush past the great room, gym, and guest rooms to the emergency stairwell on the opposite side of the condo. Sending up a silent prayer that Nik hasn't changed the code, I enter the six digits into the panel with shaking fingers. A beep followed by the words *invalid code* appear. Shit, shit, shit!

Shaking out my arms I close my eyes and focus on centering myself before opening my eyes and trying the code again. This time I hear the lock disengage and the words *access granted* flashed in green. I release the breath I was holding.

Having no time to celebrate this minor win, I slip out the door and begin to run down the stairwell until I reach the thirty-fifth floor. Lowering my head, I step into the interior of the building to use the communal elevator to descend to the garage. My eyes are on my shoes as I pray that Nik's team isn't monitoring the stairwell or elevators.

The elevator dings to announce its arrival at the basement level of the garage, and I can't bring myself to look up as the doors slide open. The anticipation of hearing Nik's voice reprimanding me has me braced for a fight.

I lift my eyes slowly to see a garage full of cars, but empty of people. Taking advantage of this kernel of luck, I sprint to the black 911, and slide in. The scent of new leather envelops me; I haven't driven this car in nearly ten months. It was too painful, but I'm momentarily surprised to feel closer to Alex now than I have during these past months.

For the second time in a matter of minutes, I get the sense that he's with me, and as a team, we will be able to find Gen.

My confidence bolstered, I tear out of the garage and press down on the gas. The quick acceleration of the car, combined with the adrenaline coursing through my body, makes me feel invincible. I feel like I could scale a skyscraper if that's what's needed to get Gen back. I just hope I can hold on to this feeling once I get to the High Line.

THIRTEEN

I MANAGE TO MAKE IT TO THE WAREHOUSE IN FIFTEEN minutes, giving me a moment to drive by the address before parking a block away. The area appears to be deserted, which isn't surprising since the clock on the center console of my car reads 3:24. I reach for the glove box and hold my breath as I release the latch. Please, please be in here. I run my hand along the contents of the compartment, pushing aside the owner's manual. My fingers clumsily pat the open space until they brush against a cold, hard surface.

I remove the steel case from the glove box and exhale the breath I was holding in relief, simultaneously sending another silent thank you to Alex as I enter the standard password we use for all things security related. I slowly lift the lid to see a Taser gun and a can of bear Mace.

I can't help the bubble of a laugh that escapes my throat as I think of all the times I teased Nik for placing portable gun safes in random places. Steel-encased Easter eggs waiting to be found. I look at the Taser nestled in black velvet padding, I suppose his foresight was spot on.

My shaking fingers pick up the Taser gun. Thank God Nik forced me to take tactical self-defense lessons that included Taser practice a couple of years ago. I slide out of the car. A cool night breeze causes the long cardigan I threw on to flap like a cape behind me. I look around to make sure I'm still the only person around before slipping the Taser inside the waistband of my yoga pants. The cool plastic presses against my spine, causing a shiver to run through my body. I continue to scan the quiet street as I wrap the front flaps of the calf-length sweater around me and set off to the address pulled up on my phone.

The short distance between my car and the warehouse disappears much too quickly. My pulse reverberates through me; a bass drum that increases with every step I take. Sweat gathers on the back of my neck, despite the cool night air, making me shiver. When I arrive at the last corner separating me from the warehouse, I steady myself before peeking around the corner. The street is quiet as I continue to watch for what feels like an eternity but is only a minute or two. I'm about to round the corner when my phone vibrates in my hand, making me jump back into place, my back pressed firmly against the brick wall I've been using as cover. I look down to see a text from an unknown number that reads *Chelsea Piers.*

"You have got be kidding me." I shake my head in annoyance before looking toward the Hudson. More games.

The beginning of Chelsea Piers is only about a two-minute walk from where I'm standing, but the multiple piers span about six city blocks, and I am quickly running out of time.

Jogging across the wide intersection toward the pier, I duck into the shadows from the trees lining a dog park. It's dark and quiet as I speed-walk to the carousel that bookends one side of the Chelsea Piers development. The well-lit pier is deserted, so I continue down the path bordering the water. The yachts used for dinner cruises moored at the next pier are dark. My breaths increase as the seconds quickly tick by. Picking up my pace, I make it to the third pier in less than a minute, only to see that it too is dark and deserted. How are there no people around? It's late, but this is New York. There should be the random homeless person, if nothing else.

My heartbeat pounds against my chest. Every second that ticks by moves Gen closer to an unknown guillotine. I am nearly running to the last pier, straining my ears for any noise that might alert me to where Gen is being held. The marina is so silent. Too silent, I realize, frantically scanning the boats littering the brackish water. Shit, shit, shit. Where are you, Gen?

Nearing the last pier, I slow my pace in an attempt to control my breathing as the thump of my heartbeat throbs in my ears. I pass a golf shop on my left and five smaller boats tied along wooden slats bordering the walkway to my right. I walk as if I'm on glass, my head moving from right to left and back as I search for movement from either side of the boardwalk.

A feeling of foreboding envelops me as I near a dock the length of the pier with four docks branching out from it, resembling a giant comb. Each dock extending from the base has several boat slips, many of which are occupied. Goosebumps spread over my arms; every instinct I have is screaming that Gen is here.

I duck behind a trash can and study the boats moored in the marina. An ostentatiously large yacht is tied near the end of the pier. Light pours out of several windows lining one floor. I illuminate my phone screen to see that I have nine minutes before my time is up, I switch my phone from vibrate to silent before returning my attention to the yacht. How am I going to get on the boat without being discovered? I look around the dock. Nothing inspires a grand rescue plan. I eye the dock and then the boat. There are really only two options: access the boat from the docks, or access the boat from the water. The dock isn't well-lit, but there is enough light to see me coming.

Shit. As much as I don't like the idea, it will have to be a water rescue.

Standing from my hiding spot, I move from one shadow to the next until I'm at the edge of a pool of light marking the entrance to the pier. My eyes scan the area around me in desperation as panic crawls up my throat. A small dinghy tied next to a larger boat bobbing in the water about twenty feet away snags my attention. The boats are bathed in subtle silver from the moon but are otherwise in shadow. Perfect.

Looking toward the yacht, I take a steadying breath before leaping through the light to the shadowed dock to my left. I land as softly as possible and immediately duck, waiting a moment before peeking around the large boat concealing me. There's still no movement from the yacht at the end of the pier.

My fingers fumble in chaotic jerks as I work on the knot tying the small boat to the dock. Once the knot is released, I crawl into the small rowboat. The acrid scent of the Hudson encases me as I grab the oars and begin to row past the abandoned boats moored for the evening.

Once past the first line of boats, I turn the small rowboat away from the shore and continue to row until I am at the last dock. Clumsily turning the boat into the third line of dark shadows, the large super yacht looms as a sentry over the others in the cul-de-sac of water. I try to row as silently as possible, but the sound of water cascading off the oar every time it raises from the water is amplified in the silence of the night.

Time for plan B. Placing the oars back in the boat, I pull the small boat up to the end of the dock, knocking into it with more force than anticipated. Shit. Grabbing onto the dock, I tug the small boat flush to the wood to prevent a second hit against the dock. Holding my breath, I listen. A male voice comes from the direction of the yacht.

Shit, shit, shit. My arm muscles strain as I use the dock to walk the boat up its length until I am nestled into a shadow cast by a large boat tied to the first slip. The voice is now accompanied by another, and both are getting louder as they near where I'm hiding. Climbing out of the rowboat and onto the narrow dock of the boat slip as quietly as possible, I walk the small rowboat to the back of the larger boat and hurriedly tie the fringed nylon line to an open dock cleat.

The voices are now directly in front of where I'm standing, the boat in the slip the only thing separating me from them. I say a silent prayer the boat is vacant as I gingerly step onto the back platform, thankfully the boat is large enough to not move when I step aboard. With rushed movements, I open the back gate and step onto the stern.

The two male voices are clear now that they are practically standing next to me. A graveled voice that sounds like a carton of cigarettes has been smoked every day for the past twenty years interrupts the silence. "I don't see her, how long are we supposed to be out here?"

"Who cares, I'd rather be out here than in there. I swear if that bitch says one more thing, I'll shoot her myself."

I hear cigarette voice wheeze out a chuckle. "Come on, let's check the boardwalk."

I listen to the men's footsteps until they fade around the corner before jumping up and silently stepping from the boat to the dock on the opposite side. With my head down, I make my way to the yacht, diving from one moored boat to the next to keep cover.

Pausing beside a large boat directly across from the vessel that holds Gen, I slow my breathing and listen. There doesn't appear to be anyone on lookout, but I know that can't be the case. I don't have time to orchestrate a grand plan for how I'm supposed to get onboard without being detected. I'm just going to have to walk on and pray I find her before I'm found. I close my eyes and take a steadying breath. As I slowly release the air from my lungs, I straighten to step away from the boat. Here goes nothing.

The tinkling sound of water dripping onto the wood of the dock makes me freeze mid-step. My head snaps to the side to look over my shoulder and my hand goes to the Taser gun at my back. Time stands still when I see a figure in black two paces away. On instinct, I draw in a breath to curse as my hand wraps around the gun, but I feel a bee sting prick on my neck before I've finished inhaling. A soft moan leaves my mouth a moment before I realize I can no longer feel my legs.

I am falling and then floating through the air as strong arms lift me. My next breath has me fighting to open my eyes. This can't be happening. I fight with everything in me to focus on my surroundings. I feel myself moving slightly as I'm cradled to a warm body. Through the haze I realize that I'm being carried, at least I think I'm being carried. Maybe I really am floating. The muffled sound of shouting and gun shots comes from behind us, or is it in front of us? Everything is shifting and I can't be sure. *Focus, Elle.* I grab on to the cacophony of noise and pull myself out of the darkness. My head rolls from the side to look up at the person holding me.

My lungs seize when the eyes I've been seeing in my dreams stare down at me. The love and intensity I remember so fondly is amplified. I try to talk, but instead of words, another soft moan leaves my lips.

Am I in heaven? Did I die? I feel myself brought closer to the warm, hard chest I'm cradled against. A low whisper near my ear says, "I've got you, baby." I vaguely register a tinge of electricity in my belly, even as a dark void threatens to smother me.

I fight my way out of the vacuum pulling me under, but it's so strong, stronger than before. Or perhaps I'm getting weaker. Either way, I know it's only a matter of time until the viscous blackness drowns me. I feel lips on my forehead and whispered words that I can no longer decipher as the nothingness wraps around me, swallowing me whole.

* * *

My head throbs in time with my heartbeat. It's this percussion of pain that clears the gauzy haze enough for me to attempt to open my eyes, but they remain sealed shut.

The murmuring of voices captures my attention over the drum echoing in my head. I try to concentrate on the words, but they sound garbled, as if I'm underwater. There's an incessant beeping near my head. I try to move my arm toward the sound, but I am a prisoner in my own body.

The dark vortex begins to pull me under again and I

welcome the reprieve when the pressure in my head begins to dissipate. I am plummeting deeper into the abyss when I hear a familiar voice. Ben! Why is he in my dream? A second voice I don't recognize responds to Ben, but I can't make out their mumbled words.

The voices become muted as I relax into the weightless warmth of nothingness, somewhere between consciousness and unconsciousness, when the sweetest sound fills my world. The voice of an angel is next to me. I envision reaching out and grabbing the angel's hand, but my arms remain unmoving by my side. The voices become more garbled before I'm lost to the blackness once again.

* * *

Beep, beep, beep, beep. Ugh … I keep my eyes closed, willing myself to fall back into blissful sleep. The pulsating throb in my head and a full bladder make that plan impossible.

Cracking my eyes open, I blink into the darkness and attempt to get my bearings. Everything is blurred. Every cell in my body screams out when I try to roll over. Shit, that hurts. It feels like I was hit by a Mack truck. What the hell happened?

Memories from last night filter through. I had a migraine—wait, no. I'm missing something. Something important, but I can't think.

I'm so tired.

The beeping increases in speed. What the hell is that noise? Turning my head slightly to the left, I see what looks like hospital equipment. Hospital equipment in my bedroom? This is an odd dream.

My eyes move down to see an IV in my hand and a gray clip on the tip of my index finger. What the …?

"Eliana."

My body goes numb, every ache felt a moment ago now gone, as a large hand sweeps hair away from my face before pillowed lips kiss my forehead.

If I had any doubt before, it has been dispelled. It's official, I'm still dreaming. That is the only explanation that would make sense. I close my eyes for a moment before opening them again. Concerned blue-gray eyes are staring back at me.

"Love, can you talk? How are you feeling?"

How am I feeling? I FEEL like I'm either hallucinating or staring at a fucking ghost.

My own eyes must telegraph this message because I see a spark of humor in the blue-gray eyes I am drowning in.

"I have a lot to explain, but first I need to know you are okay." He bends to eye level and cups my cheek. "Love?"

I glance down to sever the electric tension building between us. This can't be happening, there's no way this is real. I'm obviously still dreaming … Right?

I look back up at those piercing blue-gray eyes, so full of adoration and concern, and I feel myself splinter. My consciousness fragmenting into reality and dream. After months of agony, barely surviving, to now have my one wish, the one thing I would give up everything for, even for just a moment, now sitting beside me … I look away as the room starts spinning. This isn't happening.

Alex can't be here because Alex is dead. He's fucking

dead and this is the reality I haven't been able to accept, not truly. And now I've lost my sanity.

I hear the beep of the heart rate monitor playing in triple time.

Fingers caress my cheek. "Baby, I need you to breathe. Come on, take a deep breath."

I'm trying to register what Dream Alex is telling me to do, but my vision becomes fuzzy. I try to blink the fuzziness away, but everything blurs before fading to black. The reprieve I so desperately need returns, and I gladly allow the abyss to claim me once again.

* * *

I wake to a painfully full bladder. Moaning in discomfort, I try to roll over, but I'm stopped by a hand on my shoulder. Opening my eyes, I see Ben hovering over me.

"Good morning, doll." His blinding white grin is far too chipper for me at the moment.

"I'm about to pee the bed," I croak out, my voice sounding gritty and foreign to my ears.

Ben manages to make out what I said and his smile somehow gets bigger as he helps me sit up. "No need for dramatics."

Ben watches as I struggle to sit up before scooping me into his arms. He carries me to the bathroom and sets me in front of the toilet.

Raising an eyebrow, I attempt to respond, but my dry and unused throat makes words impossible. Ben fills a glass sitting next to the sink with water and places it at my lips. I drink greedily until my throat is lubricated.

Nodding my head that I'm finished, I point at the toilet. "Who's being dramatic?"

Ben just shrugs as if to say *what else was I supposed to do?*

"Thank you, Ben. I can take it from here."

He winks before leaving the bathroom and closing the door behind him.

I relieve myself for what must be several minutes. Shaking my head in amazed confusion that my bladder was able to hold that much liquid, I stand to wash my hands. I'm forced to brace myself against the vanity as the bathroom tilts and black dots float in front of my eyes.

There's a knock on the door before Ben opens it and moves to stand behind me.

I make eye contact with him in the bathroom mirror. "Ben, seriously, I can manage to wash my hands on my own, thank you."

He lifts his eyebrows saying *yeah, it looks that way,* without words.

Scowling at his reflection, I reply, "God, even your eyebrows are sarcastic," before looking down at the sink to wait for my lightheadedness to clear enough for me to stand without the help of the bathroom vanity. I pump soap onto my palm and begin to rub my hands together when a bandage on the top of my left hand makes me pause. My head snaps up to look at Ben's guarded reflection in the mirror. I watch his expression shutter as my eyes round in shock when a series of images assault me.

Alex. I dreamt Alex was here after I tried to save Gen.

I suck in a breath and turn to face Ben, placing my soaped hands on his chest for balance. "Where's Gen? Please tell me she's okay?"

Ben cups my shoulders. "She's fine. Finish in here and I'll get the doctor."

"Doctor?"

Ignoring my question, Ben guides my shoulders to turn until I'm again facing the sink. The weight and warmth of his large hands is comforting as I rinse my hands and reach for my toothbrush and toothpaste. Seeing that I am able to function a marginal degree, he finally releases my shoulders and leaves the bathroom.

I scrub what feels like cotton out of my mouth, feeling somewhat human when I'm finished. That is, until I see my reflection.

Oh, wow.

My complexion is paler than normal, and the purple shadows recently smudged under my eyes are now blue. My eyes track down to see that I'm wearing the sacred T-shirt I have been preserving in a Ziploc bag under my bed. I bring the cotton material up to my nose and inhale; the scent of my perfume greets me.

My stomach drops.

This was my last connection to Alex, and now it's gone.

Potent loss hollows me out and my stomach moves to my throat as I fight back tears, knowing if they start, they won't stop. I throw my wild hair into a top knot and fling open the door to see Ben anxiously waiting. Water marks from my hands are outlined on the front of his shirt.

"Feeling better?"

I clear my throat. "Starting to, thank you."

Ben reaches out to place a hand on my shoulder. "Hey, what is it?"

I look down in embarrassment. "It's nothing."

"It doesn't look like it's nothing."

I pinch the cotton of the shirt I'm wearing and pull it taught. "This was the last thing that smelled like him." I hear the pitiful defeat in my voice. "I kept this shirt in a Ziploc bag to preserve the scent." I look off to the side, unable to look Ben in the eye with my admission. "Creepy, I know, but it felt like my last connection to Alex, and now it smells like stale Coco Mademoiselle."

Ben's expression tightens before he once again shutters whatever it is he doesn't want me to see. "That's not stupid. I can see why the shirt would be comforting, but do me a favor and don't fret about this right now. We still have a lot of ground to cover."

What? I'm about to ask Ben what he means when a knock sounds at the door and he yells for whoever it is to come in. An older gentleman in a collared button down and slacks walks in, followed by Dr. Wickham.

Ben introduces the man I haven't met as Dr. Reddy and explains that he has been monitoring my vitals the past two days.

"Two days!" My eyes fly to Ben's. "I've been out for two days?"

Ben turns to Dr. Reddy to say, "I'm going to get her some water," before glancing back to me. "Would you like something to eat?"

The mention of food makes my stomach roil. "No, water will be fine. Thank you."

I walk to the bed and fluff my pillows vertically against the headboard before sliding into bed and pulling the down comforter over my now-shaking body.

Dr. Reddy sits in a chair that is usually in the sitting

room as Dr. Wickham leans casually against the wall beside him.

"Ms. Tate, as Ben mentioned, I have been overseeing your care these past two days. Your vitals are strong, but the cocktail of drugs injected into your system was far too much for your weight. Additionally, you had a negative reaction to the ketamine, which put you in a short-term, coma-like state."

What the—"I was injected with a cocktail of drugs?"

Dr. Reddy nods. "Yes, that's correct. How are you feeling? Does anything hurt?"

I mentally scan my body. Aside from feeling weak, only my head and throat are bothering me. "I have a headache that is throbbing over my right eye."

Dr. Reddy writes something in his notes before looking back at me. "Let's try acetaminophen first and move to prescription medication if that doesn't work." I nod in agreement.

Dr. Reddy's kind eyes continue to assess me. "What is the last thing you remember?"

I search my memory from what was apparently two nights ago. "I went to a club opening; the fire alarm went off and we lost my friend, Gen." I search through the gaps in my memory. "I received a phone call from a man who told me I needed to arrive at an address, alone, in order to collect Gen."

The recesses of my hazy memory are not cooperating as I attempt to place the sequence of events following Gen's disappearance. "I remember leaving home and driving to Chelsea Piers. I finally located the location, or at least what I thought was the location, of where Gen was being held." I pause to think through what happened next. "There was a large yacht at the end of a marina. I rowed a small boat to the outer docks to remain inconspicuous." I can't help but smile at that brilliant idea.

Dr. Reddy nods, and Dr. Wickham clears his throat before asking, "Is that the last thing you remember?"

I think through my failed attempt to rescue Gen, trying to close the gaps in my memory. "I was about to board the yacht when I heard a noise behind me. The last thing I remember is seeing someone in black." My hand moves to my neck, where I feel a small, raised bump resembling an insect bite.

Dr. Reddy's knowing eyes track my fingers. "And how is your neck now?"

"It's a bit stiff and sensitive where I assume I was injected?"

Dr. Reddy nods. "Soreness and inflammation near the injection site is to be expected."

I'm grateful for Ben's interruption when he returns with a tray, but I don't miss the look he and Dr. Wickham share.

Dr. Reddy reaches into a bag near his feet to pull out painkillers, placing two in my hand as he stands to leave. "I suggest you try to eat something prior to taking these as they can cause nausea on an empty stomach. I will be back to check on you this evening, but Ben has my contact information if you need anything before then."

I smile my thanks as Ben sets the tray holding a glass of water, pitcher of orange juice, coffee, and almond croissant next to me before taking the chair Dr. Reddy just vacated. "You thought of everything—this is perfect. Thank you, Ben."

My gaze goes to Ben when he doesn't provide a

sarcastic response. The blue under his eyes matches my own, and his disheveled hair looks as though he's run his fingers through it hundreds of times. My eyes track down to rest on the scruff that shadows Ben's normally bare face. Shit, I obviously put him through it the past couple of days. Which reminds me.

"So, what exactly happened two nights ago?" I look at Ben sheepishly. "I mean after I snuck out." Ben's stern face causes me to cringe. He's obviously pissed about that part of the night.

Ben exhales a frustrated breath as he leans forward and turns his head to eye Dr. Wickham. "I'm not the only one angry about your little stunt." Ben rakes his fingers through his hair in frustration. "Do you have any idea how stupid that was, Elle? I mean, what the fuck did you think you were going to do, take on a boat full of fully armed men with a stun gun?"

My eyes flair in shock at Ben's words, and he drops his gaze to the floor to rein in his temper. When he finally looks at me, my heart is ripped out of my chest by his expression. His voice is raw when he says, "Do you have any idea what you put us through?"

My stomach falls as the shame of my selfishness makes me curl into myself. I have been such a shitty friend; not even conscious of how I've taken Ben's constant support for granted these past months.

I sit forward and reach my hand out, grasping Ben's wrist. It takes a few long seconds before Ben closes his fingers around my hand and sighs. I can feel the remaining tension seep from his body as he hangs his head.

"You have every right to be upset with me. I've been so selfish these past weeks ... or months, really."

"You're damn right I do—"

I interrupt before he can continue his tirade. "But I was told Gen would be hurt if I didn't go to them by myself. I knew Nik would eventually track my phone, and I would only be alone with whoever took her for a short time before the cavalry caught up to me. But I had to show up by myself so they didn't do something to Gen. And we both know there is no way you or Nik would have let me get within a mile of that boat."

Ben looks up and the corner of his mouth lifts in a small smile. "You're certainly right about that. Nik is livid."

I roll my eyes. "Fantastic. Now, can we get to the part where you forgive me and tell me what I missed because last night—err, two nights ago, feels like a giant void. How did Gen escape?"

I feel Ben stiffen before he turns to look at Dr. Wickham yet again.

My eyes move from Ben to Dr. Wickham. "What's going on, Ben?" Before he can answer, I turn my attention to Dr. Wickham. "And it's great to see you, Dr. Wickham, but why are you here?"

The doctor smiles in his typical, professor-like way. "I'm here because you have experienced a traumatic situation. I simply want to provide support if you need it."

Well, I suppose that makes sense. I smile in gratitude before looking back at Ben expectantly. Ben nods toward the tray. "I'll forgive you if you eat so you can take some aspirin, deal?"

I rip off a piece of croissant and lean back against the pillows before replying, "Deal."

Ben takes a breath and looks around the room,

gathering his thoughts. "Nik called me shortly after I left you in your room to rest, which I knew you would never do with Gen missing." He shakes his head and gives me a look of incredulity. "I never should have left you alone."

I shrug my shoulders and shove another piece of croissant into my mouth so I don't have to respond.

Ben continues to shake his head. "You had apparently just left the parking garage, and Nik assured me he was tracking your phone and your car. He was actually already on his way to Chelsea Piers to rescue Gen, so it was convenient he didn't have to detour to also rescue you."

It's my turn to shake my head. Of course, he was two steps ahead of me.

"One of Nik's security personnel had a syringe he had planned to use on a guy nearly triple your size who was playing lookout for the yacht you were about to board. He used it on you instead so they could get you away from the scene without alerting the people who had Gen, which would have compromised Gen's extraction." Ben gives me a pointed look.

"You have got to be kidding me! Are you telling me my own security drugged me? What the hell, Ben?" My voice is shrill by the end of my rant. "Why would they do that? Why in the hell didn't they just tell me who they were?"

Ben lowers is head for a moment before raising it to look at me. My breath catches at what I see in his eyes. A tortured expression stares back at me, raw emotion bleeding out.

I grip his hand tighter, a sudden panic for my friend overtaking me. What could possibly cause his heart-wrenching expression? "What is it? Tell me," I whisper, suddenly afraid that my voice may pierce the paper-thin veil I instinctively know is insulating us.

Uncertainty flashes in Ben's eyes before Dr. Wickham speaks up. "Do you remember anything else from when you were drugged?"

What the hell, my patience for guessing games is quickly reaching its limit. Bottling my instinct to lash out, I look away as I think through the moments before I was about to board the yacht. It's a black void.

My frustration builds as I close my eyes to revisit the details I do remember. I think through the sequence of events until new images begin to filter through.

A man in black, possibility wearing a wetsuit.

The sensation of falling.

Blue-gray eyes.

Oh my God, those eyes. My own shocked eyes snap back to Ben's as a barely audible, "No" escapes my lips.

FOURTEEN

X

I F YOU LOOK CLOSELY, YOU CAN JUST MAKE OUT AN outline, slightly darker than the ink-spilled cover of black surrounding a shadow slumped against a tree. The orange light, the size of a firefly, interrupts the monochromatic shadows as it flares. I smile at this thought, the idea that I am invisible to the night. Invincible to prying eyes that could be around.

I look up at the top-floor windows of the building across the street as I think about invincibility. The need to crush something overtakes me, as it so often does these days. I feel fire ants crawling over my arms and legs as I think about her encased behind a set of windows I can't tear my eyes from. I blow out the smoke in my lungs, but the nicotine isn't fending off the feeling of bitterness that consumes me. The bitch is once again safe in her fortress.

I was so close at the docks. The plan worked—she walked right into my web, only to have her asshole security fuck it all up. How in the hell did they do it? How were they able to intercept her in the two-minute span of time I didn't have eyes on her?

Smashing the cigarette against tree bark until the

pulverized filter falls apart between my fingers, I can't help but think it's a fitting metaphor for my life. I crack my stiff neck, still sore from the battle royale two nights ago. Shit, it already feels like a lifetime ago. It's peculiar how time seems to stop when you are forced to wait for something you should already have.

Part of me is still surprised I'm alive. My saving grace was the balaclava I was wearing, and my ability to hold my breath for an abnormal amount time. Though I can't help but be further surprised that I still have the lung capacity of my formative years, back when I was a competitive swimmer, now that I smoke Lucky Strikes like they're my oxygen source.

A bolt of electricity races through me at the memory. I can still hear the shots as they were fired, feel the adrenaline of bullets zipping past me as I swam under the docks. Damn close call—too close. I need to be more prepared next time, assume her fucking security will be there every step of the way.

Headlights interrupt my thoughts and I move farther behind the tree. A black Range Rover drives by and turns into the driveway of her building. The SUV idles as it waits for the gate to lift before entering the garage.

Interesting. A foreign feeling of possibility nudges the need for destruction to the side. Thoughts of the dock are forgotten as I scan the area. When there's no sign of movement, my attention returns to the top-floor window bank as I pull the black cap, standard issue for Tate security, down to just above my eyes. I almost laugh when I think about my good fortune that a member of her security detail lost his hat in the melee. Perhaps the docks weren't a complete loss after all.

As the garage gate lowers, I feel the corners of my mouth lift when a plan begins to form. The variables of an equation coming together. With one last look at the top-floor windows, I lower my head and continue down the street, unable to remove the smile from my face.

FIFTEEN

MY HEART STOPS AS MY BODY GOES NUMB. I AM FREE-falling without a net. This can't be possible. After so many months have passed? There must be another explanation.

Dr. Wickham and Ben are talking to me, but everything is muted. I'm struck with the familiar sensation of being underwater. Their lips are moving but I can't hear what they are saying. I close my eyes to shake away the fog as I try to focus. But all I see are beautiful blue-gray eyes against my closed lids. There is no logical way this could be possible. Still, I can't help but think what if.

I vaguely register that Ben and Dr. Wickham are bent over me, fussing, but I still don't understand what they want from me. I'm too focused on blue-gray eyes and possibility. A sliver of fear runs down my spine when I realize that I allowed myself to start to imagine the possibility of a new reality. I've moved from dipping my toe in to being waist deep. Oh, God, what if I'm wrong?

I'm swirling in a maze of my own thoughts when a sharp, pungent scent causes my head to jerk back. Everything comes into focus, and I realize Dr. Wickham is holding something under my nose. I gently push his hand away. "I needed that, thank you."

I lean back into my pillow and look up at the ceiling as a collage of thoughts coalesce into one. "Holy shit," escapes my lips on a breath.

I bring my eyes back to Ben's and I see the truth staring back at me. I force the words from my mouth in a broken whisper, "Is Alex alive?"

Ben holds his gaze, raw torment dripping from his eyes as Dr. Wickham moves from Ben's side to once again stand beside the bed. He takes a breath to speak but is interrupted by a deep voice from the other side of the room.

"Yes, I'm alive."

The three of our heads snap toward the door and a punch of air leaves my lungs. I blink several times as I wait for the mirage in front of me to clear. It doesn't. The most beautiful sight I will ever see is slowly walking toward the bed, palms up placatingly, as if he doesn't want to spook a wild animal.

Time stands still as I watch in dazed amazement. Every dream I have dreamt and wish I have wished is manifested into this very moment. We lock eyes and I feel the broken, displaced pieces of my soul mend together. It's as if I had been living in a black-and-white world that unexpectedly snapped into a vibrant rainbow of colors.

Alex's legs are now against the side of the bed, his posture rigid as if he's holding himself back as he awaits my response. I remain frozen as I stare at his tense shoulders, his muscles locked in place. My eyes move from his shoulders, which are broader than they were the last time I saw him, to his breathtaking face, before locking onto tormented eyes.

Before I realize what I'm doing, I launch myself out of

the bed. My duvet wraps around my legs and I kick it off to propel myself toward Alex. He catches me in the air and squeezes my body to his. His delicious scent envelops me, and I don't care if my hold on reality has snapped, and this is all a figment of my imagination. I would rather stay in this moment forever, even if it means a padded cell, than return to the drab nothingness of one minute ago.

Alex clutches me to his chest, making it difficult to breathe, as he sways from side to side. Finally, he sets me back on the bed without breaking contact. My knees absorb my weight as I kneel on the mattress, allowing me to take a large inhale of blessed air. Alex cups my face in his hands and bends toward me until we are nose to nose. It's not until he is kissing wetness from my cheeks that I realize I am sobbing.

"Are you real?"

Alex stops kissing the tears from my cheeks and brings our faces together again. "I'm real, baby. This is real." My body is wracked with sobs, and Alex's arms wrap around me, physically holding me together as I fall apart.

Several minutes pass before I lean back and bring my hand up to his face, feeling the stubble of his 5 o'clock shadow. "But how? How can this be possible?" I manage to get out between ragged sobs.

Alex continues to caress the side of my face, placing intermittent kisses where tears continue to flow. "There is a lot I need to explain."

"That's an understatement." Ben's voice shatters the bubble Alex's presence created. I completely forgot he and Dr. Wickham were even here. I sit back on my heels, my head turning from Ben, who looks livid, to Alex, who looks like he may be about to kick Ben out. An unwelcome feeling of foreboding encroaches on this unbelievable moment as I take in the hostility between my best friend and my husband. I move from my knees to a sitting position, causing Alex's hands to drop from my face. Hugging my knees to my chest, I prepare to hear some ominous revelation that is sure to break my heart once again.

Dr. Wickham follows my gaze from Ben to Alex before shaking his head in exasperation and nudging Ben out of the way so that he can stand next to the bed. "Elle, this is quite a lot to take in at once. Perhaps Ben and Alex can leave the room for a moment so we can speak privately."

I grab Alex's hand with both of mine. There is no way I'm letting him out of my sight.

Ben laughs, and everything he isn't saying is wrapped into the sarcastic sound. I look over at my best friend, my rock, with pleading eyes. Ben sees my expression and throws his hands in the air as he looks at Dr. Wickham. "Fine, but call me when I need to put the pieces back together again." He turns to leave but stops once he's next to Alex. Hands on his hips, he angles his head. "You were gone. You left and she fucking broke. As far as I'm concerned, you nearly killed your wife."

I inhale in shock at Ben's words and watch as what can only be described as anguish flashes in Alex's eyes before he closes them. "And just when she was starting to heal, starting to get her spark back, you pull this shit. You'll be lucky if she ever forgives you for what you have done." Alex is a statue as he slowly opens his eyes, a look of torment betraying his stoic expression. Ben shakes his head and walks out the door without looking back.

Well, shit. I look to Dr. Wickham, who is staring at the

ceiling as if he is asking the good Lord for patience before turning to Alex. His posture defeated.

"Okay, what the hell did I miss while I was passed out?"

Alex leans down to kiss the top of my head. "As I said, I have a lot to explain. Ben is aware, and there's no doubt he won't forgive me any time soon." He pulls back to look into my eyes. "I just pray that you will."

* * *

Dr. Wickham sits in the chair next to the bed and leans forward in exhaustion. He places his forearms on his legs and hangs his head. I have never seen the austere Dr. Wickham look so human. A pang of remorse hits me at the defeat in his posture. I have the urge to reach out to offer comfort, but still my hand, knowing that doing so will only make the good doctor uncomfortable.

The bed dips as Alex settles behind me and pulls me to him. One of his arms wraps around my stomach and he nestles his face into the crevice between my shoulder and neck before inhaling deeply and whispering, "God, I've missed the smell of you."

I melt into him and feel warmth seep down to the marrow of my bones. I'm two seconds away from kicking Dr. Wickham out so I can show Alex just how much I have missed him. Before I'm able to voice my request, Dr. Wickham straightens his posture and returns to the consummate professional I am accustomed to.

"Elle, I believe Alex would like to explain a few things. Is this suitable? Do you feel you are ready to hear what he has to say, or would you like to process his return before layering on additional … information?"

I turn my head to look up at Alex, who gives me a sad smile before kissing the top of my head. "Love, it's entirely up to you. We can enjoy one another now and I can explain everything later if you would like more time to process—this," he finishes, pointing between the two of us. "But only you can hear what I am going to tell you. If you decide you would like to discuss my disappearance now, Dr. Wickham has agreed to wait outside in case you need him at any time during the conversation."

Despite his forced smile, the look in Alex's eyes tells me he would very much like to wait, but there's no way I can move forward until I am able to make sense of all this.

I look at Dr. Wickham. "I'm not an invalid. I can handle a conversation."

Alex squeezes my middle before untangling himself from behind me and slipping off the bed.

I raise my eyebrows as panic crawls up my throat. "Where are you going?"

A small twinge of a smile graces his lips for a brief moment before his expression turns to one of forlorn. He dips down to kiss the top of my head. "I'm just moving to the chair. I'm afraid you may not want me holding you after you hear what I'm about to say."

My stomach drops at hearing Alex's words, but if I am honest with myself, he could say just about anything at this point, and it won't change the way I feel. Nothing will change that I want him wrapped around me just as he was a moment ago.

Dr. Wickham slowly rises from the chair, clearly reluctant to leave. He looks uneasily from me to Alex. "I will be in the living room. Please let me know if she shows any sign of distress or non-response."

Alex can't hide the gutted expression that flits across his face at Dr. Wickham's words, his eyes close before he nods his head in agreement. "Of course."

Alex and I stare at each other for several long moments before he pushes the recently vacated chair closer to the bed. He sits and places his hand over mine. "Eliana, I don't know how, but I swear to you I will spend the rest of our lives making up for these past months."

The intensity in his eyes seems to surge as he awaits my response. I give him a small, knowing smile. "I know. Now what the hell happened? How are you here?"

He pauses to close his eyes once more, possibly reconsidering this conversation. "What I am about to tell you can never leave this room. I am already putting you in grave danger coming back now."

The conviction in Alex's expression and somberness of his tone gives me a chill as goosebumps raise along my arms. I study his severity, knowing I'm not going to like whatever it is he's about to say. But I have to know. I brace myself before replying, "Tell me."

Alex's eyes soften and he clasps my hand with both of his. Taking a breath, he looks away as he appears to search for where to begin before exhaling and steeling himself. "Do you remember the work I began with the government?"

I sit a bit straighter. I knew this had to be related. "The IXB project?"

Alex ghosts a sad smile. "You know, you really are too intuitive for your own good … Yes, IXB. The Office of the Director of National Intelligence became aware of a credible bioterrorism threat involving a lab-modified biological weapon created by a terror cell allegedly backed by the

Russian government. It is an aerosolized type-H botulinum toxin for which there was no antitoxin."

"Wait, aerosolized Botox?"

"Basically, except type-H is far more toxic and, as I said, was without an antitoxin."

The horrendous image of what could happen if this were in the wrong hands sends a shiver up my spine. I bring my knees to my chest and hug my legs with the arm not being held hostage by Alex's hands as I wait for him to continue.

"A small group of scientists, myself and three others, were working with the CDC to develop an antitoxin for type-H. The terror cell, or perhaps another unfriendly entity—we're not exactly sure who, somehow learned about the task force and the identities of the individuals involved."

Alex hangs his head for a moment before looking me in the eye, only continuing after I squeeze his hand impatiently.

"The CIA intercepted intelligence indicating all of our identities had been compromised, and that there was a credible threat to not only each of us, but our families. We had no other choice than to fake our deaths and go underground while we continued to develop the antitoxin."

I forget how to breathe. Oh my God, no wonder Ben is so livid with Alex. He fucking chose this. A searing fire travels from my stomach out to my hands as rage engulfs me.

I have to force words out of my now-constricted throat. "So, you are telling me that you chose to let me think you died instead of, I don't know, telling me what the fuck was going on? Instead of taking me with you?"

I see pain flash across Alex's face. "I know it appears that way, but it would have been too obvious for us both to disappear. And it wasn't supposed to happen so soon. I thought I would have more time to figure out an alternative solution."

What the hell? "What do you mean?"

"We learned the hit was already out for me and that it would—"

"The plane," I interrupt.

Alex nods. "The group somehow knew I had a scheduled trip to Paris on a private plane, which they planned to take down. This gave us the perfect opportunity for them to think they achieved their goal."

I think through the events of the night I thought Alex died. The cryptic, one-sided conversation Nik had while we were driving home. Later being notified that Alex was in a plane that went down due to the storm. Ben finding me in the fetal position after I saw photos from the wreckage being broadcast on national news; images that haunt me to this day. "But then who was in the plane?"

Alex continues to nod, as if he was expecting this to be my next question. "Really bad men. Terrorists who have done unspeakable things. They thought the government was trading them for hostages."

Wait, what? "Was the government okay with their plane being destroyed?"

"The terrorists had their own transportation out of the U.S. As you can imagine, the arrangement to trade was classified, as the U.S. does not negotiate with terrorists. From the outside, it appeared to be a private flight to Paris. A change in the flight manifest made it appear that another scientist and I were on the flight, effectively placing a large target on the plane for the Russians."

I think back to the horrific day I could never bring myself to revisit. Alex was supposed to be traveling to Europe.

Investors who were interested in Immunotech requested he accompany them to Paris to meet with the remaining partners.

Alex continues, interrupting my memories from the day I have refused to think about until now. "It was a gamble, but as was suspected, the Russian group blew up the plane. The owner of the plane, a Saudi prince, is now hunting down those involved."

I shake my head in disbelief. "Holy shit. What happened to the hostages who were supposed to be traded?"

"Delta Force took down their convoy. They were extracted and have been returned to the States."

I breathe out a sigh of relief as my forehead falls to my hands. Delta Force, hostage rescues, biological warfare. Perhaps I am still dreaming.

"Elle. Love, are you okay?"

Alex's voice pulls me out of my head. "Thank God the hostages were rescued. That's at least good news." A million questions swirl through my mind, but there is one that screams the loudest.

"Where have you been?" My voice is raw, broken, when I add, "It's been nearly ten months."

The corner of Alex's lip turns up in a sad smile, but his eyes betray his anguish. "Quite literally underground. One by one, we each managed to subvert our assassinations and make it to an underground bunker, which resembled something out of a movie. It was a small compound with a state-of-the-art lab. I was either working in the lab or working out in the gym these past months."

My eyes travel from his face to his broad shoulders and down to his arms. The definition is evident, even through his shirt. Damn, he looks good.

He smirks when he sees me ogling him. "I had incredibly limited contact with the outside world. I could only speak with Nik when one of our CIA counterparts visited because they would bring a Boeing black phone, the only secure way to communicate. I went slightly mad worrying about you during the time in between. I had to keep busy and developed a bit of a reputation with the others of being rather … agitated if I didn't release my aggression physically. I spent a lot of time in the gym."

"I see. I assume the group was able to develop the antitoxin if you're now here?"

He nods. "But the others I've been working with have remained in hiding. I refused to stay underground after my last conversation with Nik. The point of being dead was to keep you safe, and that was no longer working."

My eyes widen as my heart rate exhilarates. "Do you think whoever is targeting me is part of this terrorist group?"

Alex leans forward and tilts his head so that our eyes lock. "Absolutely not. If this was the same group …" his features tighten and he breaks eye contact to shake his head before looking back at me. "Well, let's just say they wouldn't have wasted time with kidnapping Genevieve. Whoever is targeting you is amateur, at best. But that doesn't mean they aren't dangerous."

I nod my head, his explanation makes sense, but … my muscles seize as I think through the worst-case scenario. "What about you? Won't this group come after you again when they find out you're alive?"

Alex's eyes move down, pausing at my shoulders and then my arms. Following his gaze, I am surprised to see I'm shaking. He straightens in the chair. "Hold that thought." He stands and walks to the bathroom. A moment later I hear the bathtub filling with water before he returns to the side of the bed and bends to pick me up. "Let's get you warmed up."

* * *

Alex carries me to the bathroom and sets me on the counter. The cool marble chills the back of my legs, causing my shivering to increase. Alex takes me in, his eyes tracing down my body to see that I'm only wearing an oversized shirt. His oversized shirt. I watch as his eyes warm and the corners of his mouth lift in a half-smile. Following his gaze, a dry laugh grates my throat as I recall Ben's words from earlier. I lift a shoulder. "I was devastated that this shirt no longer smelled like you. I guess I know why Ben had such little patience for my hysterics."

The warmth in Alex's eyes is replaced with torment before he looks down to regain his composure. His eyes rest on his old college T-shirt again. "I put this on you the night you were drugged." He returns his gaze to mine before continuing, "I thought the shirt might provide some comfort while you were sleeping."

My eyes flare in surprise. "How would you know that? How did you know where I kept this shirt?" I can't read the emotion that flashes in his eyes before he places his large, warm hands over my chilled arms, causing another shiver to run through me. He doesn't answer, and it doesn't appear he has plans to answer anytime soon. But I realize it doesn't matter, not in this moment when Alex is in front of me, perfectly, so perfectly, alive.

Before I can process what I'm doing, I shamelessly bury my face in Alex's chest and breathe in deeply. After a brief moment, Alex wraps his arms around me, pulling me closer to him. We stay locked in an embrace, both of us soaking the other in. I try to reconcile that he's real. That the arms wrapped around me and the chest my face is buried in belong to him. That the delicious scent enveloping me isn't from an old T-shirt. I attempt to rationalize this, but my brain hasn't caught up with my body. An unrelenting need to reassure myself that Alex is here, that this is real, consumes me.

I raise my head to look at him and the air leaves my lungs. Haunted eyes, depicting the devastation these past months have caused us both, stare back at me. The anguish is so raw it's impossible for him to hide it, even though I can see that is exactly what he is trying to do. He bends to place a chaste kiss to my lips, and his delicious scent magnifies. I'm suddenly parched for him, a lost soul in the desert, having gone days without water. But it isn't water I crave. It isn't water I need on a cellular level.

I grab a handful of Alex's shirt and pull him closer, deepening the kiss. I need him more than I need air to breathe. He is the balm to my shattered existence, and I'm done trying to act like I have my shit together.

I'm done with the pretending.

Just done with it all.

Shelving my motto for the moment, I allow a dam to break. I'm no longer thinking about what I *should* be doing, how I *should* be acting. Flames engulf me from the inside out and I have a singular focus. Alex.

Wrapping my legs around his hips, he scoops me up and walks us toward the shower. My fervor is matched by his. We are clawing at each other as if we are trying to crawl under the other's skin. I can't get close enough.

I frantically pull at Alex's jeans, trying to get the button open when he lifts me higher with one hand and undresses himself with the other. I cry out in frustration at the delay—I need him, now. Screw food and water, Maslow had it all wrong; Alex is at the top of my hierarchy of needs.

He kicks his jeans off and walks us into the shower, shielding my body against the shower spray until it warms. After a few seconds he turns us so that the warm spray rains down on me from multiple directions. I am sandwiched between the shower wall and a muscled torso when my lace panties are ripped off my body and his drenched shirt is stripped off me. The wet cotton slides against my heated skin as it's peeled off, and the thud of the wet fabric landing on the shower floor is a starting bell.

We crash into each other, finally skin to skin. My hands move to the back of his head, and I pull him against me in a bruising kiss as I cling to him. A wave of exultation crashes over me as my world returns to its axis. And then Alex's fingers begin to do magical things. I rub myself against his hand in time with his ministrations, needing more, until one finger is finally, blissfully inserted, causing me to nearly buck myself out of his grip.

My head tips back and rests on the shower wall as I focus on the coil of need winding tightly in my belly. It's so good, yet not nearly enough. Before I can voice what I want, he inserts a second finger and my eyes close as a buzzing fills my ears. I surrender myself to the moment as the coil winds tighter. As heavenly as this feels, his fingers are not what I need.

Reaching down, I push Alex's hand away before grabbing his hard length and placing it at my entrance. His deep chuckle echoes in the shower, causing me to open my eyes. The intensity in his eyes steals my breath. My fingers run through his hair before cupping the back of his neck to bring him closer. Our noses are nearly touching when I say, "I need you. Now."

He adjusts our position and begins to slowly lower me onto him. My eyes roll back in my head. The pain-pleasure of ten months without sex is enough to make me orgasm then and there. I hold my breath until he's as deep as he can possibly go. We both still as we revel in the feeling. The feeling of finally being one after months of being so empty.

Time stands still as we stare at one another in naked wonder. All pretenses are laying on the tile beneath us. The moment is beautiful and raw and so incredibly intense that a tear escapes my eye. I feel it trickle down my cheek before Alex kisses it away. And then he starts to move, and I completely lose myself. I claw at him, needing more and more. Meeting every surge with my own, the urgency increases until I see stars behind my eyelids as I combust.

Unadulterated ecstasy continues to rip through my body, from my core to my limbs. Alex adjusts his angle and continues to pump his hips, and I don't have time to catch my breath before another orgasm builds. We stare into each other's eyes, the overwhelming intensity uncontainable. Everything we have and haven't said is etched on our souls and projected through our eyes. Just when I feel like I can't handle another moment, like I'm about to combust into a million pieces, we reach a crescendo and a second orgasm rips through me. Alex's pistoling increases until he's buried, muscles straining, as he empties himself inside me.

We remain locked in the same position, both of us panting as we try to catch our breath. My forehead is resting on his shoulder and my arms and legs are draped around him as we bask in the after current. Long minutes tick by before I lean my head back to look at Alex. "I feel like my very essence left with you, and now it's back. I haven't felt this …" I pause as I try to find the right word. "Whole. I haven't felt this whole in months."

Alex's eyes soften as he sweeps away a wet lock of hair clinging to my cheek. "That's because our love is made up of a single soul inhabiting two bodies."

I smile at his adept words. "That's beautiful. Who said that, Rumi?"

Alex's dimples flash as he answers, "A deviation of Aristotle, actually." The naked intensity in his eyes amplifies before he adds, "But it's true for us. I felt the same way. It was torture not being near you and having to rely on periodic calls to Nik to know you were okay." His voice becomes gravel as he continues. "It was a special form of torture, I can assure you. If you hadn't been threatened, I never would have agreed to continue with the IXB project."

A shiver wracks my body as I think back to even a day ago. There is no way I can go back to that cold, dark place. Ever. Tears spring to my eyes as the thought of that possibility threatens to overtake me.

Alex cups my face with the arm not currently holding me up. "Baby, what is it, what's wrong?" I shake my head. I couldn't articulate this feeling if I tried.

Placing his hands on my hips, Alex gently lifts me off him. I unwrap my legs and attempt to stand, leaning against the shower wall as I regain my bearings. I feel the void of his absence. A feeling of hopelessness engulfs the joy of being with Alex as the threat of emptiness returns.

One tear becomes several before months of depression and grief cascade down my face in a cathartic baptism. A renewal I couldn't stop if I tried.

Alex ducks down to eye level. "Shit. Love, what is it? Are you hurt?"

In the recesses of my mind, I vaguely register that Alex is talking when he says, "Eliana, I need you to look at me." The white-hot sharpness of his tone sobers me enough to turn my head toward him.

"Sweetheart, do you want me to get Dr. Wickham?" The fear in his voice is unnerving. "Fuck, I shouldn't have done that. I'm so sorry. I should have waited."

I shake my head, trying to clear the fog of melancholy surrounding me. "I'm fine." I manage to squeak out. "Dr. Wickham is the last thing I need, I just … I think everything has just now caught up to me." I shiver again at the fear of the nothingness returning after feeling so alive just a moment ago.

Alex picks me up and carries me to the bath. I hadn't noticed he turned off the faucet, he must have done that on our way to the shower while I was shoving my tongue down his throat.

He steps into the tub and lowers us both into the orange-blossom-scented bath. I close my eyes as the warm water and Alex's arms chase away the fear of the desolate hopelessness creeping in once again.

My back is to Alex's front as he rubs his hands up and down my arms. He does this until my sobs soften to sniffles and then he asks, "How are you feeling?"

I cringe. This question has become one I loathe. I was asked this question so many times when we thought Alex had died, and it created an internal dilemma each time. Do I answer truthfully and share that I feel as though I'm two seconds away from rocking in a corner for the rest of my life, or do I lie and say that I'm feeling fine? I usually went with the requisite, "I'm hanging in there." This response rode the middle—it dissuaded the questioner from asking follow-up questions in effort to avoid an uncomfortable situation, yet implied that I wasn't ready to fake cheerful pleasantries.

"I hate that question."

My body lifts with Alex's chuckle. I feel him kiss the top of my head. "Fair enough, I'll try again. Tell me why you were crying just now."

My fingers draw patterns along the top of the water as I think about how to answer his question. How do I begin to explain what losing him did to me? I attempt to relax my constricted throat as tears leak to the corners of my eyes. My voice is a broken whisper when after a minute of silence I say, "I can't begin to describe what it was like to think you were gone."

Taking a breath, I relax farther into Alex. His hands move from my arms to wrap around my stomach, hugging me against his chest.

"I think I might have PTSD or something. I have this visceral fear you are going to disappear and ..." again, I pause to steady my voice, "I just ... I can't go through that again. I won't survive it."

Alex tenses beneath me before his hands move down to my hips. He lifts my body and turns me in his arms so that I am straddling him. He kisses me before pulling back to look into my eyes. The somberness of his expression steals my breath. "I will never leave you again. I promise you that. I will do everything to protect you, which may include things you won't like, but you have my word that leaving will not be an option." He cups my cheek and leans forward to emphasize his point. "Ever."

Searching his eyes, I know that his words are true. I

lean down to capture his lips in a tender kiss. Alex's hand moves to cup the side of my face as the kiss deepens. He pulls back to look at me, love shining through his eyes. He curses. "I'll never get enough of you."

I feel Alex harden, and time stands still as we lose ourselves to each other in the orange-blossom-scented tub.

SIXTEEN

A TOWEL IS WRAPPED AROUND MY BODY AS PRUNED fingers pull lounge pants and a tank out of a drawer. We stayed in the bath until the water cooled as Alex washed every inch of me, massaging bath gel into tired, unused muscles.

"Are you tired? Do you want to get back into bed?"

Looking over my shoulder, I see a shirtless Alex leaning against the closet doorway. My mouth goes dry as I take him in. Holy shit. My pruned fingers itch to trace the eight protruding ab muscles that are taunting me. I raise my eyes to clear my thoughts, only to see the same hunger reflected in Alex's eyes.

I clear my throat, but my voice is still raspy when I respond, "As much as I'd love to crawl back into bed with you, we have too much to do."

Alex's expression tightens. "You still need to take it easy today, doctor's orders. In fact, I believe Dr. Wickham is still here to check in with you."

I look up at the ceiling. The last thing I want is a therapy session right now. Especially after my cathartic cry in the shower. "I'll get dressed and meet him in the living room."

Alex nods in agreement, concern still bracketing his

eyes. "I'll let him know." He turns to leave but pauses. "I know I still have a lot to explain …" He leaves the sentence hanging, the silence stretching a beat too long before I nod for him to continue. His eyes lock onto mine, the magnitude of his gaze, of the moment, stretches. He opens his mouth to speak but pauses again before looking away and taking a breath. When he looks back at me, the previous intensity is replaced with warmth, with love, and my anticipation fades as I realize he won't be sharing whatever it was he was about to say.

He smiles and nods his head toward the door. "I'll meet you out there." He turns to walk away but hesitates and turns back to me again. "Are you sure you're okay? I know this has been a lot in a short amount of time." His eyes search mine, I'm not sure what he sees, but concern returns to his eyes.

I smile in an attempt to appease him, but I can't lie. To say this has been a lot is an understatement. "My one wish came true, I'm more than okay. It's just that I'm also still processing everything" He nods, seeming to understand that I need time, before he turns and continues out the door.

After throwing on the lounge pants and shirt, I grab what is my equivalent to a security blanket, an oversized cashmere cardigan, before leaving the closet. Shrugging it on, I instantly feel less on edge as the cozy material hugs my body in a warm embrace.

Leaving the bedroom, I follow the sound of voices coming from the front of the condo. When I enter the living room, the first thing I see is a pissed-off Nik with Detectives Rodriguez and Price. I freeze in surprise. "Officers, how nice to see you again."

Rodriguez gives me a kind smile. "Mrs. Tate, how are you holding up?"

I return her smile with a genuine smile of my own, pleased at her choice of words. Finally, someone with the emotional intelligence to understand not to ask how I'm doing. I'm about to respond but stop when I sense Alex walk into the room. He tucks me under his arm and kisses my temple. I look up at him before answering Officer Rodriguez. "I am doing much better than the last time you saw me, thank you for asking."

Alex holds my gaze. "You're off the hook with Dr. Wickham. He'll be back in a couple of hours to speak with you, if that's okay?"

I nod, relieved I can put off my session. "Of course."

The corner of his mouth quirks up before he tears his eyes from mine to look at the officers. He offers his hand. "Agent Rodriguez, Agent Price, it's nice to see you both."

My eyes trail from Alex to Rodriguez and Price in confusion as the three shake hands. "Agents?"

Rodriguez gives me an almost apologetic smile as Alex suggests we all sit.

I take my customary spot on the couch, Alex following to sit next to me. Rodriguez and Price once again choose the club chairs facing the couch. Nik, who is studiously ignoring me, continues to stand. Well, if this isn't déjà vu, I think to myself.

Rodriguez's apologetic eyes turn to me. "Price and I work for the FBI. We, unfortunately, weren't able to disclose this information during our last visit as it may have compromised our investigation."

I look at Alex in confusion.

He places his hand on my thigh. "Agents Rodriguez and Price were the FBI detail assigned to assist during the IXB operation. Their focus is on the domestic side, while the CIA worked the international angle. They agreed to help Nik find the person, or people, who are threatening you."

A snorting sound draws our attention to Price, who is clearly trying to keep a straight face. He breaks his silence by stating, "We really didn't have a choice. It was either help Nik keep you safe or he …" he pauses his explanation to gesture to Alex, "refused to stay dead."

My eyes widen at the casual familiarity of his words. Alex has clearly become close with the two agents.

Rodriguez interjects. "A lot of good that did."

I feel Alex tense beside me as he looks at the agents and then to Nik. "If the three of you could have kept Eliana safe, I wouldn't have needed to reappear so soon."

My head jerks up in indignation. "Excuse me, but I was kept safe. I am not helpless. Nik and I managed just fine, thank you." I look to Nik—his features are pulled tight in irritation, most likely at himself. "I am alive and in one piece today because of Nik. If anything, you should be thanking him."

Alex runs the hand not resting on my folded legs through his hair in frustration before nodding at Nik in acknowledgment. "Regardless, the agreement was that I could resume my life once the antitoxin was viable, which it now is."

I look from the agents to Alex as the terror from earlier grips my chest. "I don't understand. How is it your life was threatened to the point you needed to fake your own death, and now the threat has simply passed? It doesn't make sense."

Alex leans forward and turns into me, so his eyes are all I see, capturing my full attention. "Now that the antitoxin has been created, the terrorists will be far more concerned with preventing distribution than who created it. I admit, we will most likely need security for the foreseeable future, but the immediate threat has passed."

I nod, reluctantly. "I still don't understand why you didn't tell me. I mean, I get why I couldn't have gone with you, but that doesn't explain why you didn't tell me." I feel tears burn the back of my eyes.

Rodriguez interrupts, "Mrs. Tate, you are being watched, and frankly, we don't know how close to you those watching may be."

My stomach clenches as a shiver runs up my spine at her words.

Rodriguez continues, "At this point, only the people in this room, Dr. Wickham, and Ben know of Alex's return. We would like to keep it that way until we get to the bottom of who has been threatening you."

This news gives me a modicum of relief. "So, I just continue to go about my life?" I look at Alex, "How are you going to remain hidden?"

Alex graces me with his mischievous half-grin. "The same way I have remained hidden for the past three weeks."

My eyes become saucers as realization dawns. "Oh my God, you've been watching me."

It's a statement, not a question, and from Alex's expression, I am correct.

"The drunken dream I had?"

Alex's chin moves down a centimeter in confirmation. "That night was one of the most difficult of my life, coming only second to two nights ago." He looks down, breaking eye contact. "It nearly destroyed me to see you hurting, to know that I was responsible and couldn't do anything about it." The rasp of his voice tells me he is affected by the memory.

Thinking back to that night and the relief I felt when I thought Alex was with me. God, what I wouldn't have given to know that he really was there. I think through the past weeks, to the odd moments that would have given Alex's presence away. The image of a figure watching as I was shepherded into the building comes to mind.

My eyes meet Alex's. "You were there. The day Scott chased that guy away."

Nik speaks for the first time since I entered the living room. "It was Mr. Tate who first alerted me. In fact, if not for him, we wouldn't have known there was a threat."

I think back to that day, now understanding why Nik was so angry with Scott. My eyes snap back to Alex's. "You have been watching me for weeks and still couldn't tell me? You couldn't have—I don't know—given me a sign or something?"

Alex takes my hand in his. "Agent Rodriguez is right, there are only a handful of people we can trust with this knowledge. We are concerned that someone close to you may be compromised, and although we are certain this person, or people, aren't connected to my work, it's better to err on the side of caution. It would have been obvious something was off if your demeanor suddenly changed."

I'm about to argue that I could have acted as if he was still gone, but expecting this response, Alex continues to speak before I can get a word out. "Sweetheart, everyone was aware of how gutted you were when you thought I was dead." I shudder at the word, proving his point. "As horrible as this was for you—and I do realize it was beyond devastating—your devastation is what has kept you safe. There's no way someone could fake what you went through, what you have experienced. This ensured the Russians continued to believe I was gone, which was critical for this to work and for you to remain out of their crosshairs. If they suspected I was alive, they would have taken you to get to me. Regardless of how much you hate me for what I did, I would do it again because that is a scenario I cannot live with."

I see the honesty in Alex's eyes. He would do this all again, even after promising he wouldn't leave. The mended seam on my heart pulls and, "You promised," leaves my lips on a broken whisper.

Determination flashes in Alex's eyes. "Yes, and I will not go back on that promise. I swear to you. I will find another way should we ever be in a situation like this again, but I plan to ensure that doesn't happen." I nod my head, not understanding how he plans to prevent something like this from happening in the future, but at the same time trusting he will do exactly that.

Alex's grin returns. "And I tried."

What on earth does that mean. "You tried what, exactly?"

Alex's grin widens to a smile. "I tried to give you a sign."

I stare at him blankly, waiting for him to continue.

"My sweater. I left my sweater in your office."

I shake my head. "I thought I was going crazy. Why would I see that as a sign?"

Alex stares at me for moment. "Because it's your favorite sweater. I saw that my T-shirt brought you comfort." He looks down as if he's uncertain of what he's about to say. "I guess I thought the sweater might do the same."

His vulnerability causes my bite of anger to recede. I shake my head in disbelief. "I just … I wish I would have known." It's the only thing there is to say. I can't change the past but knowing that he was alive and well would have saved so much heartache.

Alex takes my stiff body in his arms, holding me until I melt into him. We stay this way for several minutes while

Rodriguez, Price, and Nik's voices provide white noise in the background.

Alex runs his hand over my shoulder and arm in a hypnotizing rhythm. "We are close, baby." His voice is low, his mouth near my ear. "This … arrangement, won't last forever. As soon as we know who is threatening you, I will publicly return from the dead and we can get back to us."

Moving my head back, I look into Alex's eyes to see resolute conviction. I bring my hand to the side of his face and guide his lips to mine, attempting to pour my understanding and trust into a kiss before pulling back. "What's your grand plan? How are you going to suddenly return from the dead?"

Alex looks over at Price and Rodriguez, who are still engrossed in a conversation with Nik, before speaking. "A play on the truth. The story will be that terrorists took me and the others, but we were rescued by the CIA. The two terrorists who went down in the plane I was supposed to be in were members of ISIS. The Russians planning to kill us will think they are responsible for intercepting us prior to the Russians blowing up the plane. Their focus will be redirected from me, to finding the antitoxin in the Middle East."

I nod my head. "That's probable. It also provides an explanation for the plane you were supposed to be in—the Russians will think ISIS sacrificed their own members to frame your death so they would have unobstructed access to the antitoxin. And the Saudi prince will go on thinking the Russians blew up his plane and the ISIS members on board."

Alex smiles, a spark of pride in his eyes that I worked it out. "Exactly."

I can't help but smile at the ingenuity. "I suppose you thought of everything."

A shadow passes over Alex's expression. "No, not every-thing. We still don't know who has been threatening you."

We both look to the other side of the room. Price and Nik are leaning over a sideboard table positioned against the wall as they watch Rodriguez sketch something on a piece of paper. "Yes, I suppose there's still that."

The look on Alex's face tells me he didn't miss the de-feated tone in my voice. His fingers move to brush a lock of hair away from my eye before cupping the side of my face. "I was being honest when I said we don't believe the Russians are involved with the threats to you, but my delayed reap-pearance until this is confirmed is for your protection."

I turn my head to kiss the inside of his wrist. "I know, and I understand. I just wish we knew who was behind this." I force a smile. "I'm getting impatient."

My smile slips as I take in Alex's sober expression. "We'll know soon, you have my word."

His words, coupled with *that* expression, erase my un-ease. If there is one truth I can cling to, it is my newly ac-quired absence of doubt that we will catch these harassing assholes.

* * *

Several hours later, I drop onto the couch as exhaustion overtakes me. The ambient music playing softly in the back-ground begins to lure me to sleep the moment my head is cradled on the couch cushion.

What. A. Day.

The corner of my mouth tips up in disbelief as I think about not only discovering my dead husband is very much alive, but he was—is—involved with a complex operation involving several government agencies.

Electricity zaps the room a moment before the cushion dips beside me. I can feel Alex's stare, but I'm too tired to open my eyes.

"What are you grinning about?" The smile in his voice causes the second corner of my mouth to join the first. "Ah, a full smile. Now I really must know what's running through that beautiful head of yours."

I sigh rather dramatically before responding. "Just attempting to sort through this ridiculousness."

"And what ridiculousness might that be?" Alex responds with a chuckle.

"Our life," I answer matter-of-factly. "Today, I woke from being drugged, after attempting to rescue my friend, might I add, to discover that my dead husband is alive and working with the Department of Justice, FBI, and CIA. Meanwhile, some unknown lunatic has me on lockdown, and we still don't know who this person is."

I feel Alex's lips against the side of my head. "That may all be true, but the team is getting closer. Give them another twenty-four hours, and they may surprise you."

My head rolls to the side and I open one eye, the incredulity on my face communicating how unlikely I believe his words to be. But as I stare at him, his mischievous grin showcasing his dimples, my heart clenches. Any annoyance I felt is replaced with utter gratefulness to have him sitting next to me. I scoot closer, and when he lifts his arm for me to snuggle under, I melt into his warmth as his delicious scent blankets me.

"Do you think their plan will work?"

Alex's fingers start tracing patterns on my upper arm.

He thinks about my question for a moment before answering. "Yes, it will work if whoever is after you plans to try something at Tate."

I open my second eye to look up at his expression. "And if the person doesn't try something at the office?"

"Then we come up with another plan," Alex states without missing a beat.

We are both quiet as Nina Simone crones softly in the background. Several minutes pass before Alex's fingers pause. "How was your discussion with Dr. Wickham?"

My eyes close again as I think about my conversation with Dr. Wickham when he returned earlier in the day. We spent well over an hour in my office while Alex, Nik, Rodriguez, and Price turned the living room into a war room as they mapped out a plan for drawing out the psycho who is after me.

"It was fine. Dr. Wickham had to tell me I was right, and I don't have to tell you how much I enjoyed that."

Alex chuckles. "What were you right about?"

My stomach somersaults when I realize we are going to have so many moments like this. Moments of me explaining what he missed while he was attempting to save the world.

"My last appointment with Dr. Wickham was a bit of an emergency. I thought I was quite literally going crazy at the time. It was the day after Theo's cardiac event." I look at Alex with an eyebrow raised to confirm he knows what I am referring to. He nods his head once. "I fell asleep in the hospital waiting room, which I'm guessing you already know. I woke because of your scent. I was convinced I was losing my mind."

"I was there, I came as soon as I heard the news. I wanted to make sure you were okay, even if I wasn't able to do much." Alex's voice is apologetic. "This happened when I was still underground. We were in the final stages of developing the antitoxin—we were so close; it was a nightmare convincing the government to allow me to check on you." I look up to see him smiling at the memory. "I have Rodriguez and Price to thank for that excursion."

I snuggle deeper into Alex's chest at the memory of waking alone in the hospital as his arms hug me closer to him. I feel another kiss on my head. "It has been a long day, especially for you. You should have taken the day to rest."

"I know you've been away, but have you forgotten who you married?" I answer sleepily as exhaustion begins to win my fight to stay awake.

Alex's deep laugh fills the room and I smile in awe, absorbing my new reality. My head on Alex's chest, feeling his heartbeat, so strong and sure. I have no doubt I am the luckiest person in the world.

* * *

I'm walking down the dark hall toward soft music floating from the living room. A silhouette, his back to the entrance, is staring out the far window. I begin to walk toward the window before my feet freeze in place; I instinctively know something is off.

Steadying my breath, I continue to approach, chastising myself for feeling uneasy. This is the same Alex. My Alex. Nearly a year apart isn't going to change that, but still, a magnetic pull is urging me to run in the opposite direction.

Forcing myself to close the distance, I reach out my

hand as the figure turns. My heart stops when Dorn's malevolent black eyes stare back at me.

I gasp and pull my hand back as a sinister smile, one I hoped to never see again, spreads across his face. "Hello, Eliana, so nice of you to join me."

Noise fills my head.

How did he get into my home? Where is security? Where is Alex?

He takes a step toward me, and I scream. With every ounce of energy in me, I scream. He wraps his fingers around my shoulder and shakes me, but I continue to scream.

"ELIANA, wake up!" My eyes shoot open to see anxious blue-gray eyes staring back at me.

Blue-gray, not black. I sit up and cradle my head in my hands as I catch my breath. I'm in bed, not in the living room.

Alex is here.

Alex is here.

Alex is here.

I repeat this mantra in my head several times as Alex rubs my back in comforting strokes until my heart rate begins to slow.

"Do you want to talk about it?" he asks, his voice strained.

I glance over at him and feel an unexpected urge to cry when I see the concern etched onto his face. Tipping my head back to staunch the liquid gathering behind my eyes, I take a breath and return my gaze to Alex. "I dreamt I was walking toward you in the front room, but you ended up being Richard Dorn, of all people." I shiver. "The look on his face made it clear his visit wasn't a social call … I just—I sort of freaked out in the dream."

Alex releases a loud, long breath. "Richard Dorn isn't getting within ten miles of you after the shit he pulled while I was away."

Nodding my head absentmindedly, I silently pray Alex doesn't discover the full extent of what Dorn has done these past months. He just returned; I don't want him arrested for assault.

Lying my head on my pillow, I focus on calming my racing heart. Alex remains upright as he stares down at me, concern still on his face. "What can I do?"

I turn toward him. "Just hold me."

His eyes soften. "Happily."

Alex wraps his arm around my middle and cradles me to him. He continues to run his fingers along my arm. "It kills me that you're having nightmares because of that asshole."

"This was actually my first Dorn nightmare, at least while I was sleeping."

"I would give anything to have been able to see you put him in his place at the board meeting. Now that is a scene I will happily have dreams about."

Laughing softly, I reply, "You would happily have Dorn in a dream? Interesting."

"Oh no, he wouldn't be in the dream, only you in all your glory, throwing down the gauntlet. Now *that* is an image that instantly makes me hard."

An uninhibited laugh leaves my lips before I lick them, suddenly knowing exactly what I need to get my mind off this stupid dream. I attempt to sound serious when I say,

"Speaking of being hard, I thought we promised to never fall asleep without making love?"

Alex cups the side of my face. "You fell asleep on the couch and were completely passed out when I brought you to bed. I didn't think you would appreciate being woken."

I shush him with my finger to his lips. "Excuses, excuses. We have months to make up for, so kiss me."

Alex's eyes become molten metal as he leans in and our lips meet. And holy wow, what a kiss it is. I surrender to drunken lust as we make up for lost time in our ecstasy-drenched bubble.

SEVENTEEN

THE MOMENT THE ELEVATOR DOORS OPEN, I SAY goodbye to Nik, step into the foyer, and kick off my heels. What a week. The comfort of being at home begins to melt away the tension in my shoulders. Excitement tickles my stomach in anticipation of my first full weekend with Alex since his return. I walk to the kitchen and set my bag on the island, my face instantly heating as images from the night before replay in my mind. I may never look at this island the same. I clear my suddenly parched throat and focus on pouring a glass of water.

It has been a week since the night of the club opening, and it has been ... well, odd. The mornings and evenings with Alex have been pure bliss. We've developed a routine of sorts. I wake in Alex's arms, which leads to us making up for months of not being together. I head to the office and Alex is secreted away to continue to support the team he left behind, albeit from the regional FBI office in New York. He has also been busy developing a plan to get Immunotech back on track, poring over the audited financials Genevieve provided me. I smile at the thought of Gen, and the memory of seeing her for the first time following her abduction.

Gen and I spoke over the phone the day I woke from

my drug-induced coma. She assured me she was unharmed, aside from a few bruises, but didn't go into detail of what she experienced that night. I told her to take as much time off as she needed, but she refused. Monday morning, she came barreling into my office and nearly lifted me off the ground with a bruising hug. We both went from tears of gratitude that the other was relatively unharmed to laughing uncontrollably at the absolute ridiculousness of being abducted and drugged, only to both show up to work bright and early on Monday. We've been eating lunch in my office this week, both of us taking advantage of the hour to just be us—friends who don't have heavy baggage holding them down.

As much as I cherish the hour Gen and I have to just be ourselves, it has been difficult to not mention Alex. I am counting down the days to his public emergence from the dead; the number of times I've almost slipped up is quickly multiplying.

We were hopeful Gen could provide intel on the people who took her, but the ringleader wore a balaclava and used a device to alter their voice, though she's sure the person is male based on size and stature. She didn't recognize any of the goons helping this mystery person, but she overheard an argument about one of them not being paid, so the assumption is they were all hired specifically for that night.

Alex and I typically return home around the same time to cook dinner together, though the food tends to be cold by the time we get to it. We're getting back into a routine of sorts, and it feels nice, even if I still have to constantly remind myself he is real and not a mirage.

Overall, my time with Alex this past week has been a dream come true. My days, however, have been chaotic. The team behind 'find Elle's psycho-stalker' decided that the culprit will most likely strike while I'm at work, as it provides the greatest opportunity for success—I have to admit, that sentence didn't make me feel warm and fuzzy when I first heard it. So, as I go about my day, there are strategically placed opportunities, times when it appears I'm alone in the parking garage or Darcy is away from her desk, to try to lure this phantom person to act, but so far, it hasn't worked.

The plotting, constant navigating of security and acting as bait hasn't been the only stress this week. Ben worked his magic on James, the owner of Bec I met during the madness at the club opening, and somehow convinced him to speak with me. James agreed to meet at my office, which was generous, but caused the meeting to start off on the wrong foot. James' skepticism of me and my intentions was highlighted by his reproachful scowl. It would have been much better if I could have met with him on his turf, at Bec, perhaps.

As awkward as the meeting began, we ended up speaking for nearly two hours. By the end of our time together, I was glad I'd trusted my gut. James shared that his wife, Rebecca, is battling cancer, hence the need for a loan to pay her medical bills. As the meeting progressed, James' scowl turned to interest as he slowly came to the realization I was more interested in helping than in sabotage. The meeting concluded with a verbal agreement for Tate to buy fifty-one percent of Bec. James will have complete autonomy to continue to operate the business as he sees fit. The best part is, as a condition of the deal, his loan will be paid, and he and his wife won't be on the hook with Capri, Inc. or Dorn. Their restaurant will remain safe.

I smile as I take a drink of water and attempt to massage the remaining tension from my neck. At least one issue has been resolved, though I still don't understand Luca's involvement. James suspected Dorn was working with someone to attempt a takeover since Dorn certainly can't run a restaurant, but he had no idea it was Luca. I felt bad sharing that information; it was clear James respected Luca as a fellow chef. I make a mental note to speak with Luca to find out why the hell he didn't tell me he was involved with Dorn.

My bag begins to vibrate, interrupting my thoughts. I grab my phone to see Alex's name.

Smiling, I press the accept button. "Are you as excited as I am to spend our first Friday in nearly ten months together?"

Alex chuckles at my greeting. "You have no idea. The only thing I've been able to think about today is having you to myself for two full, uninterrupted days. Unfortunately, I'm going to be a little late. Nik just called; he wants me to go with him to check out a lead he just received."

"What? Nik just left me three minutes ago, why didn't he say anything?"

"He mentioned that. Apparently, Scott was at Nik's door to tell him he noticed someone loitering across the street a little over an hour ago. He and another member of Nik's team followed the person to a residence in Brooklyn. The guy who was with Scott remained to make sure no one left the brownstone until we get there to question this person."

My eyes widen and I start to object when Alex interrupts. "I know what you're about to say, but there's no need to worry—we're meeting Rodriguez and Price at the residence. We won't go in until they arrive."

Exhaling the breath I took in preparation for an

argument, I mentally coax myself to remain calm. The storm of butterflies assaulting my stomach ignore my pep talk. "Please be careful. I don't like this."

"There's nothing to be anxious about, love. We just want to question the person. If it turns out they are responsible for harassing you … well, they'll be dealt with, and you will no longer have to worry."

Rolling my eyes, I mutter, "Is that supposed to make me feel better? Because it has the opposite effect."

There's a smile in Alex's voice when he says, "I'll be home in an hour, two tops. We can order in and sequester ourselves to the bedroom for the rest of the weekend."

I can't help but return his smile with my own as I reply, "Sounds like heaven."

"I couldn't agree more. Why don't you pour a glass of wine and relax? I'll be home before you know it."

That's actually an excellent suggestion, I think to myself. "Please, please be careful. And promise to call the moment you're finished."

"I promise. I love you."

"Love you too. Hurry home," I respond, my voice pitched with anxiety.

"Always."

Pressing end, I look around the quiet, empty kitchen. Perhaps a glass of wine will help me relax. I pour a glass and head to my home office. I might as well continue my preparations for the Immunotech board meeting on Monday. According to Theo, all indications are that the external audit on Dorn found a number of transgressions, many illegal, others highly questionable. He said there's no way Immunotech will be able to keep Dorn on in any capacity. Especially since TA Holdings will be firing Dorn once the full report is released. It sounds as though Dorn will be dealing with a lawsuit in the near future as well.

The findings from the audit will make my efforts to regain control of Immunotech so much easier, but I will still need to convince Edward Dooling and Elizabeth Sanders that I am their best bet. The irony is, this would all be unnecessary if Alex didn't have to remain in hiding. He could easily reclaim his role as CEO of Immunotech and chairman of the board, effectively dethroning Dorn and Edward, and we could all move on with our lives.

I begin to read over my notes, making revisions to my talking points. I'm so engrossed in the task it takes me a minute to register the dim ding of the elevator sounding from the front of the condo. Glancing at the time on my computer screen, I see that just over thirty minutes have passed since I spoke with Alex. He must have decided to come home instead of accompanying Nik. I jump up from my desk chair and rush to the to the foyer, giddy with anticipation. Eyeing the island as I pass the kitchen, the thought of an impending repeat of last night quickens my steps.

I round the corner and freeze when I see Scott instead of Alex. It takes me a moment to recover from my surprise before I say, "Scott, I wasn't expecting you. Please, come in."

We walk to the kitchen and I ask if I can get him something to drink. He declines but I pour two glasses of water to keep myself busy. "So, what brings you here …" I pause as terror grips me. "Oh my God, did something happen to Al—uh, Nik?" Shit, that was close. I hold my breath as I await Scott's response.

I watch as he fidgets, his eyes downcast, and my terror escalates. He clearly doesn't want to tell me something. "Scott?" I nearly shout. "What is it? Tell me."

He looks up but doesn't make eye contact. "Nik is fine, but he wants me to do a sweep."

"Really? That's odd."

Scott's mouth thins into a line as he nods and shrugs one shoulder. "Sorry."

"Scott, don't apologize for doing your job." I put my arm out, gesturing to the front room. "I know the drill by now, do what you need to do."

Scott leaves the kitchen and walks to the stairs. He looks back and gives me a small smile before walking up the staircase.

Well, that was weird. I walk back to my office to grab my cell phone before backtracking, stopping partway down the hall so that I have a view of the stairs while remaining out of sight. I call Alex, the phone rings until his voicemail comes on. I hang up and call Nik. The same thing happens, but Nik immediately sends a short text back.

We have him. It was Dorn. Will be back soon. Need anything?

I exhale and lean against the wall. Holy shit, it's over? I should have known it was that asshole.

After a moment of soaking in the news I walk back into the kitchen, embarrassed with myself for my paranoia. I respond to Nik with a text of my own.

Wow, I guess I shouldn't be surprised. Keep Alex safe. Just called to ask about Scott wanting to check out the condo. No worries now.

My head snaps up at hearing a noise on the stairs. I press send and set my phone on the island. "Scott, good news, I believe you are relieved of your babysitting duties," I yell up the stairs. "It was Dorn all along. Nik is with him now." I silently congratulate myself on the number of times

I have abstained from mentioning Alex in the few minutes Scott has been here.

After several moments of silence, I call out, "Scott?"

I walk to the stairs and look up just as Scott steps around the corner to stand at the top of the last flight. "Did you hear me?" I ask with a wide smile as he makes his way down. "You're relieved of your babysitting duties. That must be good news on a Friday night?"

My phone vibrating in the kitchen interrupts his answer. "Just let me grab this and I'll walk you out," I call over my shoulder as I walk back into the kitchen.

I'm about to pick up my phone when something slams into me from behind. I fly forward before I'm grabbed, saving me from cracking my head onto the marble of the kitchen island. I am picked up, my arms pinned uselessly to my side. I kick my legs out and snap my head back in an attempt to headbutt whoever is holding me, somehow knowing it's not Scott. Before I can make another attempt, I'm thrown unceremoniously onto the couch.

Ready to fight, I flip to my back and raise my fists. My eyes widen in shock at seeing the two men staring down at me. "Luca, what are you doing here?" I look to Scott who stares back at me blankly. "Scott, what the hell is going on?"

Luca's lips spread into a smile. "Ciao, bella. Did you miss me? I certainly missed you."

A shiver travels through me at the tone in Luca's voice. It's as if I don't know the man standing in front of me. "What's going on, Luca? Why are you here?"

Luca continues to stare for a beat too long before finally speaking. "Tsk, tsk, so many questions, bella. Perhaps you do us all a favor and just shut up, huh?"

The silence in the room builds upon itself, one layer

after another, as the three of us stare at each other. This continues for several long seconds until I've had enough and stand from the couch. "I don't know what's going on here, but Nik will be back to check on me soon, and he won't be pleased to see an uncleared visitor." I look pointedly at Scott, who finally displays a reaction as he looks to the floor.

Luca's smile turns malevolent. "Ah, one can hope. I would relish the opportunity to repay Nik for making my life difficult these past months. But, as you just said, he is not here." His grin widens. "And Brooklyn is quite a ways from the Upper East Side, no?"

"Months? I thought you arrived following Theo's hospitalization?"

Luca's eyes turn to ice. "Theo's hospitalization? Is that how you are referring to nearly killing him? How convenient for you to forget the reason he ended up in the hospital."

What the—"Enough with the games. Why are you here, Luca?"

Before I have a chance to consider what is about to happen, Luca's upper body turns to the side before whipping back to center, his arm outstretched. The impact of his hand hitting my face propels me backward, my body once again landing on the couch before I even feel the sting on the side of my face.

Holy shit! The pulsing sting near my eye makes this unbelievable moment entirely too real. As badly as I want to press my cold hand against the sting on my cheek, I refuse. Denying Luca the satisfaction of seeing a reaction from me. Instead, I slow my breathing and ride out the waves of pain. Fuck, that hurt.

Think, Elle, think. How are you going to get out of this? I take a steadying breath, slowly rise to my feet, and face Luca. "Well, that was unnecessary. I'm going to ask you again since I don't speak backhand. Why are you here?"

Luca is in my face in an instant before pushing me back onto the couch. For a moment I'm terrified he has a far more nefarious plan in mind as he follows me down, grabs my face, and growls into my ear, "I am here to take what is rightfully mine," before jumping up and yelling at Scott to find something to tie my hands.

Shit, shit, shit. I look around the room, still contemplating how to get out of this as Scott leaves in search of something to restrain me. I certainly can't rely on him for help. I watch Luca out of the corner of my eye as he paces the room.

I need to get out of here. Now.

The elevator will most likely take too long to arrive, but if I can somehow make it to the other side of the condo, I can leave through the emergency stairwell. The question is, how do I get to the stairs undetected?

I'm considering the best strategy when I hear my phone vibrating on the kitchen island. Luca and I make eye contact for a split second, both realizing my lifeline is only feet away. Before I can think twice, I turn and vault over the couch. My bare feet provide the traction I need for a solid landing on the hardwood floor. I don't dare look back at Luca as I run to the kitchen.

Snatching my phone from the island without slowing, I continue my sprint to the back stairwell. My bare feet slap against the polished wood as I pump my arms. I am almost to the staircase when I glance down to hit the accept button and see it's Nik. Thank God. I hear Nik's voice on the other end the instant I connect the call, even with the phone away from my ear. I take in a breath to yell for help, but only manage a yelp when I'm tackled from behind.

My body propels forward, and I lose my grip on the phone. I watch in horror as the last thing I see is my phone sliding down the length of the hall right before a crack reverberates throughout my head and everything dims to black.

* * *

My head is pounding with a pain so extreme I no longer feel the sting on my face. Instinctively, I try to raise my hands to rub my temples, but they don't move. Squinting one eye open, I see that my ankles are duct-taped to a dining room chair. I assume the same must be true of my hands. Fuck.

I keep my head bowed forward, which limits what I can see, but the throw rug indicates I am back in the living room. Voices are arguing behind me, and I struggle to focus on what they are saying. Luca responds to Scott with clear disdain. "I told you I'd take care of you, and I will. Now, kindly shut the fuck up." Followed by, "When in the hell is she going to wake up? We don't have time for this, we need to leave."

Footsteps on the floor echo in the room before they are muffled by the rug as they get closer. Two shiny black Ferragamos stop in front of me. With my head still bowed, I close my eyes and focus on maintaining slow, even breaths. Maybe I can just pretend I'm unconscious until Nik and Alex get here. Nik will know something is wrong after his call. Who knows what he heard after I answered, but he has to be on his way.

I feel a hand on the top of my head before fingers lock

onto the roots of my hair and my head is yanked up. I can't stop the moan of pain that leaves my mouth. Shit.

"Open your eyes, Eliana."

My eyes crack open to slits before the dim light makes them slam shut again. A wave of nausea overtakes me.

"You asked me why I was here. It's very simple, I am here for you."

My eyes snap open at his words. Pain and nausea are momentarily forgotten when I ask, "What does that mean?"

Luca smiles. "It means you will be signing two documents. The first is a contract and bill of sale. We are buying Bec for five million dollars."

The nausea returns, forcing me to close my eyes for a moment. "And where exactly are you planning to get five million dollars? I believe you came to me to fund this, and I haven't agreed."

Luca tightens his grip on my hair causing another involuntary whimper to escape my throat. "And why exactly haven't you agreed? Ah, that's right, you went behind my back to make your own deal with Bec's owners." The fingers tangled in my hair jerk my head back so that I'm forced to look into Luca's cold eyes before he continues. "Which leads me to the best part: the second document you will be signing is our marriage certificate. What's yours is mine, *moglie.*"

My eyes flare in surprise. "Are you crazy? How on earth does this plan work? You are delusional if you think I would agree to marry you."

Luca sneers down at me. "I don't give a fuck what you agree to. This is happening. As of last week, Scott is a registered officiant in Washington, D.C., the same place where we can get a marriage license in a couple of hours after applying online. That's all that is needed to make us husband

and wife." Luca looks off into the distance, a smile spreading across his face. "And once we are married, I get everything in the event of your untimely death."

It's in this moment I realize Luca has completely lost his mind. What kind of half-baked plan is this? "So, your plan is to marry me and use my money to purchase Bec, and then what? We ride off into the sunset or I'm dead?" I snicker. "You really are delusional." Luca manages to tighten his hold on my hair. I try not to react, but the sting is too much not to suck in a breath.

"Luca, if I don't take a pill for the raging migraine I currently have, I will be sick all over your shoes."

Luca releases his hold and jumps back a step. He stares at me for several seconds, probably trying to determine if I really am about to be sick. Apparently satisfied with what he sees, he looks over my shoulder. "Is she telling the truth, does she have medication for migraines?"

Scott answers from behind me. "Yes, she's telling the truth."

Luca raises his eyes to the ceiling as he mumbles something in Italian under his breath before looking back at me. "Where is your medication?"

I feel a sliver of hope. "It's upstairs."

He looks back at Scott, "Do you know where?"

"No, but there is a medicine cabinet in the bathroom across from the gym that has bottles of pills."

Luca impatiently motions to the stairs. "Then go get the pills."

I hear Scott stutter behind me. "I don't know what the medicine is called."

Luca throws his hands up dramatically before looking at me. "What is the name of the medication."

"I can't remember, but I would recognize the bottle if I saw it."

Luca glowers down at me. "Nice try, bella. But you are staying in that chair until we are on our way to D.C." He looks back at Scott. "Bring me all of the prescriptions."

This moment of reprieve allows me to consider Luca's words; something isn't adding up. "This all seems rather dramatic for access to my accounts, Luca. What does Dorn have to do with this?"

Luca's maniacal smile returns. "Ah, Richard Dorn. Why does he hate you so much?"

I roll my eyes, ignoring him. "What does Dorn have to do with any of this if your plan was to force me into marriage?"

Luca considers me for a moment before answering. "Let's just say my plans have changed." He crosses his arms and turns to look out the window, staring blankly at the city skyline. I am shocked when he actually starts to talk. "Theo introduced me to Dorn shortly after he joined the firm. Theo knew I was looking for funding, and Dorn was looking for investments. We had been meeting virtually for a few months before he made me an offer I couldn't re-fuse. Our arrangement brought me to New York. That was the reason I was in town the day Theo had a heart attack."

I can't help but interrupt him. "It was not a heart at-tack, it was a cardiac event. And your best friend, Dorn, did not help that situation."

Luca's glower becomes a sneer. "You think you are above everyone else, Eliana. You always have. When you were in college you were too good to give me the time of day. And after, when Theo and Margaret always placed you on a pedestal, I could never compare. Even when I was the one making something of myself, I was the success, while you wallowed in self-pity." Luca's voice pitches higher in condensation. "Poor Eliana, she lost her parents. Poor Eliana, she lost her husband." His voice turns into a growl. "Really, does anyone around you remain alive?"

If I wasn't about ready to vomit, I would actually laugh at the realization that I am in this predicament because of this man-boy's insecurity. "Luca, I have never thought I was above you. Dorn, yes, but never you. I have no idea what led you to believe that, but I had the biggest crush on you when we visited Italy that summer in college."

Luca snorts in disbelief and turns toward me. When he remains silent, I forge on. "As for Theo and Margaret, they love you like a son. This will break their hearts."

Luca's face twists in anger. "When are you going to understand this is all your fault? Everything, Every. Single. Thing. Is your fault! And it's time you face the consequences. If it wasn't for you, I would have multiple restaurants by now, but your influence over Theo royally fucked up my plan!" Spittle is flying out of Luca's mouth by the end of his tirade; his eyes are wide and unfocussed as he becomes completely unhinged.

I shake my head in disbelief, I clearly don't know the person standing in front of me. "Wow, you really are delusional."

The moment the words are out of my mouth, l realize I went too far. Luca straightens his hunched shoulders and fixes his raging eyes on me. I don't recognize the person standing in front of me; it's as if he's possessed.

Terror shoots through me at what I see in Luca's expression right before he launches himself at me. He's flying through the air, his arms outstretched, his fingers bent like claws. With my hands still duct-taped all I can do is turn my head and brace for impact.

It feels like I'm hit by a train as the chair I'm taped to flips onto its back and Luca lands on top of me. Before I can recover from the wind being knocked out of me, Luca wraps his hands around my throat and squeezes, cutting off my airway. His snarled face is inches from mine. "If you would have just given me the money, this wouldn't have happened! I wouldn't have had to go this far. But now I have no choice, because I am a dead man if I don't move forward with this."

I look up at him, completely helpless with my hands still taped behind my back and my legs taped to the chair. My eyes plead with him to let me go, but rage has completely overtaken Luca, his face unrecognizable as he glowers down at me with pure hatred. Spots float in front of my eyes and I welcome the distraction from the monster looming above me. My body begins to feel numb before becoming weightless.

I've heard people say your life flashes before your eyes when you are near death, but all I can think of is the disbelief that after everything, this is how I'm going to die. Strangled by someone I once considered a friend. The spots grow larger until there is no light and no darkness. It strikes me that there is a distinct moment when I move from fighting to allowing myself to relax into the numbing peace that fills me.

EIGHTEEN

ALEX

NIK UNLOCKS THE EMERGENCY EXIT DOOR AND WE slide through the cracked opening to enter the second floor of the dark penthouse. Our breath is labored from our run up five flights of stairs. I focus on slowing my breaths as Nik silently closes the door behind us and turns to the alarm panel. It's already disengaged. We look at one another knowingly, there's only one reason this alarm would be disengaged—someone recently used the door. I look down the hall as we wait a handful of seconds to listen. The top floor is silent.

"They must be downstairs," I whisper. Nick nods his head in agreement.

We begin to make our way down the hall when we hear footsteps on the stairs. Nik nods his head toward the gym and we both duck inside.

I watch as Nik removes his gun and moves partially behind the door. Pressing my body against the far wall, we wait. Heavy footsteps pound up the stairs. Definitely male.

The footsteps move down the hall and stop in front of the gym. I see Nik's arms extend, both hands ready on his gun. A small pool of light spills into the gym when a light from across the hall turns on, followed by the sound of plastic hitting the floor and the tinkling rain of pills. Nik moves his head to the side to get a visual.

I continue to stare at Nik, anticipating his signal, but he shakes his head no.

Plastic once again hits the floor and it's evident the person is looking for something in the medicine cabinet. Shit.

"It's someone we know."

Nik nods, not taking his focus away from the doorway.

"What the fuck, Nik? This is taking too long. We need to move. Now."

Nik gives one aggressive shake of his head.

I move toward the doorway, ignoring Nik as he continues to shake his head no, and stretch my neck to look across the hall, keeping my body covered by the wall. Whoever is in the bathroom is leaning forward, so the only thing I see are black boots. The same black boots everyone on Nik's team wears. I turn to look at Nik—his suspicions were correct.

I shift my weight to the balls of my feet as I prepare to tackle the fucker when I hear Nik's grumbled curse from behind me before he barrels past me.

Stunned, I watch as Nik jumps behind Scott, clamps his hands on either side of his neck and, after a few seconds, lowers the unconscious man to the floor.

I shake my head at seeing Scott's slack face. I had hoped Nik was wrong about Scott.

Nik stands from where he was kneeling to zip tie Scott's hands. "Help me stand him up?"

After we lift Scott's limp body, Nik bends to drape him over his shoulder in a fireman's carry. "I'm going to lock him in the guest room closet down the hall until we know what we're dealing with." He pauses to look at Scott's closed eyes and gaping mouth reflected in the mirror. "We'll question him once he wakes up." Nik moves to exit the bathroom but turns to me with a severe expression. "Stay here until I get back, this will take less than a minute."

I nod. "Hurry."

Nik turns and silently speed walks down the hall, as if he isn't carrying a man who weighs more than him.

The moment he's gone, every instinct I have is telling me to run downstairs to find Elle. Turning toward the sink, I lower my head as I try to calm my thoughts. It doesn't work.

Fuck this. I straighten and step out of the bathroom, intending to let Nik know I'll meet him downstairs. But before turning to find Nik, a loud crash, and what sounds like wood breaking, comes from the stairs.

Without thinking, I take off down the stairs. When I round the corner of the bottom floor my world stops. All rational thought evaporates when I see someone on top of Elle. I launch myself, tackling the fucker off. I straddle him and start punching with no plans to stop.

I'm in a fog of numbness as I continue to pound my fists into flesh until all I see is mottled red below me. I sit back on my heels and register the man's pulverized face and blood splattered on the front of my shirt. Shit.

The fog dissipates and awareness returns. Mortification that Elle just witnessed me losing my shit, and potentially beating this man to death, makes it difficult to face her.

"Elle, baby, are you okay—" I look beside me, expecting to see my wife scowling at me in disgust at what I just did. But my world shatters when I see Elle's lifeless form on the ground. She is pale, far too pale, as she lies with her head slightly canted to the side, in absolute stillness.

Nik careens around the corner and takes in the scene

as I dive to Elle and cradle her head. "Baby, wake up. Eliana, can you hear me?"

I check her pulse. Fuck, fuck, fuck. This isn't happening.

I gently lower her head, pinch her nose and open her mouth to perform CPR. My thoughts are frenetic from desperation, yet my motions are somehow controlled. I no longer register anything around me, as my reason for living lies motionless on the floor.

Time stands still, I have no concept of minutes, only the seconds that tick by with Elle remaining unconscious.

Nik kneels beside me and tries to move my hands from Elle's chest as I am performing compressions. I rear back, about to lash out with my fists when I notice a red box with a white heart next to him.

Thank God. I nod. "What do you need me to do?"

"Remove her clothes. Everything from the waist up."

Ripping Elle's shirt down its center, I quickly remove her bra, using my body to shield her naked form.

Nik explains where to place the pads, and we wait as the machine performs an analysis of whether a shock is needed. Finally, the device indicates all clear. I take my hands away from Elle's body and Nik hits the button to deliver a shock. We wait, my breath is held as I pray for this to work. For Elle to come back to me. But there's no response.

I continue CPR until the device indicates another shock is needed.

We repeat the process, and I continue praying like I've never prayed before. I wager, I make promises. I will do absolutely anything to see life in Elle once again. Anything to erase the pale face and blue-tinged lips in front of me.

A soul-shattering moan fills the space as we wait, and

I vaguely register that it came from me. The very long seconds tick by as I resume the manual CPR.

"Eliana, I need you. Please don't leave me, baby. I need you to fight. Fight, damn it!"

I continue the CPR, waiting for the machine to give me the all-clear signal, but it doesn't come. Instead, the line registers a tiny little blip. I jerk back and look at Nik, eyes wide. His expression matches mine.

"Eliana, can you hear me, love? Wake up, sweetheart."

My eyes are glued to the device as the heart rate line continues to register small peaks every few seconds. The last breath I took is frozen in my chest as time continues to stand still, as the entire world stands still.

Bringing my face next to Elle's, my voice breaks when I tell her I can't live without her and beg her to fight like she's never fought before.

My eyes are transfixed on her pale face as I wait, willing her to wake.

Time is suspended when one eyelid begins to quiver. Kissing her forehead I say, "I'm here, baby. Open your eyes."

An eternity passes before, finally, both eyelids flutter and then begin to open. The breath that has been frozen in my chest is released as a sob.

Elle's unfocused eyes lock onto mine when I hear. "Mr. Tate, we need to attend to your wife."

I look up, shocked to see multiple people in our home. Paramedics and police congregate in two separate groups. Several police officers are dealing with the unidentified man, who is now conscious and sitting up, blood covering his face. Rage incinerates the shock I must be in. If Elle wasn't near death, I would tear his fucking head off.

"Alex." My eyes shoot to Nik in surprise, my first

name sounding foreign on his lips. He places his hand on my shoulder to urge me back, which shakes me into action. I cover Elle's body with my own before placing the material from her ripped shirt over her chest. I caress her face and kiss her forehead. "I'll be here, love. I'm not going anywhere."

I reluctantly back away to allow the paramedics to work. As Elle is hooked up to equipment, I notice for the first time that Nik somehow untied her hands and feet while I was performing CPR. I watch as Elle is secured to a stretcher, the group wheeling her to the elevator in under a minute.

I'm blindly following the stretcher to the foyer when Nik calls out that he will find me at the hospital. I nod and leave him to deal with the aftermath of Scott and the man who is now in handcuffs.

The elevator arrives and Rodriguez and Price step out. They quickly take in the scene, my blood-spattered face and clothes, Elle strapped to a stretcher, her eyes closed, face still too pale, lips still tinged blue as the paramedics wheel her out. The two agents, uncharacteristically, move to the side to get out of our way without peppering me with questions.

We quickly move onto the elevator, my eyes not leaving Eliana's angelic face. As the doors close, Rodriguez speaks up. "Dorn is in custody. He told us about Luca Vacanti's involvement, that's why we're here."

My head snaps up to look at the agents as my eyes flare at hearing Luca's name when they continue. "We'll take care of everything here."

I nod my head once as the elevator doors close.

NINETEEN

ELIANA

WAKE TO AN INCESSANT BEEPING THAT MAKES ME WANT to bury my head under my pillow. I idly wonder if this is Groundhog Day, and if so, whether I really want to wake up. I decide I don't and allow my eyes to remain shut.

Beep. Beep. Beep.

My agitation grows with every minute I'm unsuccessful in tuning out the maddening sound until I give in and slowly peel my eyes open. White, sterile walls and medical equipment greet me. Well, shit. The fact that I'm in a hospital room and not at home this time isn't a great sign. I try to turn my head to identify the offensive beeping, but a searing pain slices my throat.

What should have been a scream, but is only a mute breath of air, leaves my lungs. Fuck, that hurts. I pat the area around me, attempting to locate a call button, but I'm interrupted when blue-gray eyes look down on me. I smile at the sight of Alex. A hoarse, high-pitched keening noise comes out of my mouth instead of my greeting.

Alex grabs my hand and stoops to place a chaste kiss on my forehead where he lingers to breathe me in. "Try not to talk, sweetheart. I'll get the doctor." Alex smiles when he sees my eyebrow raise. Chuckling, he brushes my hair back. "I know, it's cliché, but your vocal cords are injured."

Alex's head disappears from view and I try to think through the events that led me here. The vivid image of Luca's enraged face looming over me while I felt myself slipping from my body is the last thing I remember. After that, there's a void. A void that was filled by a dream about my parents. They were hugging me and telling me how proud they are of me.

I close my eyes. The dream was everything. The pure joy and belonging I felt, as if I was right where I needed to be. Sunshine had flooded my soul. At least until the pull of consciousness stole my parents away once again.

Tears sting the back of my eyes, and my nose starts to tingle as I think about the goodbye we were finally able to say to one another. My mom embracing me and rubbing my back as she explained that it wasn't time for me to join them and that I would be waking up shortly. I didn't want to leave, and I recall the sheer panic that filled me as I clung to her, telling her I wasn't ready to let go. Not yet. My father interrupted by hugging us both and telling me they would be right there, wherever there was, waiting for me when it was the right time, but that this wasn't it.

I fought the pull that I knew would separate us, but it was too much, the force too great. The warm, insulated love and belonging evaporated, being replaced with a white-hot stake down my throat.

My thoughts are interrupted when a handsome gray-haired man in a white coat comes into view. "Mrs. Tate, I am Doctor Ted Johnson. I would ask how you are feeling, but it's best for you to rest your vocal cords. Are you able to nod or move your head at all?"

I attempt to nod, and the pain shoots down my neck.

Dr. Johnson types something into a laptop sitting on a cart beside him. "Alright, how about blinking. Are you able to blink once for no and twice for yes?"

I blink twice before rolling my eyes, I'm not an imbecile.

Dr. Johnson fights back a smile and continues to tap the keys of the laptop before returning his attention to me. He pours water from a plastic pitcher into a large, mauve-colored plastic cup with a clear plastic straw. "Would you like some water?"

I blink twice and Dr. Johnson brings the straw to my lips. I take a small pull, and cool water hits my tongue. I attempt to swallow but nearly cry out at the pain. Alex is immediately at my side, and I realize everything I'm feeling must be telegraphed on my face.

Dr. Johnson pulls the cup back. "Do you want more?" I blink once. *Hell no, get that cup out of my face.*

The doctor places the cup somewhere next to my head before continuing. "Occlusion of a carotid artery may cause neurological deficits, so I'm just trying to assess your current state. We ran a CT while you were unconscious, which showed extensive vascular injury." Dr. Johnson pauses as if he's assessing whether I understand what he is saying. I blink twice, urging him to continue, and he smiles once again.

"We need to keep you for observation to ensure your condition continues to improve and doesn't reverse course. We will manage your pain with medication as you continue to heal. You should regain limited use of your voice in a few days. Does all of this make sense?"

My eyes widen in alarm. How in the hell am I supposed to communicate if I can't talk or move my head?

I raise my hand and mime writing, to which Dr. Johnson looks pleased. "We will get you a pad of paper and a pen so you can communicate."

Satisfied by his answer, I move my eyes from Dr. Johnson to Alex, who looks like he has been on a five-day bender. He clasps my hand and brings it to his mouth for a kiss.

Dr. Johnson stands. "You are in far better shape than I expected, Mrs. Tate, but we aren't out of the woods just yet. Get some rest, you will need your strength these next few days."

After Dr. Johnson leaves, Alex pulls a chair next to the side of the bed and bends toward me. "Elle …" His voice breaks as he lowers his head to regain composure before once again looking at me. "I can't begin to describe what I am feeling right now. Seeing your exasperation with the doctor. I didn't know if I would ever see that spark again."

Alex lowers his head again, his uneven breaths giving away how emotional this has made him.

I blindly reach beside me until my clumsy fingers brush against Alex's ear. I raise my hand to run my fingers through his hair before he clasps my hand in his, bringing it to his mouth for a kiss.

Alex positions himself so that I can see his face and looks into my eyes. My breath stutters and my stomach squeezes at the brokenness I see in his eyes. I cup his cheek, giving him a look that I hope telegraphs that everything will be fine.

He covers my hand with one of his. When he speaks, his voice is as broken as his eyes. "I thought I lost you, that after everything I did to try to keep you safe, all the anguish I put you through—after the pain you were somehow miraculously able to survive. After all of it, I thought I lost you."

It's torture watching Alex swim in remorse and pain and not be able to reassure him that I will be okay. I mime writing again and provide a *Find something for me to write with, now,* expression. I watch as Alex looks around the room, but apparently there aren't any options because he finally takes his phone out of his pocket and opens the notes app before handing the phone to me.

I type my message and hand the phone back to Alex.

> *This is NOT your fault.*

> *I will be fine—well, once I can talk again, that is.*

> *Where's Luca?*

Alex's expression turns murderous. "The only reason he isn't dead right now is because I needed to be with you." He pauses to rake his hands through his hair in agitation. "He's in custody. You will never, and I mean never, have to worry about him again."

I reach my hand out for the phone.

> *Does Theo know? He and Margaret must be devastated.*

Alex lets a half-smile grace his lips. "Theo and Margaret are here. They came as soon as they heard. I think they're still trying to process how someone they viewed as a surrogate son almost killed their surrogate daughter. They've completely cut Luca off."

I reach for the phone again.

> *And Dorn?*

Alex's murderous expression returns. "We were

interrogating Dorn when Nik got your text. I didn't realize the text was from you at the time. Rodriguez, Price, and I continued to question Dorn; he was baiting us. It wasn't until he asked if I knew where you were while I was sitting there with him that I knew you were in trouble. Nik walked in at that moment and told me we had to leave." Alex shakes his head at the thought before continuing. "Rodriguez and Price stayed to continue questioning Dorn. His face as we left, his smile and his parting words will stay with me for as long as I live."

What did he say?

"He told me to tell you 'Hello' if I made it to you in time." Alex wipes his hand down his face. "I saw it in his eyes—he didn't think I would find you, at least not alive." He stops talking to look up at the ceiling for long moments before finally looking back at me. "If I had arrived a moment later …" He shakes his head, unable to finish the sentence.

I grab his hand and squeeze to get him to look at me. We stare at each other, communicating without words. Me telling him he needs to stop blaming himself. Him telling me he is still shattered from finding me nearly dead. This continues until finally, I see some of the tension leave Alex's shoulders as he bends to kiss my forehead.

"Dorn is in custody as well. Rodriguez and Price found a treasure trove of evidence on his laptop. He had you under surveillance from the time you started working again after my disappearance. Several photos of you littered his bedroom walls. This was personal for him, the guy was obsessed."

What the hell? My eyebrows scrunch together as I

process what Alex is saying. Photos on his wall? That's next-level creepy.

"Rodriguez found the man Dorn was paying to keep tabs on you, and he admitted to placing a tracking device in your purse."

What! I grab the phone.

What the hell??? How'd someone get close enough to place a tracking device in my bag?!

"He said he planned a run-in with you at the office." Alex lifts his shoulders as if to say that's all he knows. I think back. When on earth would someone have had access to my bag at the office? My eyes widen in realization—the guy who ran into me while I was waiting for the elevator with Ben.

"Scott alerted Nik to Dorn so that Luca would have a window of time when Nik would be on the other side of town. The tracker in your bag let Scott know when you arrived home. When Scott was supposedly sweeping the condo, he let Luca in through the emergency exit. You were incredibly smart to let Nik know about Scott's surprise visit. If you hadn't done that, Nik wouldn't have known that we needed to get to you."

I can't believe Scott was in on this!

Alex's eyes soften when he sees that I'm hurt by Scott's betrayal. "Scott didn't know Luca's plan. He agreed to help Luca because Dorn was threatening Scott's sister. Luca attempted to play Dorn by giving Scott the information he needed to take Dorn down. He convinced Scott that he would be seen as a hero for alerting Nik to suspicious behavior. Nik would arrive at the address Scott had followed this 'suspicious' person to and see that it was Dorn. Scott knew Nik would have Rodriguez and Price with him, and he knew they would find incriminating evidence. Dorn would be arrested and would no longer be a threat to Scott's sister."

Holy shit. I have a million questions, but by the end of Alex's explanation, my eyes are heavy. Pain medication must be flowing through my IV, because as shocking as this information is, and as badly as I want to dissect everything I just learned in this moment, I can't as I fight to keep my eyelids open.

Alex smooths my hair back with his hand. "Sleep, my love. I'll be here when you wake up."

I think about telling him to get some sleep himself, but before I can motion for the phone, my eyes close and I'm floating.

* * *

Sitting up in the hospital bed I've been occupying the past three days, my makeshift office scattered around me, I review the contract for the acquisition of Bec on my laptop.

Two knocks on the open door cause me to look up to see my beautiful best friend leaning casually against the doorjamb. I feel my lips stretch into a smile so wide, it's painful. I motion for him to come closer.

Ben raises his eyebrows. "You sure you have time for me?" He takes in the documents littered on the bed, my laptop perched on the tray over my lap, and the stack of files on the cart beside me. "You do realize you were technically dead three days ago, right? You don't think you should take this time to, I don't know, *rest*?"

I lift one shoulder as if to say *what else am I supposed*

to do in response. My enthusiastic gesture for him to come closer becomes a demand as I jab a pointed finger toward Ben and then point at the chair next to the bed.

Ben raises his hands in the air in surrender as he straightens from the doorway and walks to the bed. Once he's closer, I notice the strain visible on his face. I grab his hand and squeeze. I see Ben's composure slip before he wraps his arms around my shoulders in a side-hug, effectively hiding his face. I cradle one of his arms just under my collarbone and we hold each other for several minutes, me pretending Ben isn't crying as he regains control of his emotions.

After several minutes, I grab the pad of paper next to me and begin to write as Ben continues to hold my shoulders.

I love you, Ben. I'm sorry I worried you … again.

I promise this will be the last time.

I rub Ben's arm before patting it to get his attention. When he leans back, I hold the pad of paper up for him to see. He reads it and stares for a moment before deep, boisterous belly laughs erupt from him.

What the hell? I raise a questioning brow, which causes Ben to laugh even harder. I push his shoulder and raise a hand, a gesture that screams *what is your problem?*

It's a full minute before Ben is able to regain control of his laughter. When he does, he kisses the top of my head. "Oh, Elle. I love you, too, but you are out of your mind if you think this is the last time you will have me worried." Ben shakes his head as if affronted I even made the suggestion. "With all the shit you're now wrapped up in, I don't believe for a second this is the last scare I will have to go through—that this will be the last time Jackson will have to take an emergency flight back to New York to hold me together, or that this will be the last time I go over forty hours without sleeping." His voice is raised by the end of his tirade, and he pauses to take a breath.

I grab the pad of paper.

> *I know you have no reason to believe me, but I swear, this will not happen again. Also, it's not fair to fight with someone who can't talk—can we table this argument for when I regain use of my voice?*

Ben reads the note and places his hands on his hips as he looks up at the ceiling. Searching for patience, I have no doubt. When he finds what he's looking for, he lowers himself into the chair and leans his torso onto the bed. I watch as his face begins to relax, the pinch becoming a little less severe, even if he does look exhausted. The purple smudged under his eyes a tell-tale sign he wasn't lying when he said he hadn't slept.

Ben grabs one of my hands and I place my other hand over his as we stare at each other. The past days are catching up to us both. We stay this way for long minutes of comfortable silence until Ben speaks. "There is a waiting room full of people who want to see you. I should probably let some of them have their turn—the hospital is only allowing two people in your room at a time. I was actually supposed to get Jackson if you were awake."

I nod in understanding and grab the pad of paper.

> *Tell Jackson I am forever in his debt for supporting you during this—and I'm sorry his trip was cut short because of me. Speaking of significant others, have you been taking it easy on Alex?*

Ben reads the paper and I see the answer on his face before he responds. "Have I been taking it easy on the man who continues to put your life in danger? I think you know the answer to that, doll."

My stomach sinks. I realize it will take time to repair their friendship, but it is difficult to know that the two people I'm closest to can't be in the same room together. Ben's eyes soften when he sees how his words have gutted me as I nod in acceptance. He kisses the top of my head as he stands. "Give it time, Elle. These things don't happen overnight. Now, is there anything else you need from the office? Anything Nik wasn't able to grab?"

I shake my head no.

"Okay, Jax and I will be back later this evening. Text me if there is anything you need."

I nod again and give Ben an air kiss.

"Love you, doll. We'll be back soon. Try to stay out of trouble in the meantime," he adds with wide eyes, as if the concept of me staying out of trouble is improbable.

I shoo him away and he turns to leave. Once he's gone, I lean back on my pillow. What will it take for Ben and Alex to get past this? Perhaps a group vacation? It's difficult to hate someone in paradise. I am mentally cataloging vacation spots when I hear Margaret and Theo's voices outside the door before they enter the room. Margaret rushes to the side of the bed, clasping my hand in both of hers. "Eliana—" She stops speaking to search my eyes. "How are you feeling?"

I answer by lifting one shoulder as if to say *I've been better* before dropping her hand to grab the pad of paper beside me.

My throat is beginning to feel better, it's just annoying not being able to talk.

I watch as Margaret reads the line I just wrote before looking at my neck. She winces and her hand moves to her own neck when she sees the purple collar bruising my skin. She shakes her head in disbelief as tears fill her eyes. "I still can't believe Luca is capable of doing this." Her voice is raw with grief.

The tears in Margaret's eyes spill over and drip down her cheeks as Theo puts his arm around her and nestles her into him, kissing the side of her head.

Theo turns his head toward me. "Eliana, words cannot express how sorry we are. We can't help but feel responsible since Luca was in town because of us."

I shake my head at Theo and pick up my pen.

Luca was already in town when you were admitted to the hospital. He was in New York to meet with Dorn. None of this is your fault. I knew Luca just as long as the two of you and I never suspected he could do something like this.

Theo reads my note and nods, though his expression remains the same. "The detectives have been interviewing him—he shared that Dorn had been blackmailing him. Dorn planned to pull his investment in Luca's restaurants, which included the locations in Italy, if Luca wasn't able to get you to invest." Theo shakes his head in confusion. "It's odd, according to Luca, Dorn demanded that it had to be you. Luca had to get you to invest, no one else. The detectives are trying to get Dorn to disclose why that was, but he isn't cooperating."

What on earth? I shake my head and raise both shoulders in a *your guess is as good as mine* gesture.

Theo places his hand over mine. "Whatever the reason, thank God Alex got to you in time."

A muffled sob leaves Margaret as Theo continues to comfort her. I reach out and take her hand. Haunted eyes meet mine before she bends to wrap her arms around me. I return her squeeze as her tears wet my shoulder. When Margaret straightens, Theo pulls her into him again and I grab the pad of paper.

Please don't cry, I will be fine, promise.

Margaret nods her head as she continues to run a tissue under her eyes. "I know sweet girl, it's just that we could have lost you. And then for Alex to be alive! It's all a bit of a shock."

I have no idea what they've been told regarding Alex's magical reappearance, so I just smile and nod in response.

Theo kisses Margaret's temple. "To think he was being held by terrorists." Theo shakes his head in disbelief. "You two need a vacation."

My shoulders shake in silent laughter, and when I look to Margaret to gauge her response, I am happy to see she, too, is laughing, I suppose it would be difficult to maintain a straight face at Theo's deadpan delivery. Truer words were never spoken.

Margaret and I are still smiling when Theo continues, "We should let you rest, although it looks like you are working more than resting." He raises his brows as his eyes pointedly scan the documents strewn across the bed.

I smile and raise my arms to hug them both goodbye.

It's obvious Margaret doesn't want to leave as she stalls,

finding excuses to stay in the room. "We'll be back tomorrow, but if you get bored or need us for anything today, just text. I'll have my phone on me."

My smile widens and I nod in agreement as I give them the same air kiss I gave Ben.

After Theo is finally able to lead Margaret from the room, I slump back into the stiff hospital pillows and close my eyes as exhaustion settles over me. My thoughts return to vacation spots. Bali is too far, and Hawaii is too … obvious. Perhaps the Maldives? I'm dreaming about huts over cerulean water when an unmistakable scent makes my mouth water. I open my eyes to see a paper bag with Stella's logo sitting on the stack of files beside me.

Deciding sleep can wait, I sit up and open the bag to see chocolate croissants, the only thing I've been able to eat small pinches of, individually wrapped in tissue. I shake my head in wonder. I have no idea how he does it. If there is one thing the past days have taught me, it's that my husband can be a ghost when he wants to be. It's no wonder he was able to stay hidden, even when he was no longer underground.

I pick up a tented notecard resting on top of the croissants and see Alex's orderly script. He has been bringing me croissants accompanied by sweet messages, quotes, or yesterday, a three-page love letter. I think it's a ploy to get me to eat—the hospital-provided liquid meal replacement is repulsive and nearly impossible to choke down. I open the card and read.

> *My love for you is infinite. It is without time, limitation, or reason. So much so, the word itself is inferior to the reality of how I feel—because how could I ever describe the gravity of what we have, of what we are when we*

*are together? A meager four-letter word does not do it
justice. What I can say is this: You are more necessary
than the air I breathe. I can continue on without air,
but I cannot continue on without you.*

I feel a tear slide down my cheek as the overwhelming emotion invoked by Alex's words spills out of me.

"None of that now."

My eyes snap up in surprise to see Alex standing in the doorway, his sexy half-smile and dimples on display. If I could talk, I would tell him to lock the door and strip. My expression must give my thoughts away because Alex walks to the side of the bed and bends to kiss me. My hand moves to the back of his head to deepen the kiss.

Alex chuckles before leaning back to look at me. "I thought you were sleeping, I didn't want to wake you."

I pull his head down for another kiss in response before scooting over and patting the bed beside me. Alex slides in and wraps me in his arms. The beat of his heart against the side of my face as I lie on his chest is a hypnotizing rhythm that has me fighting to stay awake.

Alex runs his hand over my hair in soothing strokes. "There are still a lot of people waiting see you, but I think you should rest. They can come back tomorrow."

I try to nod my head in agreement, but I'm not sure it actually moves before I stop fighting the exhaustion and allow sleep to take me.

* * *

Sunlight filters in through the window and cuts an angle across the other side of the room that makes me wish I was outside, soaking in the warmth. I smile at the little hummingbird fluttering near a spray of flowers in a lone planter on the small terrace outside my hospital room. I can almost feel the warm sun blanketing me, as it did so long ago when my mother told me to look for the hummingbirds in life. If I close my eyes, the sweet scent of honeysuckle almost replaces the chemical tang of bleach.

Joy, love, and healing. With eyes closed, I rest the palm of my hand against my breastbone. It may be my imagination, but I swear I can feel her warmth. "From here to eternity," I whisper before returning my gaze to the window. The hummingbird appears to be levitating, its little wings fluttering so rapidly they are invisible.

"This day is now officially perfect."

My gaze moves to the doorway to see Alex walking toward the hospital bed, his eyes on the hummingbird.

I smile up at him. "I couldn't agree more."

Alex loses the joyful spark in his eyes at the rasp in my voice. I sound much better than I did eight days ago, in the sense that I can actually speak, but the ever-present gravel in my voice is a painful reminder of just how lucky we are.

"My voice will continue to improve. Dr. Johnson said I should be back to normal in another week or so."

Alex sits on the edge of the bed and moves a lock of hair away from my eye as he returns my smile.

I wait for him to reply but he just stares at me. A million-dollar smile graces his face, showcasing his panty-dropping dimples. "Are you ready to get out of here?"

I return his smile. "You have no idea."

Alex lets out a breath of a laugh. "You act like you're bored out of your mind and haven't been working from this room the past week and a half."

I return his smile with a smirk. "Doesn't matter, I am so ready to be home." I reach out to grab his hand. "With you."

The love that pours from Alex's eyes makes me skip a breath before he adds, "Agreed. The nurse should be here any moment to discharge you."

Studying Alex, I imagine what it will be like to be with him publicly again. His return from the dead has been seamless so far. No one has questioned the story Alex and the feds have crafted, and now that we know it wasn't the Russians who were after me, it was time for him to come out of hiding. Which reminds me ...

"How was the board meeting this morning?"

Alex grins, "I wish you could have been there. It felt so incredible to knock Edward Dooling down a peg or two." Alex's smile grows. "I think even Elizabeth enjoyed seeing someone else call the shots while Edward was unable to do anything about it. The old man didn't know what to do being out of his element."

A raspy chuckle escapes my throat. "I can only imagine how much that must have grated under his skin."

Alex's expression turns conspiratorial. "The group is in agreement—if you want it, and I really hope you do, you still have a seat on the board. Everyone was incredibly impressed with your diligence in uncovering what Dorn was up to."

I think about it for a moment, but my heart isn't in it. I need to focus on Tate and my portfolio of investments. We already have plans to expand Bec to two additional locations, one in Vegas and the other in Los Angeles, and I have three investments ready to IPO, one of which is Immunotech.

Smiling at Alex, I shake my head. "The only reason I fought to be on the board was to save Immunotech. Now that you're back," I bring my hand to the side of Alex's face, "I can focus on Tate, and you can resume your role as CEO and take over as chair."

Alex turns his head to kiss my wrist. "Whatever you want, love."

I tilt my head in thought. "Well, when you put it that way, there is one thing I want."

Alex smiles before replying with, "Name it."

"I explained that TA took controlling interest of Immunotech while I was grieving. It was only meant to be temporary until I was able to once again function."

Alex's expression shutters as he nods.

Ignoring his expression, I continue, "Tate needs to repurchase the shares from TA to once again have controlling interest. Particularly since I suspect Immunotech will go public within the next year."

Alex's eyes widen in surprise. "Seriously? That's three years ahead of what we were projecting."

I nod my head. "It's going to happen, and I want Tate to be the lead firm when it does."

Alex kisses my wrist once again. "My beautiful, brilliant girl. Consider it done."

A throat clearing from the doorway interrupts us. "How's our favorite patient? Are you ready to bust out of here?"

My smile widens at seeing Dr. Johnson. "Definitely."

The doctor walks to the bed and sets a small bag of prescription bottles on the rolling tray I've been using as a desk before explaining my discharge instructions.

Within fifteen minutes, I'm changed into comfortable clothes and sitting in a wheelchair, standard hospital procedure I wasn't able to argue my way out of, as Alex pushes me toward the black SUV waiting in the circular drive.

Nik jumps out and opens the back door. Nik, Theo, Margaret, and Ben have all stopped by the hospital every day since I was admitted, but seeing Nik outside of the hospital, after everything we have been through this past year—Alex's supposed death, Genevieve being taken, and my own near-death experience—causes tears to collect at the corners of my eyes. I owe so much to every person in my life, but especially Nik. I give him a brief hug and whisper my thanks before he and Alex help me climb into the back seat.

As we pull out of the hospital's driveway, I stare absently out of the car window, remembering the last time I left the hospital, after Theo had been admitted following my argument with Dorn. I was just starting to realize things weren't as they seemed after finding the camera in Theo's hospital room, which Rodriguez and Price learned Dorn paid to have planted. He admitted he'd decided to take advantage of Theo's health scare by approaching me as soon as I was alone in the hospital. He apparently attempted to get to me while I was sleeping in the waiting room, but an unknown man, whom he thought was security, was paying vigil, ruining his plans. I now know the man was Alex. Thank God he was there.

I always suspected Dorn was the devil incarnate—now I know he truly is. For him to threaten to pull his investments in Luca's restaurants if Luca wasn't able to get me to invest was abhorrent. I mentally shake my head in disgust when I think of the reason behind all of this: an irrational obsession held by an unstable man.

In addition to evidence proving Dorn paid to have a

camera planted in Theo's room, Price and Rodriguez found documents and correspondence on Dorn's laptop showing he had set the stage for embezzlement charges to be filed against me as soon as I invested in Luca's business. His ultimate goal wasn't money, but rather to take me down. All this nonsense was to set the stage for him to pull the rug out from under Tate, Inc. as soon as I was involved. He's maniacal.

A breath of disbelief is punched out of my lungs as I reflect on the events that followed, all because of two weak men. Dorn's obsession, which stemmed from a bruised ego because I got the position at T.A. Holdings instead of him after business school. And then Luca, who simply allowed greed to wrap its long tentacles around his heart, effectively strangling it. Both men will be sitting in prison for a long, long time because of the unfortunate decisions they made.

A pang of sadness that Luca got caught up in all of this hits me, until I remember he led the group responsible for taking Gen. My empathy for Luca evaporates when I think of his ridiculous plan to play Dorn by attempting to take me to God-knows-where, all to somehow access my money. I still don't understand how he thought his plan would actually work, unless he was going to demand a ransom for my return. An extreme move if so, and all because of his greed and Dorn's obsessed stupidity.

The two idiots had been working together ever since Theo introduced them when Luca needed to raise capital for his restaurant, though I hadn't realized Dorn had invested in the restaurants Luca had opened in Italy. Luca would have done anything to keep his business afloat, which Dorn capitalized on. Luca's ego must have been too big to ask me for actual help; he instead relied on Dorn, who managed to wrap Luca into his web of lies and deception.

As the SUV nears the end of the long hospital drive, I admire a row of lush green shrubs, standing about five-feet tall and adorned with pink buds. I smile, not at all surprised to see the darling little hummingbird hovering beside one of the buds. A feeling of peace settles over me as I realize that everything really will be okay.

Alex shifts next to me. "Ah, there it is." Knowing he's referring to my smile, I turn it to him. He kisses the side of my mouth. "How are you feeling?"

I take a moment to think about his question. The truth is, the emotion I feel is overwhelming. I'm certain my heart is about to burst out of my chest in a kaleidoscope of color; a blinding spotlight that's too much for one person to contain. I lean in to kiss him, and truly mean it when I reply, "I feel like I'm the luckiest person in the world."

EPILOGUE

THE SCENT OF GARLIC AND SPICES WAFTING FROM THE kitchen causes my mouth to water as I try to concentrate on Gen describing her date last night. She has been seeing a guy she met in her Krav Maga class, which she began taking following her abduction. The relationship is still fairly new, but the sex is apparently amazing, and she isn't shy about giving me the details. Every detail. She's animatedly explaining something involving a handstand when Margaret joins us. The shock that flashes across Gen's face when she notices Margaret listening causes me to laugh out of my nose as she attempts to recover by pivoting to describe a yoga pose. Winded, Gen stops her rambling to take a fortifying gulp from her glass of Sancerre.

Margaret gives us a knowing look before winking and taking a sip of her wine. Gen's eyes meet mine as we both try to bottle our laughter. This, of course, results in the two of us doubled over. When we are finally able to get ahold of ourselves, I straighten and smooth out my dress. Margaret just raises a shoulder. "I wasn't born yesterday, girls," she says, effectively raising another fit of laughter from the three of us.

Theo and Alex join our trio, humor lighting their faces

as Theo wraps an arm around Margaret's shoulder and kisses her cheek. "It sounds as though we're missing all the fun."

Alex steps behind me and hugs my body to his. He nuzzles my neck as he inconspicuously whispers, "With Genevieve in the mix, I can only imagine what the three of you were laughing about."

The vibration of his voice against my ear is an electrical current to my core, and I begin to calculate how we might slip away from the group before dinner. I turn my head to the side and wink. "My lips are sealed, but if we manage to slip away before dinner, I can demonstrate."

Hunger flashes in Alex's eyes. I raise my head as he bends down for our lips to meet in a kiss. A kiss that ends far too quickly when we are interrupted by Ben's voice.

"My God, it smells good in here." I look over to see Ben and Jackson enter the room. Ben walks to me and grabs my hand as he mutters, "Alexander" in acknowledgment before pulling me from Alex's arms to embrace me in a hug. I snuggle into Ben, his clean linen scent always so reminiscent of home.

"You could at least try to be cordial," I mutter under my breath.

Ben smirks. "That was me being cordial, doll." I shake my head in incredulity. They say time heals all things, but this past year has not softened the sharp edge of blame and guilt now marring the once-strong friendship Ben and Alex shared.

Jax gives Alex the standard male hand slap and back pat before turning to me. I move from Ben to hug his partner. "I've missed you, Jax. You're spending too much time globetrotting these days."

Jax laughs. "Not you too. I've been hearing nonstop complaints from Ben."

Well, shit. Leave it to me to stir the pot. Knowing a subject change is needed, and quickly, I motion to the terrace. "James and Becca are outside, I know they would love to see you. Here …" I move to grab two glasses and fill them with champagne from an open bottle. Handing one to Ben and the other to Jax, I usher them to the patio.

Ben spears me with a knowing look before replying, "I know what you are doing, but I need to talk with them about the Miami opening anyhow, so you're off the hook."

I just smile and raise my eyebrows in an expression that says *well, get to it.*

Alex nestles me back in his arms as Ben and Jackson retreat to the terrace. I look up at him, an apology in my eyes, but he just smiles. "That was actually an improvement. At least he acknowledged me this time."

A huff of frustration escapes my lips as a sigh. "I think now is the perfect time to take the group trip we've been putting off."

Alex continues to smile. "Whatever you want, love."

Before I can pull out my phone to email Darcy to ask her to book the damn thing, my attention is pulled to new voices coming from the foyer. I peel away from Alex when I see Nik and Stella walk into the room.

I can't stop the goofy smile I feel spread across my face as I take in the handsome pair. Nik, who could pass for a taller Jason Statham, has his hand on Stella's back. His eyes are alight with adoration whenever he looks at the modern-day Marilyn Monroe beside him, which is to say always. I can't help but marvel at how Nik and Stella's initial attraction the day they met, following the infamous board meeting, has blossomed into a whirlwind romance. And to think, my hospital stay was the catalyst for the two coming together.

Nik visited Stella's café every morning to pick up croissants for Alex. As Stella describes it, Nik began showing up earlier and earlier each day, until he was waiting at the locked front door at six in the morning so he could help Stella open. I melt a little every time I hear their story.

Stella radiates joy as she hands me a platter of mini desserts. "Sugar, if you aren't a sight for sore eyes." Stella envelops me in her arms and my body goes lax. She really does give the best hugs. After she releases me, I turn to Nik. His hand hasn't left Stella's back. I snicker at him, and he gives me a look that dares me to comment on his attention toward his girlfriend. I raise my hands in mock innocence, and he just shakes his head before bypassing me to escort Stella into the kitchen to greet the others.

My eyes follow the pair and I take a moment to absorb the scene; it's not often all my favorite people are in one place at the same time. Theo, Margaret, and Gen are laughing about something near the dining room table as Nik and Stella walk over to say hello. My gaze pans to the floor-to-ceiling glass separating the dining room from the terrace to see James and his wife Becca in conversation with Ben and Jax. The four are relaxed on the outdoor chaise lounge and chairs.

My heart melts when I notice James staring at his wife in wonder as Becca laughs at whatever Ben is saying. Becca has been in remission for six months now and has been a godsend with the business. She has been the driving force behind Bec's explosive growth. We had originally planned for two additional locations in the first year, but here we are, about to open our fourth. She and James have become dear friends to Alex and me this past year. Hmm, maybe we should invite them on our *operation make Alex and Ben friends again* vacation. They would provide an excellent buffer.

Seeking out Alex, I find him leaning against the wall, his eyes on me. My chest warms when our eyes connect. Even after a year of having him back, a myriad of emotions makes me lose my breath for a moment as we stare at one another, communicating without words. I'm about to motion for him to follow me upstairs, but I'm rudely interrupted.

"You two are so annoying when you do your telepathy thing," Gen bellows from the kitchen. I feel my face heat in embarrassment as our guests stop talking and turn their attention to us. Alex's eyes soften when he sees my reaction. Straightening from the wall, he walks to me, his signature sexy smirk in place as he scoops me into his arms, bringing his mouth to my ear. "If they're going to look, let's give them something to watch." His lips meet mine and I forget we have an audience. All prior embarrassment is seared away by the heat his kiss creates as I become liquid in his arms.

Whistles and applause bring us back to reality, and none too soon, as Bec's head chef announces dinner is ready.

We are all laughing as we make our way onto the terrace, where Becca has beautifully set up our outdoor table for the group to dine alfresco. Linens, crystal glasses, clusters of lavender, and strands of white lights, which have begun to twinkle overhead now that the sun is setting, provide a slice of Provence in the heart of Manhattan.

Once we are all seated, the laughter and cacophony of noise that results from multiple conversations and people talking over one another completes the setting. Drinks are topped off and Alex raises his glass, looking at me before saying, "A toast to my brilliant wife as we celebrate her one-year anniversary of life." He turns to address the group. "We owe so much to each of you for your support and assistance this past year." Alex makes eye contact with each person as he addresses them.

"James and Becca, you have provided the creative outlet and unflinching friendship Elle has needed in order to move forward, thank you. Theo and Margaret, you stepped in as Elle's surrogate parents when she lost her own. You have always been there for us, but your ability to always know just what Elle needs and when, through the months leading up to Luca's betrayal, while the world thought I was dead, and the months following. You truly are family, and I can't thank you enough for what you have done for Elle." A lump forms in my throat when Margaret looks to me, placing a hand over her heart before picking up a napkin to dab her eyes.

"Genevieve, your support of Elle and your ability to bring levity to any situation, which we all need at times, is invaluable. Thank you for being you." The table laughs as Gen winks and responds, "You can count on me to make sure you all loosen up once in a while."

Alex moves to Ben and Jax. "Ben, even if I had a lifetime, it wouldn't be long enough to express how thankful I am that you are in Elle's life. There is so much I need to say, but it boils down to the fact that I am so fucking grateful Elle has you. Not only for the past two years, but for the many trials that are yet to come. I owe you everything." Ben looks down as he considers Alex's words before looking back at Alex and nodding. I feel a ray of hope that the two may be able to move past the guilt and blame that shrouds their relationship. That is, until Alex continues. "Jackson, thank you for putting up with your mercurial spouse and supporting him through sleepless nights and endless energy devoted to Elle." Ben glares at Alex as my eyes widen. Right … perhaps they need more time.

Alex looks at Nik across the table. "Nik, we quite literally owe Elle's life—" Alex looks down in thought before looking back at Nik. "Actually, we owe both of our lives to you. To tell you thank you feels like an insult, because it is such an inadequate word, but we will spend the rest of our lives showing you how grateful we are." Smiling, I raise my glass with the others to toast, but Alex looks down at me.

"Eliana, you are the strongest, most capable person I know. Tonight, we celebrate your life and the joy you bring to all of ours. I love you, sweetheart."

I can't speak past the lump of emotion that continues to grow in my throat, so I smile in gratitude and raise my glass once again. A chorus of cheers and santé echo around the table before we drink and dig into the food that was placed in front of us during Alex's speech. After a few bites, Theo raises his voice to be heard over the conversations that have resumed. "I understand we may have another reason to celebrate in the not-too-distant future."

Smiling in response, I tilt my head in acknowledgment, knowing that he's referring to Immunotech's impending initial public offering. Following weeks of negotiating with the SEC that resulted in many sleepless nights, we filed to go public last week, which was the start of public speculation of when the company would IPO. We begin the whirlwind roadshow next week. If all goes to plan, and the market remains stable, Immunotech will be public in two to three weeks.

My smile brightens. "One can only hope we are all celebrating in the near future." I feel Alex's hand on my leg before he gives me a reassuring squeeze.

Theo's eyes twinkle, and I know what he's about to say before he opens his mouth. In unison, we both reply, "Hope is not a strategy." I lift one hand to stop him. "I know, I know. But in this case, I think it's fair to add a dash of hope that the market remains stable."

Theo chuckles and nods. "Very well."

I'm about to tease Theo that he must not be feeling well to have acquiesced so quickly when Nik excuses himself to take a call, answering his cell the moment he stands to walk away from the table. A familiar pit of dread forms in my stomach. This past year has been relatively uneventful, but security has tripled, and I'm still not allowed to run outside. There have been situations that have been … odd. I don't know if it's my paranoia, or if the team continues to hide things from me, but every couple of months, there is heightened security for one reason or another.

Nik walks to the corner of the patio, far enough away to not disturb the dinner, but close enough to keep an eye on the table.

I turn to Alex. "Will we ever have a normal life again?"

Alex puts his arm around the back of my chair and leans toward me to conspiratorially whisper, "Love, we have never had a normal life."

"Obviously, but I was unaware of that fact until last year." He rubs my shoulder and is about to reply when his gaze moves to the skyline over our shoulders. I follow his eyes to see a drone hovering above the terrace right before a pop rings out in the night, and the flying apparatus explodes into pieces.

What the fu—Alex has me on the ground, his body covering mine before I have time to register that the pop was a gunshot. I try to lean up to see what's going on, but Alex's weight has me pinned. I feel his heart beating heavily against my back when he barks, "Stay down." The demanding tone of his voice makes me want to jump up in spite, but I force myself to relax under his weight.

Several seconds tick by before Nik's voice cuts through the buzz of adrenaline in my ears, followed by a commotion over the terrace. I turn my head to see Nik walk to the ledge to look over the side, a phone still to his ear. Raised voices filter to us from below. Nik watches before turning back to the table, shaking his head in annoyance when he does. He runs a hand down his face before speaking. "Is everyone okay?" I hear murmurs from our guests before Nik continues, "My apologies for startling everyone. Please feel free to return to your chairs."

Alex's weight is blessedly lifted off me, but before I can push myself up, he has me cradled in his arms and places me back in my chair, his body shielding mine from behind. I internally roll my eyes at Alex's overprotectiveness. I've learned to excuse it this past year because I have been overprotective of him as well. We have a mutual understanding to allow room for these antics while we each work through our deep-seated fear of losing each other with Dr. Wickham. If it makes him feel better to act as a human shield between me and the harmless night sky, so be it.

I look around the table to see pale faces and wide eyes. Nik is now stooped next to Stella, I assume making sure she is okay, before he straightens. "The kid in the unit downstairs thought it would be entertaining to spy on our dinner party. The team is down there now questioning him. I apologize for the scare."

Murmurs and nervous throat clearing fill the night sky as we all try to shake off our residual panic. I know I need to say something to try to salvage this dinner, but I'm at a loss for words. I'm wracking my brain for a way to fix this when Ben speaks up. "Well, at least one thing remains constant." Ben pauses and we all look at him expectantly, waiting for him to impart a kernel of wisdom. "There is never a dull moment when these two are around." He gestures to Alex and me. Laughter echoes around the table, effectively dissolving some of the tension.

Gen raises her glass. "Cheers to that. I wouldn't be having the best sex of my life if it wasn't for these two." She nods her head toward Alex and me. "I never would have enrolled in Krav Maga classes and met the Adonis currently rocking my world if I wasn't abducted."

The table erupts in laughter as Nik and Theo shake their heads in mock abhorrence while fighting to maintain stoic expressions. I love my friends. Only Gen and Ben could manage to successfully dispel the lingering cloud the drone incident cast over the dinner. Conversations begin to once again flow freely, and Alex returns to his seat next to me, though he pulls my chair closer to his and wraps his arm around the back of it.

I lean into him as I watch our friends. "As I was asking, will our lives ever be normal again?"

Alex kisses my temple. "Not likely. At least not in the short term."

The gravity in his tone makes the pit return to my stomach. I look over at him to search his eyes, but his focus is across the table. I follow his gaze to catch him and Nik staring at one another before Alex's expression smooths as he turns back to me.

The anxiety and suspicion must be displayed on my face because he leans in to bring the two of us to eye level. "There is nothing to worry about right now. You know us, we're overly paranoid." His eyebrows raise as he looks at me in an adorably pleading way. His plan works because with his face so close, obscuring everything around us, I do feel my anxiety subside. "Let's try to relax and enjoy tonight, okay? I want you to be able to take this in, allow us to celebrate you. We can meet with Nik to ask any questions you would like tomorrow. Deal?"

Well, when he puts it that way, how can I say no? I feel my smile widen in agreement. "I suppose that's not too much to ask." Alex closes the distance between us, but I place a finger to his lips to stop him before adding, "At least for tonight."

Alex's lips meet mine before he pulls back to reply, "That's all I ask." We both settle back in our chairs, his arm still around the back of mine as we take in the laughter and boisterous debate between Gen and Ben over whether *Sex in the City* should put out a third movie. Ben is arguing that Carrie Bradshaw dresses like an Upper East Side four-year-old who has full access to her mother's designer wardrobe. Gen is currently rebutting Ben's claims by listing the many merits of *Sex in the City* and Carrie Bradshaw's fashion sense. I feel myself relax as I join the others in laughing at their banter.

The remainder of dinner is enjoyable, but I can't fully let go of the feeling that this normality is a fragile crystal bubble that could easily shatter at any moment. As much as I try, I can't shake the feeling.

After eating far too many of Stella's mini cakes, tarts, and truffles for dessert, our guests begin to leave, and none too soon, because Alex's fingers have been teasing the inside of my thigh for the past twenty minutes, and I am squirming in my seat.

Theo and Margaret are the first to say their goodbyes, but not before I promise to meet them at Stella's for coffee next week. They are followed by Becca and James, and then Ben and Jax. I tell the group to expect packets on vacation destinations, as well as potential dates, in the next few days.

Nik walks Stella to us to say goodbye, and I once again snicker. I never thought I would see him so wrapped up in another person, but I'm beyond happy he is. It's almost a relief to not worry about his life and whether he is happy outside of work.

Nik watches Stella hug Alex and me goodbye before saying, "I will be back up after Stella's settled, but the team will remain in place."

Alex shakes his head. "Go enjoy the rest of your evening. The three of us can meet tomorrow."

Nik contemplates this for a moment before nodding. "Fine, I'll be back tomorrow. The team will notify me if I'm needed before then."

Alex smiles before replying, "Fair enough." He walks Stella and Nik out and I turn to the table to see the multiple dishes we still need to bring in. Genevieve is lounging casually in her chair as she refills her wine glass. I walk to my spot at the table to grab my wine glass before taking the seat next to Gen. We both sit in silence as we stare at the table.

"Thank you for what you did tonight. The dinner would have been wrecked if it wasn't for you and Ben."

Gen grabs my hand as we both continue to stare at the table in thought. "It's what I'm good at." I smile at her reply. Gen's good at many things, but not caring what others think, which allows her best authentic self to shine through, is her superpower.

Gen squeezes my hand. "How are you holding up? You seemed to be on edge during dinner."

I feel myself nod at the table. "Yeah."

Gen waits for more, but when I don't continue, she turns to look at me. I shake my head before speaking. "I've had this feeling ever since Alex returned that his involvement with the antitoxin, the IXB project, and the government groups involved isn't over. It's an intuition I continue to bury, but it's always resurfacing. I mean, how could it possibly be over that easily?"

Gen nods in agreement. "I know what you mean, I've thought the same thing. Though, it wasn't necessarily over that easily. I mean, it was a pretty elaborate coverup if you think about it."

She isn't wrong, of course, but something just doesn't sit right with me. "And the drama with Dorn and Luca just happened to occur at the same time of Alex's disappearance, but the two aren't related? I doubt the two incidents are mutually exclusive."

Gen nods again before replying, "But how would the two situations be connected?"

I look out at the twinkling lights that make up the Manhattan skyline and shake my head. "I have no idea."

"Why do you two look so solemn? This is a night for celebration, remember?"

And just like that, the pit in my stomach is filled with warmth when Alex walks up to the table. I smile at him, "Long night, that's all. Thank you for arranging this, it was magical."

Alex walks up behind me to put his hands on my shoulders and begins to massage my tense muscles.

My gaze returns to the table. "I should start taking these dishes in."

Alex continues to massage. "No need, Bec's chef is still here, along with Stephens and two additional security detail. They agreed to clear the table for us."

Gen grins at Alex and me, a mischievous glint in her eyes. "That's my cue to get lost."

Alex replies with, "Thanks, Gen," as I say, "Don't be ridiculous," at the same time.

Gen laughs. "Trust me, it's time for me to meet up with the Adonis anyhow."

We rise from the table and begin to make our way into the condo when it strikes me that I actually don't know Gen's new sex-buddy's name. "Out of curiosity, what's Adonis's real name?"

Gen smirks. "I was wondering when you were finally going to ask." His name is Adon Islee, drop the lee at the end and you get Adonis."

Laughing, I reply, "Of course, it is. Only you could find both a literal and figurative use for your guy's nickname."

We are at the elevator when Gen winks and presses the button. "What can I say, I'm talented."

I hug Gen. "You, my friend, most certainly are."

We say our goodbyes and Gen steps onto the elevator. As the doors close, she calls out, "I'll call you tomorrow."

The look on her face says what she doesn't: So we can continue our conversation.

Nodding my agreement, I wave as I call out, "Text me when you get home." Gen returns my nod as the elevator doors shut.

I turn to find Alex, but stop when I see he's once again leaning against the wall. The predatory look on his face causes my stomach to take flight in anticipation.

"I know tonight didn't go as planned, but did you have a good time?"

Walking to him, I slip my arms around his hard stomach and raise my eyes to his. "I had a wonderful time. Thank you so much for arranging everything. I loved having everyone together."

"Good. What would the woman of the hour like to do now? Are you tired?"

My breathing increases as I run my hands up the muscled ridges of his abdomen. "Definitely not tired."

The hunger in Alex's eyes flares as he bends to kiss me. I lose myself in the kiss, and before I know it, my legs are wrapped around his middle and my back is against the wall. Alex leans back. "I believe you mentioned demonstrating something involving a handstand?"

My head goes back as I laugh. "You heard us earlier?" I swat his bicep in mock reprimand.

Alex just grins as he begins to walk us down the hall. "You did offer to demonstrate whatever it is you and Gen were talking about, did you not?"

"Oh, I'm happy to demonstrate. The question is, do you think you can handle it?"

The growl that leaves Alex's throat as he picks up speed would have made me laugh had he not started kissing my neck. We pass the kitchen and I wave apologetically to Stephens and two members of Nik's staff who are bringing dishes in from outside.

Alex is nearing a run when we enter our room. He throws me onto our bed and follows, crawling up the length of me. He stills once he's suspended above me; the intensity of his stare makes me squirm before he says, "I don't know how it's possible, but I fall more in love with you every day."

Returning his soul-searching stare with my own, I caress his cheek. "I know exactly what you mean. I don't know how to properly articulate how I feel, but it's as if something within us becomes more intertwined every day."

Alex smiles, the ever-present intensity in his eyes is a drug that consumes me. I'm lost in his gaze until he lowers his head and begins to worship my body, slowly undressing me as I remove his shirt, and he helps me remove his pants. Everything feels amplified. Every touch, every worshiping kiss. When we finally join together, I have to concentrate on not detonating. We have left earth and are on another planet. The experience is ethereal. The only appropriate description is otherworldly.

We have had every kind of sex. Hot, passionate sex, where there was an itch, a need to crawl under each other's skin to be sated. Sweet and slow sex, where the climax was a marathon buildup that explodes from a deep, dormant place. Lazy morning sex that is sweet and unhurried, like huckleberry pancakes on a Saturday morning. But this … This is something else entirely.

The feeling of coming together as one is indescribable. We both climax in record time, an omnipresent cocoon of love wrapped around us. We stay connected, Alex supporting his weight over me, as we both try to catch our breath. We stare at each other, the look of surprise on both our faces.

My eyes widen. "Holy shit. That was intense."

Alex smiles with his eyes as he shakes his head. "That was—I'm at a loss for words." He rolls to the side, bringing me to his chest. I snuggle into him, wrapping my leg around his.

I have no words for what we just experienced. "That was weirdly intense," I repeat.

Alex's muscles tighten as he lifts his head to look down at me. "Is that good or bad?"

I manage a chuckle. "Good. Very good."

He kisses the top of my head before relaxing again. "Good."

We are both silent for several minutes as we bask in the afterglow, each lost in our own thoughts, when Alex breaks the silence. "It was nice having everyone together tonight; we should do that more often."

I nod my head against his chest. "I can't imagine a better way to have spent today." We both tense when I mention the reason for the dinner and Alex begins to trail his fingers up and down my arm in soothing strokes.

His voice lowers when he says, "You and Gen looked pretty serious when I interrupted your conversation tonight. Was that because of the drone incident?"

I think about his question for a moment before shaking my head. "No, not necessarily. I just can't shake the feeling that our year of normality has been on borrowed time. Do you ever feel like the IXB drama isn't finished?"

Alex's arms bring me closer to his chest. "Whatever the future holds, we will manage our way through. I love you too fucking much for us not to." My eyes shoot up to his at the emotion in his voice. I suck in a breath when I see a cyclone of turmoil swirling in his eyes.

"I know. We can get through anything together," I raise my hand to stroke the side of his face. "And I love you too. So much."

Alex's eyes clear as his gaze penetrates my layers until I'm certain he can see my soul. He must like what he sees because his face warms and the crinkles on the side of his eyes smooth as he kisses my forehead.

With all the things not said, the omissions and half-truths that forever changed the two of us, I feel the truth of his words down to my marrow when he says, "Regardless of what's thrown at us, we'll face it head on. It's me and you. Forever."

Propping myself up to reach his lips, my eyes search his, finding conviction and unconditional love. His eyes search mine, likely finding the same thing. Because he's right, it doesn't matter what's yet to come. All that matters is we will face it together. I ghost my lips to his and whisper softly against them, "Forever."

The End

ACKNOWLEDGMENTS

A, for being the best muse—and for supporting the many, many weekends of me being glued to my laptop. I am the luckiest to have you in my corner. Love you forever.

Archie and Lucy for mending broken hearts.

You. Without readers like you, Elle and Alex would be on a shelf. How sad would that be? Very. So, thank you.

My power posse. May every woman be lucky enough to have such strong women as friends. Women who celebrate each other's wins as if they are their own—and will drop everything to help when needed. If iron sharpens iron, you all are the sword from Kill Bill.

My amazing family for always being my biggest fan club. Always. I won the genetic lotto with you.

ABOUT THE AUTHOR

Landry Yves fell in love with writing the moment she discovered it provided a creative element that was missing from her life. With a background in business, she became addicted to escaping spreadsheets and PowerPoint presentations by losing herself to words. Landry lives in Los Angeles with her husband and pups.

Connect with Landry at:
landryyves.com

www.ingramcontent.com/pod-product-compliance
Lightning Source LLC
Chambersburg PA
CBHW021230310726
48971CB00006B/1757